W9-AAN-065

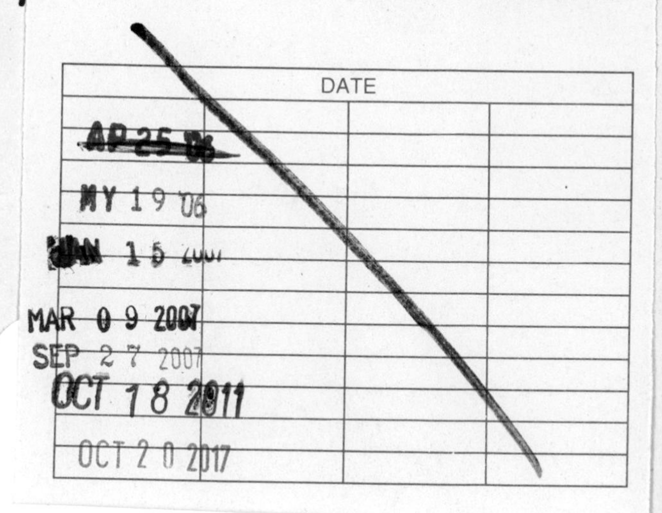
DATE
MY 19 '06
MAR 0 9 2007
SEP 27 2007
OCT 18 2011
OCT 20 2017

The GOOD, the BAD, and the UGLY Men I've Dated

Shane Bolks

An Imprint of HarperCollins*Publishers*

 For information address HarperCollins Publishers Inc., 10 East 53rd Street, New York, NY 10022.

HarperCollins books may be purchased for education, business, or sales promotional use. For information please write: Special Markets Department, HarperCollins Publishers Inc., 10 East 53rd Street, New York, NY 10022.

FIRST EDITION

Interior text designed by Elizabeth M. Glover

Library of Congress Cataloging-in-Publication Data

Bolks, Shane.
The good, the bad, and the ugly men I've dated / by Shane Bolks.—1st ed.
p. cm.
ISBN 0-06-077310-3
1. Dating (Social customs)—Fiction. 2. Female friendship—Fiction.
3. Class reunions—Fiction. 4. First loves—Fiction. I. Title.

PS3602.O6544G66 2005
813'.6—dc22 2004020638

05 06 07 08 09 JTC/RRD 10 9 8 7 6 5 4 3 2 1

For Courtney Burkholder and Tina Hergenrader.
Thanks for pulling me out of all the black holes.
You're Jedis in the truest sense of the word.

Appreciation and love to:

Evan Fogelman, for not rejecting me twice and convincing me that Avon really did want to buy this book.

Mom and Dad, for being my biggest supporters and loving me no matter what.

WHRWA and NWHRWA, for your sage words of advice and your rah-rah-ing during the Dark Times.

Linda Andrus, Laura Faulkenberry, and Marti Kristynik, for laughing in all the right places and steering me on the right course.

The GOOD,
the BAD,
and the UGLY
Men I've Dated

Chapter 1

A long time ago, in a suburb far, far away . . .

In my opinion, there are three truly great philosophers: Aristotle, Confucius, and Yoda. I didn't know about Aristotle and Confucius until high school, but I grew up steeped in Yoda's ideology.

My education began at age seven, when my step-father, Dan, and my mother, Sunshine, took me to see *Star Wars*. The first of two life-altering events that year, it set off a chain reaction, the effects of which still alternately inspire and irk me. It's been twenty-five years, but my memory of the first time I watched *Star Wars* is more vivid than this morning's commute on the el.

Those scrolling white words. That riveting John Williams score. The blackness—the utter blackness—of space in the first shot. Suddenly *I* was part of that galaxy. *I* was on Princess Leia's rebel cruiser. I *was* Princess Leia.

In the real world, I was a geeky kid with glasses and crooked teeth, living in the Chicago suburbs. But during those two hours in *Star Wars* world, I was a princess—beautiful, witty, and poised. I was a rebel with a mission. I was part of the galaxy's last stand against the Evil Empire. I was—

"Rory? Rory! Are you listening to me?"

I blink, transported from saving the universe to saving room for dessert. Momentarily disoriented, I stare at the crowded dining area of Cosí on Michigan Avenue in downtown Chicago.

"Earth to Rory." The woman seated across from me, a titian-haired beauty who resembles a real-life princess, raises an annoyed brow.

"Sorry. I was daydreaming."

She snorts and digs into her salad, stabbing a cucumber with her plastic fork. "I'll just bet you were. And I know *who* you were dreaming about, too. I mean, of all the people to come walking into your office."

Hunter Chase. That's the second momentous event. On my first day of school, I tripped over a loose piece of carpet in Mrs. Allman's first-grade class. I went sprawling, my skirt over my head, my tin lunch box flung in a corner. All the kids howled, and I went beet red. But when I stood up, Hunter Chase handed me my lunch box. "You okay?" he said, and he wasn't laughing.

I fell in love. How could I not? But my adoration of Hunter was based on more than his kindness that day. He was one of those kids that teachers look at and say, "Now that kid is going to be someone."

In a classroom full of knobby-kneed, snotty-nosed, rambunctious seven-year-olds, Hunter Chase *shone.* Shone as brightly as the burst of light from the Death Star when it explodes in Episode IV, as brightly as the dual suns on Luke Skywalker's home planet, Tatooine. Like a tractor beam, his very essence drew me to him. Every day I waited for him in the back of the room, standing among the cubbies where we stored our lunches and the hooks where we hung our winter coats. When he walked in, my little heart beat faster, and I inevitably gravitated toward him.

Unfortunately, so did all the other kids. Five seconds after Hunter Chase arrived, a circle formed around him, shutting me out. As usual.

"So tell me again," Allison says now through a mouthful of salad. "What did you do when you saw him? Were you completely freaked out?"

That's the understatement of the millennium.

"I almost fell over. He was walking down the hall with Mr. Yates and some of the other account execs from Dougall Marketing, and when I saw him, I almost tripped over my feet."

That's not exactly true. I actually did trip over my feet, spilling hot French vanilla cappuccino all over my crisply pressed white Oxford button-down. I yelped when the coffee scalded me and slammed my leg into a file cabinet, snagging my pantyhose in the process. It was first grade all over again.

Hunter and Mr. Yates had glanced over at the commotion, but I didn't need my figurative lunch box handed to me a second time, so I'd ducked behind the file cabinet, hoping they wouldn't see me.

"You *almost* fell over, huh?" Allison says. Her eyes, trained by her years as an interior designer, assess me, taking in the rumpled jacket of the navy suit I've buttoned snugly over my stained white Oxford. "I think your reaction was a little stronger than that. You sounded like you were having an orgasm when you called me this morning."

"Allison!" I hiss, glancing around Cosí. "Keep your voice down, okay?" Creator! I hate it when people stare at me.

She picks up a breadstick and rolls her eyes. "Give me a break. No one here cares whether you have an orgasm or not." She grins, flashing perfect white teeth. "Well, except me. By the way . . . how long *has* it been since you've experienced *la petite mort?*"

"Not very long, for your information." I sit up straighter. "Just last night, in fact." Well, that's not exactly true, either, but there was the opportunity for an orgasm, so that pretty much counts.

Allison sits forward. "Ooh, *do* tell! Did you pick up some hunky mimbo at Bardo's, then drag him home and ravish him?"

Right. Like that would ever happen in Rory World. The guys who frequent bars like Bardo's don't go for girls with straight, limp hair, mud brown eyes, and a face that blends into the woodwork. "No," I tell her. "Tom came over. Tom. Remember him? My sort of boyfriend."

Allison sits back and picks at her lettuce. "I've actually been doing all I can to forget about Tedious Tom. God, Rory. How can you *stand* him?"

"Tom's not so bad," I mutter. I fumble for my veggie sandwich and take a small bite.

"Rory, he wears a pocket protector! I mean, he's like a bad caricature from *Revenge of the Nerds.*"

I put the sandwich on the plate and push it away. "In case you haven't noticed, Allison, *I'm* not exactly Princess Leia. Han Solo isn't knocking on my spaceship."

"Oh, please. You could do much better than Tedious Tom."

"I happen to *like* Tedi—" I glare at her. "*Tom.* He's a nice guy."

"Nice." Allison throws her fork into her salad bowl. "What you mean is *boring.* "

"No. Tom's not boring. In fact, we had a pretty exciting

night last night." I fold my arms, resting my elbows on the table.

"Oh, really?" Allison arches a brow. "So, tell me about this *exciting* night. Did he take you out to some kinky new sex club? Did you answer the door wearing spiked heels and nothing else?"

I reach out lazily and poke at the bread on my sandwich. "Not exactly," I mumble. Knowing Tom, if I greeted him wearing nothing but heels, he'd ask if I was cold and offer to get me a sweater.

"So? What then?" Allison asks.

I study the menu posted behind her.

"Did he take you to a romantic restaurant? Light candles all over the house and feed you grapes on a bed of rose petals? What?"

I stare at her. "Who the Dark Side are *you* dating?"

"Rory just answer the fuc—"

"Fine! There was no Don Juan routine. We'd planned to go out, but Tom got busy and came over kind of late so . . ."

Allison narrows her eyes. "He got busy? Doing what?" She raises a finger. "And, so help me God, Rory, if you say playing video games with his loser friends, I will hit you over the head with this breadstick."

I rub the bridge of my nose where my glasses pinch. I can feel a headache starting.

Allison slumps back in her chair. "Oh. My. God. That's it, isn't it? He got busy playing Pac-Man—"

"They don't play—"

She holds up a hand. "—or whatever games the nerds play now and forgot about you."

"He didn't forget. He was just late. And he was very sweet about it. He even brought me flowers."

Allison blinks, unimpressed. "What kind?"

"I don't remember."

"Yes, you do. What kind?"

"Carnations," I whisper.

"Jesus, Rory! You have got to be kidding! And you still slept with the guy?" she shouts.

"Will you *please* lower your voice? I told you, he was sorry, and the flowers were really very sweet." Well, they were wilted and turning brown, but the thought was sweet.

Allison runs an exasperated hand through her long curly locks. "I just don't understand it. I mean, is he that good in bed? No!" She waves frantically. "Don't answer that. I don't want any carnal images of Tedious Tom imprinted in my brain."

"Look, Allie," I say. "He's a nice guy, okay? He's not my dream man or anything, but this is real life, not a fairy tale. Sometimes you just have to settle for what you can get."

Allison shakes her head. "No."

"What do you mean, no?"

She pushes her plate to the side and leans over, palms flat on the table. "I mean, no. I'm not going to let you settle."

"I don't see as how you have any say in the matter. I like Tom. I'm content with Tom. I'm settling for Tom." I sit back, crossing my arms defiantly.

"No, you're not."

"Yes, I am."

"Nope." Allison shakes her head again. "You deserve romance. You deserve passion. You deserve . . ." She pauses dramatically, leaning forward. *"Hunter Chase."*

"Oh, yeah, right. Like Hunter Chase would ever be interested in *me*." Once he saw what a nerd I am, he'd sprint the other way.

"Girl, by the time we get done with you, Hunter Chase

is going to be falling all over himself just to be in the same room."

"What do you mean, 'by the time we're done with you'?" A shiver of apprehension runs down my spine.

Sitting back, Allison grins smugly, a queen on her throne. She picks up her scepter—a salad fork—and points it at me. "You, Rory, are going to get the man of your dreams."

A statement like that calls for dessert. Pushing our entrées aside, we reach for the good stuff—a huge chocolate chip cookie for me and a white chocolate macadamia nut cookie for her. Then we break our cookies in two and trade halves.

"So here's what you're going to do," Allison says after we've both savored our first bites of dessert.

"Eat this cookie and go home?"

"Sure. If you want to kiss your chance with Hunter good-bye. *Forever.*"

I narrow my eyes and take another bite. "All right. I'm listening."

"Finally. Tomorrow you implement Phase One. I'm calling that the Get Him to Notice You Phase."

"And this is Phase One of how many phases?"

"Four." Allison spots a waiter cleaning tables and waves him over. Cosí is a deli-type place. The staff dishes your food at the counter and leaves you alone. If I'd summoned him, he would have laughed, but, no surprise, when Allison crooks her finger the waiter rushes to our table. No one ignores Allison. She's gorgeous. And confident. And, on top of all that, smart.

I watch Allison run a slim, pale hand through her hair before ordering a vanilla latte. The waiter watches, too.

What I wouldn't give for Allison's hair. It's a heavy mass of red curls that falls to the middle of her back, while I'm cursed with a limp brown mop that resembles a wet cat in the Chicago summertime humidity. Luckily, it's still early March.

"Anything for you, Rory?" Allison asks. I shake my head, and the waiter promises to bring her latte right out. She smiles. What I wouldn't give for her perfectly straight teeth. Who am I kidding? With her looks, personality, and career, I'd trade places with Allison in a second. A nanosecond, if I'm being honest. It's always been this way. In junior high and high school she was one of the Popular Girls. I'm talking head cheerleader, homecoming queen, voted Most Beautiful. (Two guesses who Most Handsome was. That's right, Hunter himself.)

But despite all her good fortune, I've never been jealous of Allison. I've often wondered why she, being who she is—beautiful, popular, and sought after—wanted to be friends with me, being who I am—plain, nerdy, and a social failure. I asked her once in ninth grade, and she gave me this look like I was crazy. "Who *wouldn't* want to be friends with you, Rory? I mean, you're smart and funny."

"Funny?" I said.

"Yeah. In a quirky sort of way."

"Great."

She put her arm around me. "Rory, the reason you're my best friend is because, unlike most people I know, you're really my friend. You don't make up stuff about me or say one thing and mean another. I don't know many people like that."

I realized then, and now, that I could say the same about Allie. She is who she is. She doesn't play games and pretend that she's not beautiful and sought after, but she's not stuck up about it, either. Allison is the kind of person who doesn't have anything to prove—to herself or anyone else. She dates when she feels like it, stays in when she doesn't.

She was engaged for six months to a great guy—rich, handsome, charming—then broke it off because she wasn't ready for marriage. As far as I can tell, she's never regretted the decision or looked back. I admire that in Allison. She's not afraid to take a risk. I would have been terrified of ending up alone, of never finding another guy as great as that one. Another guy, period.

The waiter walks away, and Allison turns back to me. "Then, after Phase One is in full swing, we move on to Phase Two. I call it Proximity."

"And the last two phases?" I ask, humoring her. Obviously with a job like hers, she tends to think of projects in phases, and I suppose this plan to snag Hunter is her new personal project.

"Phase Three is the Nostalgia Phase—I'll talk more about that later—then Phase Four is the biggie. That phase we implement on Reunion Day—Lincoln High School, Class of 1990's fifteen-year reunion. The day we've been looking forward to our whole lives."

I laugh. "More like dreading the last five years. I was a complete klutz at the ten-year reunion."

"Well, that's not going to happen this time. This reunion is going to be Rory Egglehoff's big night. The night Hunter, your dream date, sweeps you off your feet." She leans back to allow the waiter to set down her latte.

"*He* sweeps me off *my* feet? There's a lot of prep work."

Allie waves her hand and blows on her coffee. "Of course, but *he* won't see that. He'll think he fell effortlessly in love with you. Then, after you have him, you can relax—" She gives me a sharp glance over the rim of her mug. "Well, relax *somewhat,* and let *him* do all the work."

"Sounds too good to be true. What if it doesn't work? What if he shows up at the reunion with a date? What if he doesn't go? What if I trip and go sprawling in front of everyone like last time?"

"You won't," Allison assures me. "I promise, everything is going to be perfect."

"Maybe if you were the one who's supposed to carry this off, but we're talking about me here. Truthfully, what are the odds of this working?" I know I shouldn't ask. It can't be good, but I let Allison conjecture for me anyway.

Allison's red hair spills over her shoulder as she cocks her head to the side and considers. "Well, if you really go for it . . ." She gives me a narrow, relentless look. "I mean, go all out, starting with Phase One—clothes, hair, makeup—I think your chances are pretty good. Maybe . . ." She taps her finger to her chin. "Sixty percent chance of success?"

I crumple, inside and out. "That's a forty percent chance of failure. Anyone with half an ounce of business sense would tell you this venture's too high-risk."

Alison nods. "Yep. But what you, as an investor, need to decide is: Is the payoff worth it?"

Two days later, it's time to put what I've dubbed the Ultimate Jedi Plan into action. After raiding Allison's closet and submitting myself to the tortures of the straightening iron and the eyelash curler, I'm finally ready.

Sort of.

"Blast it!" I hiss as my hand collides with the paper coffee cup.

"What's wrong? Did he walk by again?" Allison asks on

the other end of the line. I'm attempting to balance the phone on my shoulder while simultaneously mopping up the spreading coffee with a wad of Kleenex and rescuing my new HP 12-C financial calculator from a soggy demise.

"No." I snatch a file just as the river of cappuccino threatens it. "I spilled my coffee again."

"Jeez, Rory. Calm down."

"I'm *trying*, but he's in the office next door. *Next door*, Allison." I toss the wad of wet Kleenex in the trash, miss, and have to pick it up and do it again. I plop back in my chair. My heart is pounding and my hands are shaking worse than if I'd downed three double espressos instead of a small French vanilla cappuccino. Make that *half* a small cappuccino.

"Okay, take a deep breath. You sound like you're going to hyperventilate."

I suck in air and focus on exhaling slowly. "Hoh-purrh. Hoh-purrh." I sound like Darth Vader making a prank call.

"Are you breathing?" Allison asks.

I nod. "Hoh-purrh. Hoh-purrh."

"Rory? Are you all right? What's that sound?"

"It's me breathing," I say.

"Take it down a notch. You're scaring me.

"Hoh-purrh. Sorry. Hoh-purrh."

"Stop freaking out, okay? Now's your chance to put the plan into action."

I shut my eyes and rub my throbbing temples. "Allison, will you stop with the stupid plan already? I mean, I can't even be in the room next to Hun—" I shift my glance to the open door and lower my voice. "Hunter Chase," I whisper, "without suffering heart palpitations."

"Obviously, you're going to have to get over that."

I roll my eyes. "Right. It'd be easier to make the jump to

light speed with a damaged hyperdrive than to remain calm around Hun—*him.* "

"You know," Allison says, sounding contemplative, "this is one time I think a *Star Wars* comparison is appropriate."

I almost drop the phone. "Really?"

Allison hates my constant references to *Star Wars.* She's had to put up with them since second grade, so I can hardly blame her. One of the shakiest moments in the early years of our friendship was when she confessed that, though she liked *Star Wars* and thought Luke Skywalker was cute, the movie didn't have enough kissing. I forgave her for that slight because Sunshine told me that everyone has to make compromises sometimes, then pointed out that Allison—and my whole family, she'd muttered—had to compromise by putting up with my *Star Wars* obsession.

"Think about Luke Skywalker," Allison says. "Remember when he was in warrior training with the little green Muppet?"

"Yoda. And he's a *Jedi Master.* " Little green Muppet! Some people have no respect.

"Whatever. Anyway, remember the part when Luke had to go into that dark slimy cave?"

"Yeah." I don't like where this is going.

"Well, don't you think Luke was scared to go into that cave? Remember how he brought his light thingy—?"

"Saber. Lightsaber," I correct automatically.

"Yeah, he brought his *lightsaber* in with him even though the green dude told him he wouldn't need it."

"Well, I'd want my lightsaber, too, if I had to go into a cave and face the Dark Side of the Force! It's not like Luke was weak or anything."

"Rory!" Allison yells, exasperated. "Shut up and pay attention, okay? I have to get back to these fabric swatches, and I'm meeting with a client in twenty minutes."

"Sorry," I mumble, but I don't mean it. Allison should know better than to disparage Luke.

"Anyway, Luke was scared to go into the cave, right? But he went in anyway, didn't he?"

I fiddle with the phone cord. "Yeah. He went in anyway."

"Why?"

I sigh. "Because he had to."

"Why?"

This feels like elementary school. "Allison—"

"*Why,* Rory?"

"Because he wanted to be a Jedi knight and that was part of the training."

"Right. And he must have wanted it pretty bad to go into that cave and live on that gross planet—"

"Dagobah."

"What*ever!* Anyway, my point is—are you listening?"

"Hmm-mmm."

"My point is that sometimes when we want something, when it's really important, we have to do things we don't want to."

I tap my fingers on my desk and stare down at my blunt-cut fingernails. I had a feeling that was her point.

"If Luke could go into that cave and face the black side of the force—or whatever it was—*you* can walk down the hall and say hello to Hunter Chase."

Blast it. She's right—again. What am I so afraid of? Hunter Chase has nothing on the Dark Side of the Force.

"Fine," I say. "I'll do it."

"Yes!" Allison screams, and I can almost see her arm pumping in the air. "And remember what we talked about?

n is to titillate Hunter, just give him a glimpse of the sexy Rory Egglehoff."

"The new sexy Rory Egglehoff?" Who is *she* talking about?

"Right! Hook him today, and then reel him in. By R Day, we'll have him right where we want him. He'll be begging you to be his date to the reunion."

I smile, picturing Hunter *begging* me to be his date. Hunter giving me flowers. Hunter opening the car door for me. Hunter on one knee before me . . . Creator! For a moment Allison even got *me* caught up in the fantasy.

"Allison, this is never going to work—" I begin, slamming myself back to reality.

"Rory! Attitude is everything. Remember Luke."

Remember Luke. Remember Luke, I chant, still gripping the phone cord.

"Now get up."

I stand.

"Square your shoulders and march into that office."

My shoulders slump and my stomach tenses. Remember Luke.

"Are you with me, Rory?"

"I'm with you." But my voice squeaks on the last word.

"Good. Then hang up the phone and go."

I nod, but just as I'm about to replace the phone on the receiver, I hear Allison call my name. "Rory? One more thing. Put on some lipstick before you go in there, okay? And maybe a powder. Do you still have that Bobbi Brown blush I got you?"

I sink down in my chair. I've got a bad feeling about this.

Chapter 2

*Ten minutes later, powdered, lipsticked, and contact-*lensed, I'm flattened against the wall between my office and Mr. Yates's, trying not to hyperventilate.

Remember Luke. Remember Luke. Remember the Alamo.

Blast it! Where did *that* come from? Think positive. I look good, wearing a short gray skirt and cashmere sweater I bought for a hot date that fizzled and black designer boots Allison loaned me. The high heels click with authority when I walk. I *am* the new elegant, sophisticated Rory. Then I notice the inkstain on my jacket, and I remember something else that happened when Luke was training on Dagobah. He went into the cave and when he was face to face with Darth Vader, he saw his own face under Vader's mask.

I shudder. Who am I kidding? I'm not Luke Skywalker. I'm C-3PO—awkward, rigid, and scared of everything.

Forget this. But before I lurch back to my office, Mr. Yates and Hunter—oh, Creator, he's gorgeous—step into the hallway.

"Rory," Mr. Yates says, spotting me immediately. "How are you?"

I swallow. My throat is suddenly as dry as the desert of Tatooine. I can't speak. I can't move. I can't do anything but stare at Hunter Chase. With his dark curly hair, sapphire eyes, and lean, athletic body, he puts Han Solo to shame. Then, like Han would to Princess Leia, Hunter gives me a cocky grin.

My heart jumps in my chest, slamming against my rib cage so hard I swear I feel a rib crack.

"Rory, did you need something?" Mr. Yates asks. My heart's beating so hard, the sound mutes his voice, giving it an underwater quality.

"Wh-what?"

"Did you need to see me?"

I pry my eyes from Hunter and stare blankly at Mr. Yates. "Y-yes," I stammer. My mouth feels like it's been injected with Novocain.

He raises his bushy salt-and-pepper brows expectantly and prods, "What did you need?" His eyes drop to my empty hands.

Blast it! What was I thinking? I've brought no files with me, and now my mind is a complete blank. I can think of nothing—absolutely *nothing*—to ask Mr. Yates. In fact, all I *can* think is that Hunter Chase is standing three feet away from me, smiling his sexy smile at me. *Me!*

"Do you two know each other?" Mr. Yates asks, looking from me to Hunter.

"No," Hunter says at the same time I answer, "Yes."

Mr. Yates chuckles. "So which is it? Yes or no?"

I peek at Hunter and see that the sexy grin is gone, and he's scrutinizing me. I clear my parched throat. "Yes. We—

we—" My breath deserts me, and I suck in more air before continuing. "We went to school together."

"Wonderful!" Mr. Yates says, folding his hands over the jolly belly straining against his navy suit jacket. He looks at Hunter. "Did you go to college together or do you go way back?"

Since Mr. Yates is looking at Hunter, I do, too. But Hunter—horror of horrors—is looking at *me.* He's staring, brow furrowed in confusion because, obviously, he doesn't remember me.

The cappuccino churns in my belly. This is worse than seeing Darth Vader in the cave. Worse than Darth Vader wearing *my* face. *Why* did I listen to Allison? I knew this was going to be a disaster!

I feel sweat break out between my breasts and on the small of my back. It trickles down my skin in icy rivulets. At the same time, my face heats, and the contrast makes me even more nauseous. My desiccated throat burns with acid. Swallowing the rising bile, I answer, "We went to high school together."

Hunter frowns and looks at me more closely. "You went to Lincoln? What was your name again?"

"Rory," I mumble.

"Rory . . . Rory." He runs a hand through that thick dark hair, then glances at Mr. Yates and shakes his head.

"You don't remember Rory?" Mr. Yates bellows, and I cringe at how his voice carries. "How could you forget our Rory? Rory Egglehoff—best accountant at Y and Y."

I start, surprised by the compliment. But I'm distracted when Hunter's face breaks into a dazzling grin, showing off straight white teeth that, unlike mine, have never known the feel of braces. "Egglehoff? Were you in my first-grade class?"

Mr. Yates glances at me and, like C-3PO's mute cousin, I nod again. Could whoever's programming my hard drive please give me some lines?

"Wonderful! Wonderful!" Mr. Yates says. "Chase here is an account executive at Dougall. We're going to be working very closely in the next few weeks to set up a stellar ad campaign. The guys at Dougall promise me that once the public sees their work, we're going to be swamped with clients."

Hunter nods confidently. "Good news for you, huh Rory?"

I nod again. What is wrong with me? Why can't I speak? Mr. Yates gives me his "win one for the Gipper" look. "Keep your nose to the grindstone, Rory." He unclasps his hands and begins to move away. I try desperately to think of something, *anything*, to make up for this mortifying start.

I was supposed to hook Hunter. Intrigue him with the sexy, grown-up Rory Egglehoff, then reel him in. Instead, Hunter's swimming away. Allison will kill me if I let him go.

Remember Luke. No. Not Luke. Be . . . Princess Leia. Yes!

"See you later, Hunter," I cringe. Lame. *So* lame.

Surprisingly, Hunter turns back. "Good to see you again, Rory Egglehoff." He flashes me a grin. "You sure have changed."

"Then—and you are not going to believe this, Allie—he looked me up and down."

"He did *what?*" I hold the phone away from my ringing ear.

When her squealing dies down, I say, "He ran those impossibly blue eyes *all over* my body."

"Ooh," Allison coos. "Did it make you hot?"

I laugh. "Hardly. I blushed and ran into my office."

"Rory!"

"I know." I snuggle into my couch cushions. Nothing Allison says tonight can extinguish the warm, cozy feeling zinging through me. Hunter's perusal made me feel . . . I tap my fingers on the yearbook beside me and glance at Hunter's picture on the open page.

It made me feel . . . Beautiful? Desirable? Like Princess Leia. Well, maybe not *that* great, but like a woman, not a nerd. An attractive woman.

Allison's still oohing and ahhing, but I cut her off. "Allison, I have to go. Tom's going to be here in—" I glance at the clock on my DVD player. "Fifteen minutes."

"Tom?" Allison says. "Tom? Why the hell is he coming over? What about Hunter?"

I sigh. "He gave me a *look,* Allison. That's it. Tom and I have a chance at a relationship."

"Yeah, if you don't mind dating a dork."

"He doesn't mind dating a nerd, so I guess we're even."

I hang up, then pull the yearbook into my lap. Junior year at Abraham Lincoln High School. I loved that year. Doesn't everyone? You're old enough to drive, stay out late, and earn a paycheck, but not quite to the point where you have to stress about colleges and SAT scores.

Not that I didn't stress. I wouldn't be Roberta Joplin Egglehoff if I didn't stress, but during junior year, college is still sort of a fantasy. It's something golden and beautiful in the future. I flip through the yearbook looking for familiar pictures. There's Allison with the rest of the varsity cheerleaders. My sister, Stormy, at the PETA table in the cafeteria. My friends Dora and Sam from Science Club at one of our competitions. And then there's me with the rest of the math honor society, Mu Alpha Theta. I was vice president that year.

The next dozen or so pages are the sports teams. We had everything: football, baseball, softball, basketball, soccer, tennis . . . I didn't play any of them. Hunter Chase played just about all of them. There's Hunter with the varsity football team. He was the quarterback, which, I understand is something of an accomplishment for a junior. There's Hunter with the baseball team. I love him in that baseball hat.

I smile and run my hand over another picture. He looks so young, his grin more boyishly appealing than sexy. But I'd thought he was sexy. I went to every basketball game that year—okay, not away games, you can only take a crush so far—to see Hunter Chase run around in shorts.

I flip a few more pages and reach the section with the individual pictures. The Cs are on the third page, and there's Hunter. Hunter Zachary Chase. The picture's in black and white, but I remember Hunter wore a blue shirt that day. It was my favorite because it made his sapphire eyes appear turquoise.

Our English teacher, Mrs. Morton, had taken us to the auditorium for picture day. After I was done, instead of going to sit in the seats with the rest of my friends, I hung around the photographer, standing in the shadows and waiting for Hunter's turn. He wasn't in my class that year, but he had English the same period, and his class had come down with ours.

He stood in line, laughing and joking with his friends—other popular jocks with names like Chaz, Cody, and Mitch. They were goofing around, like guys that age do, and the cheerleaders and drill team girls in front of them were pretending to ignore them, all the while tossing their hair and probably praying one of the guys would start teasing *them*.

But when it was Hunter's turn, when he stepped away from his friends and the girls, when he sat on that little black stool, the hazy blue background behind him, I saw something I'd never seen before. I think it was something few people outside of Hunter's family had ever seen.

Cody went before Hunter. He was always a total spaz, and right when the photographer took the picture, he puffed up his lips and crossed his eyes. The photographer yelled at him, but Cody laughed it off, walked away, giving his buds a thumbs-up.

So, when Hunter sat down, the first thing the photographer said was, "I hope you're not a knucklehead like your buddy." He shoved a black rectangle into the camera. "Your mom is paying for these pictures, and she wants something to send to your grandma and grandpa."

Hunter had been sort of grinning up until that point, maybe still laughing at Cody's joke, maybe thinking about how he could top it, but when the photographer mentioned his mom, Hunter's grin vanished. It wasn't a big mystery why. Everyone knew Hunter's mother left his father when we were in sixth grade. She went to California or Aruba or something because, as the rumor went, she "just wasn't cut out to be a mother and a wife." Everyone at LHS knew Hunter's mom hadn't wanted him. Everyone but the photographer.

"You understand what I'm saying, young man?" the photographer asked, positioning the camera.

"Yes, sir," Hunter had answered. All amusement drained from his eyes. Then he squared his shoulders, set his jaw, and looked directly into the camera's lens.

"Are you going to smile?" the photographer asked.

"No," Hunter said.

The photographer nodded and snapped the picture.

I'm looking at the picture now, and the look in Hunter's eyes has the exact same effect on me as it did then. It makes me shiver because the pain in Hunter's eyes is so visible, so *raw.* He looks incredibly vulnerable, like a little boy, and yet so old, ancient almost. It's the look of a man, not an adolescent. The look of someone who has suffered loss and come through to the other side. The look of someone who is determined to succeed, to make his life mean something.

And now I know why I've pulled out this particular yearbook. Today when I saw Hunter at Yates and Youngman, I saw the manifestation of this picture. I saw the man I'd only glimpsed in Hunter on picture day.

And that was the Hunter that turned my childhood crush into love.

Chapter 3

I'm still staring at Hunter's picture in the yearbook when the intercom buzzes. Blast it! Tom.

I glance at my clock and see that, for once, Tom is on time. Tonight I wish he were late. I'm not quite ready to put my memories of Hunter away. Closing the yearbook, I stand, check my new skirt and sweater for wrinkles, and stroll to the door to buzz him in. All day I've felt like a real-life princess, and now I straighten my shoulders and smooth my hair to preserve the magical feeling. Even the Y&Y offices had a fairy-tale aura about them today. Amazing how a few words and a look from the right man makes everything from your stapler to your salad fork seem enchanted.

I didn't duck my head or hunch my shoulders when I walked the halls today. I even had the courage to forgo the granola bar and package of almond M&M's I usually scarf in front of my computer screen to brave the cafeteria. I'm pretty proud of myself, too. I had a salad and fruit—*so* healthy—and was daring enough to join a table of my coworkers, even though I didn't know any of them very well.

So, buoyed by the successes of the day, I stopped in a boutique I always pass on the walk home. The skirt and sweater displayed in the window the last few days was fabulous—sophisticated, with just the right mix of fun and flirty. It's the kind of outfit I lust after but am always too much of a coward to buy.

But not today.

Today I marched into that boutique, found my size, and plunked down my credit card. I didn't even wince much when I heard the total. It's criminal to charge that much for an outfit—but it's worth the price to look as good as I feel. Tom is going to fall over when I open the door.

I pause a moment longer, seized by the grip of panic. I hope this outfit is okay. I'm not sure where Tom's taking me. Creator, I hope he's not in a suit or something. With a last deep breath, I unlock the door and fling it open. "Hey!"

"OMG." Tom pushes past me, cell phone attached to his ear. "OMG! This I have to see. Just give me a minute." He pulls the phone from his ear and rounds on me. I'm standing abandoned in the half-open door, staring at him.

"Rory, I need to use your computer. Like now. This is an emergency."

"Uh, okay." Tom barely waits for my reply before putting the cell to his ear again and striding into my room. I close the door and follow in time to see him click the mouse furiously and start searching the Internet.

I watch him, alternately amused and annoyed. But mostly annoyed. He's hunched over the keyboard, cell phone balanced on his shoulder, fingers typing and clicking with rapid-fire speed, the brown eyes behind his wire-rimmed glasses intent on the screen. I glance down at my new outfit. I don't know why I even try. As usual, Tom's wearing beat-up Converse sneakers, jeans that end above his ankles, and a T-shirt. This one reads: "Accountants Do It with Form (1099)." At least he can't wear the pocket protector with a T-shirt, I think, and then frown. What do I care if Tom wears a pocket protector?

Still, it would have been nice if Tom had at least shaved or brushed his hair. Patches of stubble dot his face, and his hair is going seven different directions. I look closer, wondering when he last remembered to wash it.

"Yeah, yeah, I see it," Tom says into the phone. "No, this is unreal, man."

I peer over Tom's shoulder and see that he's logged into an online interactive game he likes to play with his friends. He's moving a muscled warrior through a forest and directing the character to shoot wolves.

Thank the Creator Stormy isn't here to see this. She'd have PETA here with protest signs, a media frenzy, and virtual reality bloodied fur coats before you could say, "Save the Computer-Generated Wolves."

"Uh, Tom?" I say.

No response, just more furious typing. As a last-ditch effort, I send him telepathic messages. Look at my new outfit, Tom. Look. *Look.* "Tom? How long do you think—"

He waves a hand. "Shh. I'll be off in a minute. This is the crucial level."

I bite back a retort, and he half turns in the chair. "Five minutes, babe."

I narrow my eyes. I think we all know what five minutes really means.

"I promise," Tom says imploringly. "This really is an emergency."

An emergency? I slide my heels off and pad back into

the living room. Since when did computer games rate as emergencies?

Sighing, I plop on the couch. I suppose everyone makes compromises in relationships. Though after only four months, it seems a little early to be making so many. I turn on the TV and flip through the channels. Nothing but reality TV shows are on, so I hit play to start the DVD.

The swirling snow of the planet Hoth mists my screen as the Empire's gigantic and seemingly indestructible Walkers attack the hopelessly outgunned rebels.

The Empire Strikes Back. I love this movie. Of the original trilogy, it's my favorite, probably because it's the most romantic. I love the repartee between Han and Leia. So many snappy comebacks, so many great lines.

My favorite scene is later in the movie when they're alone on the *Millennium Falcon*. In a moment of tenderness, Han takes Leia's hand. She's trembling, and he—arrogant, gorgeous man that he is—knows it's because of him. Predictably, she denies it, calling him a scoundrel. Then Han sort of murmur-whispers that he thinks she *likes* scoundrels. Ooh, I shiver just thinking about it!

On the screen now, Luke's speeder crashed and an Imperial Walker looms ominously. I frown. *What* is Tom doing?

"Tom? I'm getting hungry." I look down at my skirt and sweater. Might as well forget it. "Want me to call and order a pizza?"

There's a long pause, and I'm about to ask again, when he finally answers, "No. I'm going to take you out. Just give me two more minutes."

I roll my eyes and reach for the afghan draped on the arm of the couch, dragging it over my cold toes.

When Tom finally emerges, Han is being lowered into

the carbon freeze pit. Leia's face is burnished by pain and the orange lights of the ominous chamber. Chewbacca howls in protest, and I swipe a trickle of wetness from my eye.

"Hey, babe. What'cha doing?" Tom lopes into the living room, shoving his cell phone into his jeans pocket.

"I'm Rory, not babe, and I'm watching a DVD." I hit pause.

He smiles knowingly. "*ESB* again?"

I grin back. "Yeah."

"Hey, that reminds me. The tickets for the extravaganza go on sale tomorrow. You're still going, right? If not, I need to let Grant know so he can fill your spot in the costume show."

I pull the afghan tighter around me. "I don't know, Tom. I'll feel stupid. I hate parading around in front of people."

"Oh, come on, babe. Grant is counting on you."

I groan. I am such a pushover sometimes. One little guilt trip, and I cave completely. "But it's the same day as my high school reunion."

"The extravaganza will be over by five. We'll have loads of time to make the reunion."

We? *We?* I don't remember asking Tom to go to the reunion with me. That—if Allison's Ultimate Jedi Plan works—will be Hunter's job. I don't mind going to the Second Annual Creatures and Features Sci-Fi Extravaganza with Tom. I don't even mind playing Princess Leia in the costume show, but I'm not sure I want Tom as my date to the reunion.

It might not be a bad idea to hold Tom in reserve. If, for some reason, the Ultimate Jedi Plan doesn't pan out, I may need a date. I can decide later if a bad date is better than no date.

"Well, if you aren't going to go," Tom continues in a

whiny voice, "you should be the one to tell Grant he has to start scrambling to find another Leia."

I sit up in mock indignation. "*Another* Princess Leia? Who can play Princess Leia better than me?"

"Carrie Fisher."

I roll my eyes. Tom has no sense of humor. "Besides her, Tom."

He glances at his watch. "Hey, it's a little late on a week night to go out. How about that pizza?"

I look at my watch: 8:49. Tom had been playing that stupid computer game for over an hour. He pulls out his cell phone again. "Pepperoni and mushrooms sound good?"

I grimace. Why can't he ever remember that I don't eat meat? I'm not a fanatic about it, but I do take it seriously. Not as seriously as Stormy and Sunshine, but I try to do my part for animal rights and the environment. Tom should know this.

Before I can "gently" remind him, he's on the phone with Domino's. "Yeah, a large pepperoni with mushrooms, breadsticks, and a six-pack of Coke. Okay, Pepsi. Whatever."

"Tom, I don't want pepperoni. You know I don't eat meat."

He stares at me, a Gomer Pyle expression on his face. "Hold on a sec, okay?" he says into the phone. "What's that, babe?"

Babe. I hate that.

"I don't want pepperoni," I repeat. "I don't eat meat, *dude,* remember?"

He frowns as if the memory is annoying. "Hey," he says into the phone again. "Can you make that half pepperoni and mushroom and half just mushroom? Yeah. *Vegetarians.*" He shakes his head.

While Tom gives the delivery guy my address, I go to the

bathroom and exchange my skirt and sweater for jeans and my old Northwestern sweatshirt. I look in the mirror and dab on some lipstick, but I don't know why I'm bothering. Tom didn't even look at me tonight. Through the door, I hear him asking the total, and a shaft of annoyance spears me.

Is this the best I can do? Is this all there is? Hunter the Unattainable or Tom the Tedious? And yet tonight, Tom isn't even tedious, he's rude. I throw the container of lipstick into the sink. Thinking back, I can't recall the last time we even went out. All we ever do is watch DVDs, get takeout, or go to Grant's, and I spend an evening watching them play computer games.

Maybe Allison is right. Maybe I need to ditch Tom.

"Hey, Rory!" Tom calls. "Get out here. It's the best part! Luke's about to get his hand lopped off."

I shake my head and open the door. On the other hand, where am I going to find a guy who appreciates fine films this much?

It's 1:07 A.M., and Tom's snoring keeps me awake. Why did I agree to let him stay over? I'm never going to get any sleep.

I slink out of bed, grab my old terry-cloth robe, and wrapping it around my naked body, tiptoe to the kitchen. Methodically I pick up the pizza boxes and pop cans, shoving them all in the recycling bin. Then I turn on the faucet. I have a dishwasher, but sometimes cleaning can be therapeutic, and I need some serious cleaning therapy tonight. That was the worst sex ever. And I mean *ever.* Maybe the worst in the history of mankind—or humankind, as Sunshine would say.

Despite the picture I've tried to paint for Allison, sex

with Tom has never been great. Okay, it's never even been good. Not that we've been at it for a long time. We've been seeing each other four months but didn't go to bed together until about a month ago. Tom and I had actually known each other for a year and a half when we started dating. He's also a CPA at Yates and Youngman but was hired the year before me. We got to know each other when we were assigned to work together on an account.

I wish there was some romantic story behind how Tom and I started dating—something to tell our kids, if we ever get that far—but, like the rest of our relationship, it was less than stellar. We'd been putting in long hours, eating and practically sleeping at the office, and when the project was complete, we just kept seeing each other.

It was all very laid back and relaxed. No big declarations. No roses and champagne. No frills. Kind of like Tom.

Kind of like Tom in bed.

Now, I've never been one of those women who expect the earth's tectonic plates to shift during sex. I don't expect extinct volcanoes to erupt, mountain ranges to burst from the plains, or seas to rise from the desert, but I do expect the occasional orgasm. Notice I say *occasional.* I'm not demanding. I just think I should get some satisfaction on occasion. Say, the best three out of five?

Is that really too much to ask?

Apparently, because Tom's batting zero for about twelve.

After the pizza came and we finished watching *ESB,* I figured Tom would go home and I'd go to bed. It's Wednesday night, and we both have to work tomorrow. Tom had other ideas. He reached for the remote before I did and flipped the channel to the FX station. A rerun of *The X-Files* was on. Normally I love *The X-Files.* I might have even watched it after Tom left, but it annoyed me that he just assumed control of my remote.

He assumed as well that I wanted him to stay.

Scully was stewing over another of Mulder's crazy ideas, and I was stewing over Tom's behavior, when I heard him yawn and felt his hand on my shoulder. I gave him a sidelong look. Please tell me he didn't just use a junior high move to put his arm around me. Please tell me he's further along in sexual etiquette than to resort to the old yawn and stretch.

I glanced at him, and he smiled down at me. I think the smile was supposed to be sexy, but it came off as more of a leer. I turned back to the TV. A few minutes later, his hand started caressing my shoulder then moved to my neck. It was a nice feeling, and I sort of loosened up.

I knew what he wanted, and when, during the commercial break, he kissed me—or rather slobbered all over me—I didn't say no. Looking at Tom and his perpetually chapped lips, you wouldn't think he's a wet kisser, but he is. One of the wettest. I mean, sometimes when we're kissing, the saliva runs down my chin. Okay, it's not that bad. But I swear on at least one occasion I've had to catch the drool with my finger and wipe it away.

Short of saying, "What's with the water fountain in your mouth?" I've tried to fix this problem through every subtle method I know. I've varied the way I kiss, pulled away when he got too sloppy, whispered to him to take things slowly. So far nothing has worked.

So, a few minutes later, with *The X-Files* theme in the background, I'm once again wiping spit off my chin. Now that he's spread his spit over me, I guess Tom feels like it's time to move on to other pursuits. I don't even need all my fingers and toes to count the number of times we've done it, but already I have Tom's "moves" memorized. If there was a cheat sheet, this is how it would read:

1. Slobber all over face.
2. Slobber on neck. But not enough to make her feel anything.
3. Grab boob and push it around.
4. Push shirt up, fumble with bra, slobber over boobs.
5. Unbutton your pants and put her hand inside.
6. Breathe hard and say something like, "Oh, yeah."
7. Take off her pants (or lift skirt). Fumble with panties.
8. Put on condom.
9. Push your willy (his word, not mine) around down there until she finally helps you get it in.
10. Thrust three times, freeze, shudder, and collapse.

There you go. Tom's Guide to the Ultimate Sexual Experience.

And now at 1:23 A.M., I wonder why I'm putting up with it. In the beginning I could have claimed I thought things would get better. That Tom and I just hadn't established our rhythm, hadn't perfected our technique. But if twelve times isn't the charm, nothing is.

I have to accept that there's no hope for this relationship. It's going to be carnations, sweatpants, take-out pizza, and prom night sex from here to the end.

Blast it. Allison was right. Tom is a Wookiee.

"I told you, didn't I?" Allison says, taking a sip of her appletini. We're at her favorite bar, a trendy place in Lincoln

Park, sipping expensive drinks and eating cheap appetizers. "I told you he was a dork."

"Dorks I can live with," I say, leaning my chin on my hand and poking the congealing cheese on the potato skins in the basket between us. "Wookiees, I cannot."

"Dork. Wookiee. Same thing."

"Not really."

Two girls in short black skirts and tops baring one shoulder stop near our table to gab. I raise my voice and lean toward Allison. "A dork may be socially inept, but he can be sweet and attentive. He can bring you flowers and take you out for romantic dinners, moonlit walks, picnics—"

"Whoa!" Allison pushes my mojito to the far side of the table. "I think the alcohol may have affected your brain. You're going into fantasy mode."

"Okay," I say grudgingly. "That might be overdoing it a bit, but my point is that a dork can still be a Jedi Knight."

"Your knight in shining armor."

The girls standing next to us erupt into giggles and grab hold of each other. Their movements shake the table, and I reach for my drink to steady it. "Right," I say to Allison. She flashes the gigglers an annoyed look, but they don't notice. I wonder how they can manage to stand there and talk, looking like they're having the time of their lives, when they must be freezing their asses—partly visible at the hems of the short skirts—off. Even dressed in the navy wool crepe suit I wore to work, I'm a little chilly.

"So what makes a Wookiee a Wookiee exactly?" Allison polishes off her appletini and runs a finger along the rim.

"Allie, I have told you this a million times. Don't you pay *any* attention to me?"

She grins. "Of course I do. Just not when you talk that spaceship stuff."

"This isn't just *Star Wars* stuff." I give her a stern look. "This is a life strategy. This is a relationship metaphor, so pay attention."

"A metaphor?" She picks up a potato skin and pulls off a string of cheddar cheese. "I may need more than over-cooked potato and greasy cheese to get through this." She takes a bite, then a deep breath. "All right, I'm listening. Enlighten me, oh Master Rory." She nods her head in mock obeisance and I frown, but I can't hold my smile back for long. The half-naked girls finally spot some male targets and move away, so I'm free to deliver my instruction in peace.

"A Wookiee is a loser. A follower. A—a—"

"A slacker," Allison adds through a mouthful of potato.

"Right." Sorry Chewbacca. I love him and his loyalty to Han, but he's got no goals of his own. And all that hair and howling—he'd make a terrible boyfriend. "A Wookiee has no initiative. He's not going anywhere. He might be thirty-five, but emotionally he's stuck at thirteen. He's got no depth."

"And he doesn't know how to treat a woman," Allison says, putting the half-eaten potato skin on her napkin and warming to the subject. "He brings you Russell Stover instead of Godiva, takes you to White Castle, not Morton's—"

I shake my head. "That stuff is just superficial. Where you go to eat isn't important. A Jedi treats you like you're the most important person in the world. When he looks at you, you know he really sees *you*. It would be great if he did all that romantic stuff, but even if you were sitting in a booth at Big Boy, you'd have a great time because you'd be with him. He makes you feel special."

A Jedi knight, like a knight in a fairy tale, is wise and brave and good. He's strong and powerful with fathoms of depth. Definite boyfriend material. "A Wookiee appears to be a Jedi at the beginning of your relationship, but pretty soon his lightsaber is gone and you're stuck with a lot of hair and grunting."

Allison is staring at me. "Yeah, I know what you mean. It's like opening the shipment of art deco pillows you ordered and pulling out plaid ones instead."

"Right," I say. "But let's not mix metaphors, okay?"

Allison has this thing about plaid. One of her first design jobs was for a wealthy Scotsman, and he insisted his entire house be done in plaid. Allison claims she's still haunted by flashbacks of crisscrossed wool.

"So, Rory, if you believe all this stuff about Wookiees and Jedis," she says finally, "why go out with Tedious Tom? I mean, it must have been pretty obvious he wasn't your dream man."

I shrug. It probably *would* have been obvious to Allison and probably *should* have been to me, but it wasn't. A classic case of trying to turn a Wookiee into a Jedi, or—as Allison would say—a plaid into a paisley.

I reach for the last potato skin. "I don't know. I guess I was just feeling like maybe there *aren't* any Jedis left in the dating universe. I'm thirty-two, ready to settle down, and all I have to choose from are Wookiees." I take a bite of the potato skin. "Tom seemed like the best of the bunch—or do Wookiees run in herds?"

Allison leans back and studies me. "I can't believe you, of all people, would fall for that tired myth, Rory. It must be that left-brained thinking you do all day. It's warped you."

"Thanks," I mumble, sucking the grease from my fingers, then picking up a napkin. "I knew I could count on you."

"You *can* count on me. I came up with the plan, and I think it's time to ratchet it up," she says, eyeing my suit.

I narrow my eyes. "Ratchet it up?"

"Yep." She nods, and her dainty silver earrings flash in the dim lights. "Finish your drink. We have to stock up on Jedi-hunting supplies."

Chapter 4

I surreptitiously tug the hem of my miniskirt lower while trying to read Mrs. Stoddard's appointment book upside down. Is that Dougall Marketing or McDonald's penciled in for today?

"Yes, I will give him the message," Stodgy Stoddard says into the phone. She eyes me warily, then slams the appointment book closed.

Blast it! My first crack at snooping, and I've already failed. How am I ever going to make it to Phase Two—the Proximity Phase—when I can't even get past my boss's ancient secretary?

Mrs. Stoddard ends her call and, folding her skinny, veined arms on the desk in front of her, narrows her squinty eyes at me. "Can I help you, Miss Egglehoff?"

"Um, is Mr. Yates in, Mrs. Stoddard?"

She raises one gray eyebrow, or rather the skin under the pencil outlining where an eyebrow would be if Stodgy hadn't plucked all the hair out back when that look was in style. "As you can see, Miss Egglehoff—" She gestures to the open door of Mr. Yates's empty office, clearly visible just behind her gleaming desk. "And, as I'm sure you heard me tell Mrs. Yates a moment ago, Mr. Yates is *not* in at the moment."

"Oh, um, hmm."

She blinks, her expression that of a patient bulldog. "Would you like me to give him a message?"

My gaze flicks to the appointment book. If I could only get a peek inside—better yet, if I just knew where Mr. Yates was at the moment. It's almost noon. Is he lunching with Hunter even as I waste time with Stodgy Stoddard?

"Miss Egglehoff?" Mrs. Stoddard asks again. Her patient gaze falters, and her eyes sweep over me disapprovingly. I can almost feel those slate gray orbs burning into the V of my sheer white blouse. I fight the urge to close a button so the top of the lacy camisole doesn't show.

"No. I'll stop by later. It's not anything important."

"I see." She gives me another long, gray look, then picks up a sterling silver pen and begins making notes on a memo pad.

I stare at the closed appointment book again, my fingers itching to open it. I need a distraction. One little distraction. One little peek.

"Was there something else, Miss Egglehoff?"

I jump. "No! Sorry, my mind must be somewhere else today."

She nods and looks back at the memo, and I swear I hear her grumble, "As is your taste in clothing."

I glance down at my outfit—tight black miniskirt, sheer rayon blouse with a thin lacy camisole underneath, and, to top it off, black spiked heels. My hair is curled, sprayed, and brushed into something resembling a style, and I'm wearing about a pound of makeup. Actually, compared to Allison's other ensembles, this one is pretty conservative.

"Floozy," I hear Stodgy mutter. Cheeks burning, I turn to leave and smack hard into Mr. Yates.

"Oof! I'm sorry! I—" But I don't finish because right behind him, smiling that sexy, crooked smile, is Hunter Chase.

"Are you all right?" Mr. Yates takes my elbow to steady me.

"Oh, I'm fine." My voice is a high-pitched squeal in the quiet office. Behind me, I feel Stodgy's glare; in front of me, I see Hunter's smile. The blood thrums in my ears. I want to flee Mr. Yates's oversolicitousness and Stodgy's knowing look, but I can't. I have to solidify Phase One. I step back, out of Yates's reach, and angle toward Hunter. "I hoped to review the MacKenzie account with you, Mr. Yates, but you're busy."

I toss my hair—hopefully still looking sleek and sophisticated—and give Hunter what I pray is a sultry look. Every shy, nerdy pore in my being rebels against this bimbo behavior, but I force myself to continue. I am Princess Leia—or Princess Leia if she were completely plastered and trying to act sexy. Running a finger along the lace at the top of my camisole, I shift my weight, put hand on hip, and purr, "Mr. Chase. How good to see you again."

From the corner of my vision, I see Mr. Yates's eyes widen. Hunter inclines his head. "You, too, Ms. Egglehoff."

Then, to my utter surprise and shock, he steps forward, takes my newly beringed hand, and kisses it. If my eyes were any wider, I'd have 360-degree vision. He looks up and winks. "Since we're being so formal," he says by way of explanation.

In the dim background—that's anything in the world that isn't Hunter Chase—I hear Mr. Yates chuckle. "Oh, now, Rory, you're going to give Hunter the wrong impression about Y and Y. We're all friends here." He pauses but

Hunter hasn't yet released my hand, so I don't even glance at my boss.

"That's—that's not to say that we're not also a *serious* firm." Mr. Yates sounds concerned now. "After all, we are dealing with people's money. Wouldn't want to give the impression that we're casual about *that.* "

What *is* Yates talking about? His voice sounds like the drone of the engine room on the USS *Enterprise.* But Hunter must be listening because he finally releases his warm hold on my fingers and turns to Mr. Yates. "I understand completely, George. Y and Y is serious, professional, yet still approachable."

"Yes, yes. Exactly! Do you think your people can do something with that—what do you call it—that *angle* in the marketing campaign?"

"Sure." Hunter nods with casual confidence. "No problem."

"Don't you think that's precisely the image we want people to have of Y and Y, Rory?"

At the sound of my name, my head snaps up, and I realize I've been staring at my hand, loving the way it tingles and pulses from the touch of Hunter's lips.

"Absolutely," I say.

Mr. Yates beams. "Well, Mr. Chase—oh, now you've got me doing it—*Hunter,* sounds like you're on the right track."

Oh, yes, he's on the right track all right. I wish he'd take that mouth he just used to kiss my hand and make tracks straight to my lips. I wish . . .

Hunter winks at me. "Thanks for the vote of confidence, Ms. Egglehoff."

"Oh, call her, Rory, Hunter! We're all friends here."

Hunter gives me a slow grin, and I swear his sapphire eyes glide appreciatively from my chic hair to my slinky black heels. "Rory," he says.

I almost faint at the low, deep way he says my name.

"Let's go to lunch and discuss this further," Yates says, and my heart flip-flops, cartwheels, and tumbles like a cheerleader on the football field at halftime.

"Dave should be at the restaurant by now," Hunter says. He holds out an arm, indicating I should pass through the door first. My heart beats double time. Two, four, six, eight, who do we appreciate . . .

I leave Mr. Yates's office in a daze. I cannot believe this. I've barely began Phase One, and already I'm having lunch with Hunter Chase. This is going to be too easy.

As we near my office, me turning my head half a dozen times in the hall to make sure Hunter and Mr. Yates are still behind me, I pause. "Just let me get my coat," I murmur over my shoulder. "I'll only be a second."

But just before I walk through my office door, I glimpse the confused look on Mr. Yates's face, and my body jolts into complete paralysis. Not just my body—my whole being. I suddenly understand how Han Solo felt when he was put into carbon freeze.

Oh, Creator. Oh, *Force.* No, please no. I shake my head. "I'm—I'm—" I flounder, trying to think of some way out of this, some way to make it look like I haven't just invited myself to a lunch where no one wants me.

"Oh, Rory, you didn't think you were . . ." There's embarrassment and—is that pity?—in Yates's eyes.

"No, no!" I say, trying to affect indifference but sounding shrill. "I was just—just—"

I don't want to look at Hunter, but I can't seem to help myself. Are his eyes filled with pity, too? But wait. He's not even looking at me. "George, I'd love for Rory to come along. She could meet the team. Maybe throw a few ideas our way."

Yates frowns at him, then looks at me. I wish I were a speck on the wall. No, I wish I were an atom of a speck on the wall. Hunter is trying to save me, but I'm humiliated.

"I don't know . . ." Yates hedges. He'll never go for it. He's about to throw some Darth Vader at Hunter's noble Jedi intentions.

"She might be bored with all the marketing talk," Hunter says, "but we can probably find something to entertain her." He winks at me again, and I feel my face flush. Why does he have to be so nice? Why couldn't he just ignore me or laugh? This is only going to make me want him more.

Finally Yates speaks up, and his words are my death knell. "I'm sorry, Rory." Mr. Yates pats my shoulder, and I wish I could slither under the carpet and hide. Forever. Yates isn't really going to do this to me, is he? We're all pretending I'm not an idiot, so tell me Yates isn't really going to *point out* my egregious error.

But he is.

My gaze meets Hunter's again.

"This just isn't an area where Y and Y needs your help," Yates says. "Maybe we can do lunch next week. Talk about the MacKenzie case then, okay?"

Fighting back tears of humiliation, I whisper, "Sure."

And then I *do* slink into my office. Just before I close the door and burst into tears, I hear my Jedi Knight say, "Next time, Rory."

"And then heee-heeee-lowwww-"

"Rory, I cannot understand you. Take a deep breath."

"I ca-a-a-an't." I slam my forehead on my desk.

"Yes, you can," Allison says, cool and collected, on the other end of the line.

I manage a gasp, inhaling the smell of the furniture

polish coating the wood desk. I take another breath. And another.

"Rory! Are you hyperventilating?"

"Hhrrhh! Hhrrh!"

"Oh, my God! Put your head between your knees, and *calm down* so you can tell me what happened."

I put my head between my knees—no easy task in the short, tight skirt—and try to slow my breathing. I hear a man's voice in the background on Allison's side, and she says something about drapery treatments before talking to me again. "Better?"

I nod.

"I'm assuming Phase One didn't go well? No, not on the bay windows! Hang the valance over there. Sorry," she says to me, "I don't know where Miranda gets these people."

Miranda is Allison's boss, and I realize Allison must be on-site, or whatever they call it in the decorating business when they go to the house and do the makeover.

"S-s-sorry," I wheeze.

"What?" Allison says. "Rory, I have to go in a moment, so tell me what happened. Did you see Hunter?"

"Y-yes," I gasp, partly because I still haven't caught my breath and partly because the waistband of my skirt is cutting into my stomach.

"But that's good, right? Did you talk to him? Did he notice your new look? What did he—no! That curtain rod goes in the bedroom. Where are the—oh, never mind!" Her voice trails away. "Take five, and I'll get them. Rory?" Her voice is clear again. "I've got five minutes. Talk."

Five minutes? I'm not sure I can adequately describe one of the most humiliating moments of my life in five minutes. But my breath is sort of coming back to me, and it's nice and dark and safe with my head under my desk, so I decide to give it a try. "I saw Hunter," I manage. "And it was good. We were flirting, but then I messed everything up. I—I and he—he—heeee—"

"Rory?" a deep voice asks from my doorway. I slam the back of my head against the bottom of the desk.

"Blast it," I hiss.

"What's wrong?" Allison asks. "Is it Hunter?"

"Rory? Where are you? Are you crying?"

"No," I whisper to Allie, swiping the tears from my cheeks. "Tom. Gotta go."

"Ror—" I hear Allison say before I pull the phone away from my ear and raise my head.

Tom is standing in the doorway, frowning. "What are you doing under your desk?"

"Nothing," I say and replace the phone on its base. "Just looking for something." Furtively I reach into the drawer with my purse and feel around for a tissue.

Tom glances at the phone. "Who were you talking to?"

"Um—payroll." My hand fastens on a Kleenex.

Tom blinks. "Why? What's wrong with your paycheck? Is that why you're crying?"

"I'm not crying." I twist the tissue between my fingers, wishing he'd leave.

But Tom takes a step forward. "Yes, you are. Your eyes are all red." He walks to the edge of my desk and peers at me more closely. "And your cheeks are wet. What's wrong?" Then his gaze slides to my lacy camisole and he rises on tiptoes to try and get a look at the rest of my outfit. Men. I slide my chair under the desk, trying to hide.

"It's nothing, Tom. Just allergies." He's as annoying as one of those pesky Ewoks. Shoo, I think. Shoo.

"Allergies?" Tom says. "I didn't know you had allergies."

I huff. "Tom, I have a lot of work to do." I reach out to

straighten the papers on my desk, but it's clear, papers filed in the appropriate tray or cabinet, as always. Blast it!

Tom shifts and pulls his tie away from his skinny neck, which not only makes him look like a complete nerd, it draws attention to his abominable choice in ties. This one is decorated with Marvin the Martian.

I think of Hunter and his wardrobe. Even in his business attire, Hunter looks sexy. Today he wore crisp navy slacks that hugged his butt with just the right amount of tightness, a light blue Oxford shirt with the sleeves rolled up to show his bronze arms, and a dark blue tie. I don't know much about men's clothing, but the tie looked like silk, expensive silk, to me.

Now, Tom? I shake my head. Tom's black pants are faded to drab charcoal and too short for him. His brown socks peek from the gap between his pants cuff and his brown loafers. His shirt is wrinkled and dingy white, and I've already mentioned the green cartoon-themed tie.

Tom or Hunter? Is there really a choice here?

"I thought you might want to go out to lunch," Tom says. "We could walk down the street to that café you like."

I sit back, speechless. Tom usually eats at McDonald's or Sbarro on the first floor of the building where Y&Y leases offices. We haven't gone out to lunch since the first week we were dating.

"Unless you have other plans," Tom says, eyeing my outfit again. "You look really nice today."

"Um, thanks." Amazing. I can count on one hand the number of times Tom has complimented my appearance.

"*Really* nice," he says, and now he's practically leering. I think I liked it better when Tom didn't compliment me. My brain scrambles for an excuse to turn him down. I don't want to go out to lunch with Tom. I want to go to lunch with Hunter.

But Hunter would never be interested in lunch with me, especially after the fool I made of myself earlier. He must think I'm a total nerf-herder.

I look up at Tom. He's pulling at his tie again, his wiry, chicken neck straining. His leer has waned, but he's still smiling at me appreciatively.

I stand. "Okay, let's go."

"Wowza!" Tom grins as I walk around the desk. "You really do look great. What's the occasion?"

I smooth my hair. "Nothing special." It's not a lie. As of this moment, Hunter is no one special. I'm going to forget all about him. Tom is the one. Tom thinks I'm pretty. Maybe he's just a Jedi disguised as a Wookiee? "Oh, hey," Tom says as we reach the door. "Aren't you bringing your purse?"

I glance at my desk. My purse is still in the bottom drawer, and I don't feel like going back to get it.

"I mean, you've got money, right?" Tom says. Then, like a comic book character, he pulls out his pockets, spilling several pieces of lint on the floor. "I'm broke."

Chapter 5

The break room. Y&Y's version of Tatooine's Mos Eisley Cantina and just as much a hive of scum and villainy.

I casually walk by, slowing as I pass the door, trying to catch a glimpse of the situation inside. For a week I've been despairing of ever seeing Hunter again, but then I heard two of the Go-Gos—I mean, assistants—talking and fluffing their poufy eighties hair in the restroom. When one of them mentioned a sexy marketing man in the break room, I ran so fast I almost ripped Allison's tight brown designer BCBG . . . CDEF . . . whatever . . . skirt.

It's worse than I thought. The Go-Go wannabes are draped over Hunter like he's Han Solo. He stands next to the Fruitopia vending machine, looking like he just discovered treasure in the *Millennium Falcon*'s cargo holds.

Blast it! What am I going to do? I can't let the Go-Gos bebop off with Hunter. I lean against the wall and take a deep breath. This is it, Rory. Your last chance. Rory Strikes Back. Return of Rory.

The guy from the mailroom walks by and gives me a

quizzical look, and I feel like Icky Egglehoff, my nickname in middle school, all over again.

Wait a parsec. What if I don't go in there as Icky—or even Rory? Han loved Leia. What if I go in there as Princess Leia? Yeah . . . I'm not Roberta Joplin Egglehoff, boring CPA. I'm her Royal Highness, Princess Leia Organa of Alderaan. *Senator* Leia Organa. It's worked for me before.

I straighten my shoulders and stiffen my spine. I can almost feel my hair twisting into the famous buns, feel the weight of them resting on top of my ears. And Allie's designer outfit has turned into a flowing white dress made of some kind of outer space material. Okay, now what would Princess Leia be thinking right now?

"Get that walking carpet out of my way!"

I smile. Change that to "Get those big-haired hoochies off my man," and we're in business.

"Hunter!" I say, feigning surprise while striding regally into the break room. I pause and angle sideways, like Allison showed me, so he can get a good view of my thigh as revealed by the skirt's slit. "You should have stopped by and said hello."

Hunter looks slightly taken aback, but at least his attention is now focused on me, not the Go-Gos. "Oh, sorry, Rory. I meant to . . ."

My heart jumps into my throat and I want to say, *Really? Really?* You wanted to see *me?* But I don't, thank Yoda, and then I notice the Go-Gos are looking at me like they'd like to tear my hair out—rip the buns off the sides of my head. But I'm not going to give them the chance.

Unfortunately, I'm out of things to say, and now that I'm standing beside Hunter, my brain is getting fuzzy and the blood is zinging in my ears.

I'm Princess Leia. I'm Princess Leia.

"So, Hunter, have you seen anyone from high school lately?" I ask. Oh, lame. So lame.

"Oh, you two went to high school together?" one of the assistants says, trying to move in.

"Yeah," Hunter answers and then, instead of rolling his eyes and making gagging sounds at my lame conversation, his face actually lights up. "Yeah, I did see one of our old crowd," he says to me, ignoring the Go-Go, who immediately begins to pout, but doesn't—I notice—release her hold on his arm.

"I saw Mitch the other day at the Billy Goat Tavern. He's doing great, married, has kids and everything."

"Really?" I say, not caring about Mitch but amazed that Hunter is talking to me as if I'd actually known Mitch. As if I'd been part of the Popular Crowd.

Hunter takes an enthusiastic step toward me, and the Go-Gos shoot photon torpedoes with their eyes.

"Yeah. Mitch." He shakes his head. *"Mitch."*

"Unbelievable," I say. "Who would have thought?"

"I know." Hunter shrugs, and there's a pause. Oh, blast! Once again, I have nothing to say. Any moment the Go-Gos are going to strum their guitars and reclaim Hunter's attention.

"What about you?" Hunter asks. "Have you seen anyone from school?"

"Um—" Ewok shit! Why did I ask this question? Except for Hunter, I haven't seen—"Allison!" I yelp. "Allison Holloway. I see her all the time."

Hunter takes another step toward me, and the zinging in my ears turns to a steady zum-zum-zum.

"Allison. How is she? You two were good friends, right?"

"You remember that?" The adrenaline zooming through my body could fuel a Star Destroyer. I'm standing just a few inches from Hunter, the Go-Gos are forgotten, and we're talking. Hunter Chase and I are actually having a *conversation.*

"You two were as tight as Pat Summerall and John Madden."

I nod, pretending I know who he's talking about.

"What's she doing now?"

"Interior design."

Hunter folds his arms across the pale gray Oxford he's wearing, and I notice the sleeves stretch under his biceps. "Really? And how is that going for her?"

"Hunter, my *man.* " A blond clone of Hunter strides into the break room. "It's after five, bud. Let's hit happy hour."

Hunter grins and gestures to his counterpart. "Rory, this is Dave, one of my team from Dougall. Dave, an old friend of mine from high school, Rory Egglehoff."

I note with glee that Hunter does not bother to introduce the Go-Gos. They must notice it, too, because they start to back away from him, pretending to be deep in conversation with each other. Princess Leia wins again!

Dave sticks out his hand. "Hey, Rory. Great to meet you."

We shake, and when he squeezes my hand, I feel like one of those unfortunate Imperial generals Darth Vader dispatches with an invisible death grip about their necks. "Nice to meet you, too." Trying not to wince, I give him what I hope is a friendly smile.

"So, Rory—" Dave releases my hand and, cocking a golden brow, glances mischievously at Hunter. "I'd love to hear some stories about old Hunt here. You know . . ." He winks at me and lowers his voice conspiratorially. "Some juicy stuff I can use to blackmail him later."

"Um—" I say, wracking my brain for something gossipy

about Hunter. *Was* there ever gossip about Hunter? He was perfect.

"What do you say, Rory?" Dave says. "Want to join us for happy hour?"

I blink, stunned.

"Hey, that's a great idea. How about it, Rory?"

I turn to Hunter. Is he actually inviting me to go out with him? Is this like a *date?* I want to dance, give high fives, and scream, "Sha-zamm!" But I remind myself that I am Princess Leia, majestic and stately.

"Well," I hedge. Oh, Creator, don't let them take it back. "I have a lot of work to do . . ."

"Aw, come on, Rory. It's Friday," Hunter says. "And we haven't had a chance to catch up yet. Can't you cut out early?"

Hunter wants me to "cut out early"? Hunter wants to be with *me?*

I brace myself against the flood of emotions and attempt to stay calm. Allison would say I'm blowing this all out of proportion, but blast her! So what if I am? "I suppose just this once." Ooh, that sounded nonchalant. Very Princess Leia.

"Great." Hunter grips my arms and gives me an encouraging shake. "Lobby in ten, and I'm buying the first round."

"I'm in a real-life sports bar," I tell Allison on my cell phone in the dingy, one-stall women's restroom. I'm trying not to look too closely at the floor. The bottom of my shoe sticks to the surface when I walk. "I mean, a real uh—*authentic* type of place."

"A hole in the wall, you mean," Allison says. Her cell phone cuts out in the middle of the sentence, but I piece her words together.

"It's not quite *that* bad . . ."

"Oh, Rory, please. You're in a dump with two drunk guys. Don't romanticize it," Allison says, though it sounds more like, "Rory, ple . . . dmp . . . two dr . . . ys. Don't rom . . . cize it."

"They're not drunk, and I'm not romanticizing it," I protest. My heel makes a slurpy sound when I pry it from the gummy bathroom floor. "But you have to admit that this is a step in the right direction. I mean, I'm out with Hunter Chase!"

"So, make the most of it."

"How do I do that?" Using the wall for balance, I study the sole of my shoe. It's got some weird white gunk on it.

"*Flirt,* Rory! Be fun and sparkly like we talked about."

I sigh. Flirt. Be sparkly. How? Princess Leia doesn't flirt. No one in *Star Wars* flirts. I need a how-to book—*Snagging Han Solo: Princess Leia's Guide to Men.* "Are you sure you can't come down here, Allie? I could really use your help, and Hunter would freak if he saw you."

"Sorry, but I'm already at Narcisse, and Bryce will be here any minute. Besides, you need to make Hunter want to see more of *you.* Get him all to yourself and lay on the charm."

Lay on the charm. O-kaay. "But what if you and Bryce—?"

"Rory, pay attention, I *can't.* " She sighs. "I really like this guy, and tonight is sort of a special—hey, Bryce just walked in. I have to go. Call me tomorrow."

I wonder what she'd been about to say, what was so special, but then the cell phone beeps and dies, and my one lifeline dies with it. I'm standing in the dark bathroom, gunk on my shoe, devoid of role models—real or intergalactic—and the Jedi of my dreams is on the other side of the door. It's a good thing we're in a bar because I need a drink.

"Want a beer, Rory?" Dave asks when I return to the smoke-filled bar. Dave and Hunter are sitting at a table, and I have to pass a half-dozen flickering TV screens and even more shouting beer-bellied men to reach them.

"How about—" I'd been about to ask for a mojito, then think better of it. "How about a rum and Coke?" I say instead. Surely this place can handle something as basic as that.

"Coming right up." With a nod, Dave strides to the bar. I glance at Hunter, who seems absorbed in the Bulls game on one of the TVs. I don't want to bother him, so I pretend to watch as well, but my attention soon drifts about the room. On the silent screens mounted throughout, I catch glimpses of boxing, golf, car racing, tennis, and—is that fishing?

"Goddamn it!" Hunter slams his palm on the table. "Did you see that?"

"Ah—"

He shakes his head and takes a swig of beer. "I don't believe this!"

"I guess I missed it," I say apologetically.

He shrugs. "No big deal. You're probably not all that interested in sports, huh?"

"I try to keep current," I say.

Hunter finishes his beer and leans back in his chair. "I've always loved sports. Some of my best memories as a kid were hanging out with my dad, watching the big game."

It's dark, but for a moment I think I see a flash of pain in his eyes. Is he thinking about his mom? I can imagine little Hunter and his dad, two wounded men, sitting silently in their living room in front of a blaring TV. Maybe that helped shut out the pain. Hunter was only in sixth grade when his mom left. How old is that? Eleven? Twelve?

"You were pretty close to your dad, weren't you?" I ask.

Hunter raises his eyebrows in surprise. "Yeah, I was. I just wish I could have been a better athlete. I played just about every sport, but I never really excelled at any."

"I know."

"Well, *thanks.* "

"Oh, no!" I lean forward and grasp his corded forearm, resting on the table between us. "What I mean is, I remember you played a lot of sports. And you were great. Quarterback of the football team, number nineteen."

Hunter raises a brow. "You remember my jersey number?"

I flush. "Oh, um, lucky guess."

Hunter looks skeptical. "Yeah, well, quarterback probably should have gone to Jeff Martin, but the coach liked me."

Jeff Martin. I'd had a few classes with the guy. He wasn't too bright, but Hunter was right, he was an excellent athlete.

"But what about that basketball game senior year where you scored a three-pointer in the last second?" I say to Hunter because, after all, who cares about Jeff Martin? "You won that game for us. The team must have dumped three coolers of Gatorade over your head."

Hunter stares at me, and suddenly I notice the heat of his arm under my fingers. It's almost like I'm resting my palm on one of the small red-netted candle jars lighting the bar's tables. I snatch my hand away, shocked that I've been touching him so intimately. Touching him at all.

But Hunter keeps staring at me. "You remember that game?"

"Um, sure," I say and shrug as if *anyone* would.

"You were at that game? We played it in Peoria. That's a couple hours from Chicago. My dad didn't even go to that game, and he went to *all* my games."

Oops. I forgot the Peoria part. So, okay, when I said I didn't go to Hunter's away games earlier, I lied. I went to one . . . or two . . . or most of them. "Really?" I murmur and pretend to scan the bar. Where in the Dark Side is Dave with that drink? "Do you think Dave got lost?" I keep searching the bar, avoiding Hunter's gaze. I can still feel it—intense, shocked, and *hot* on my face.

"Rory."

I feel Hunter's fingers on my sleeve and melt.

"I can't believe you were at that game."

I give him a sheepish look and stare down at the scarred wooden table. "A friend of mine was going, and I just went along for the ride. Nothing else to do, I guess." This is a complete lie, of course. I had to drive all by myself, got lost three times, and ended up breaking down in tears on the way home. But Hunter doesn't need to know that, especially since his hand is still on my arm. Mmm, his touch is so warm. Warm enough that trickles of heat penetrate my overly sensitive skin through Allie's sweater.

"So, did I miss anything?"

We both start as Dave hands over two beers and the rum and Coke. Hunter reaches for his beer. "Nah. Just catching up."

"Oh, yeah?" Dave looks at me, and I gulp half my drink. Hunter isn't touching me anymore, but I still feel the burning spot on my skin where he clasped it a moment ago. It's like he's branded me or something.

"So, Rory," Dave says between swigs of beer. "I bet all the guys had crushes on you in high school. What's the story? Did you break Hunter's heart?"

I gape at him. *Me* break Hunter's heart? *Me* with guys chasing after me? "Not exactly."

"What is this, the Spanish Inquisition?" Hunter says.

"No, it's the Dave Inquisition." He turns back to me. "So, Rory, are you going to give me the dirt on old Hunt here, or do I have to resort to torture?"

"I'm sure sitting here with us bozos is torture enough," Hunter says. Then he looks at me. "Go ahead, Rory, tell him something so he'll shut up." He grins, and Dave leans forward expectantly.

My head swims with the pitch and sway of panic. Or maybe I just drank that rum too fast. "I hate to disappoint you—"

"Aw, come on, Rory!" Dave shakes my arm playfully. "You gotta give me *something*. This guy's the office wonder boy. Don't tell me he was perfect in high school, too."

"Well, not perfect . . ."

"Aw, shit." Dave sits back and groans.

Hunter laughs. "Sorry, Dave. Chalk up another for me." He tosses his beer back and gives his buddy a cocky smile. Hunter's a good guy, but even good guys can get too full of themselves. What was it Han said to Luke before Luke blew up the Death Star? "Great, kid! Don't get cocky."

"Actually, I *do* have one story," I say, and both Hunter and Dave look away from the TVs in surprise. "But it's not from high school," I add.

Dave scoots his chair closer. "All the better. I love good junior high angst. Puberty. Hormones raging."

"Sorry. It's from elementary. First grade." I sip my drink again. It's strong, and the rum hits the back of my mouth hard.

"You two really *do* go way back," Dave says.

"We were both in Mrs. Allman's first-grade class," I begin, still looking at Hunter. He raises both eyebrows. I've surprised him again, I'm sure. "And for Valentine's Day—"

"So this is a *romantic* story." Dave elbows Hunter good-naturedly. "Good choice, Rory."

Hunter is smiling, but the arrogance has been replace by curiosity.

"Anyway, she gave each of us a folder, probably a file folder or something, to decorate with our names and hearts and flowers—or race cars." I glance at Hunter and he slants me a sideways grin.

"Then we hung them up on the wall. On Valentine's Day each of us went to the wall and put valentines in the folders. When it was my turn, I was sort of nervous because even though Mrs. Allman was reading to the class, I felt like everyone was watching me, and I hated being the center of attention."

The more I talked, the more real that day became to me. The smell of glue and construction paper permeated the room, mixed with the scent of heart-shaped cookies and soggy rubber boots. The room seems enormous in my memory, like a big white cavern with soaring ceilings. And the wall of folders is endless. I begin to stuff my valentines in the folders, turning every three or four seconds to see if the other kids are watching me. My face is hot, my lower back lined with perspiration. I'm wearing a long-sleeve red shirt with a pink heart on the front, and I pull the sleeves up to my elbows because I'm so warm.

"So, I'm sort of in a hurry to finish, but when I get to the end, I have three valentines left, and I knew I'd made enough for everyone to get only one."

"So you figured you'd skipped someone," Hunter says. "And you were worried their feelings would be hurt if they didn't get a valentine from you."

I turn to Hunter and nod. I'd almost forgotten he and Dave were there.

"Beautiful, smart, and virtuous? You're something, Rory."

. . .' I stare at him. Hunter thinks I'm beautiful?

. . ." He grins.

"Oh." I struggle to pick up the thread of my story. "Oh, so I went back and started checking all the folders to be sure each one had a card. The only problem was that I was the last person to go, and the folders were pretty full by then, so I had to sort of dig through them, and it took me a long time."

I tug on my sweater, like I did my red Valentine's Day shirt in Mrs. Allman's class, trying to free the damp material from my hot skin. "I guess I'd made it to your folder"—I look at Hunter—"when Mrs. Allman asked me what was taking so long. She didn't say it mean. I think she just wanted to hurry me up so she could move on with the lesson. But she startled me, and I must have tugged on your folder just a little, and . . ."

"It fell on the floor," Hunter says. "God, I remember that now. I haven't thought about it in years."

"Well, now you know who to blame."

Hunter frowns. "Blame for what?"

"What happened next." I can't believe he doesn't remember.

Hunter shrugs and finishes his beer. "You put the folder back up again?"

I blink several times and shake my head. Unbelievable. He really doesn't remember. And he probably didn't even care that much back in first grade. I, on the other hand, was mortified. I'm even more mortified to realize that, apparently, I just wasted like twenty-five years feeling guilty for embarrassing Hunter, when he'd forgotten the whole incident by naptime.

"Well, yeah, I put the folder up, but everyone laughed."

He reaches out and touches my arm. "Kids suck. Even in first grade they get off on embarrassing each other."

I shake my head again, willing him to remember, to understand. "Yes, but they were laughing more at you than me."

He sits back. "Why?"

"Because *your* folder is the one that fell. And they said, 'Hunter has *sooo* many valentines' and 'Everyone *luuves* Hunter.' "

Dave chuckles. "Well, it could have been worse. They might have sung the kissing song."

My face heats, and I stare down at the table. "They did."

Hunter and Roberta sitting in a tree, K-I-S-S-I-N-G . . .

Hunter's looking at me, a thoughtful expression on his face. He knows.

"I hate saying this, Rory," Dave says, "but that sounds more embarrassing for you than for Hunt. I thought you were going to tell me something really juicy and damaging about him. You know, like when he wet his pants or something."

I bite my lip and give Dave a shaky smile. "This is the best I can do on such short notice." Neither Hunter nor Dave say anything, so I break the silence with, "But I coul tell you about the time *I* wet my pants."

Both guys laugh. "You're a trip, Rory," Dave says, Hunter nods agreement. I smile, pleased I'm not boring t to tears, but inside my heart is thudding. I revealed too tonight. The way Hunter is looking at me, he has to ha ured out that I had a crush on him for years. Seeing barely remembers me, he probably feels sorry for m

I sip the water from the melted ice cubes in my ing to dull the bitter taste in my mouth. I've blown it.

I gulp the last dregs of my rum and Coke, then say, "Well, it's getting late." Obviously not true since it's barely nine o'clock. "I better go." I can't wait to get out of here, home to my empty apartment where I can wallow in fathomless depths of self-pity and chocolate chip cookies.

Hunter sets down his beer. "I'll walk you to your car."

"You don't have to do that." Why does he have to be so nice? I know he'd rather grab another round with Dave than walk out in the cold with me. "The car's just around the corner," I say, reaching for my purse and slinging it on my shoulder.

"No problem." He stands, and I gape at him. I've given him the perfect out. Why doesn't he take it?

"But I don't need—"

"I'll be back in a few, Dave," he says, effectively cutting off any further argument.

He takes my arm, guiding me through the room. Outside, I point him in the direction of my car, and we walk in silence for a minute or so. The night is cool but comfortable, and the light breeze feels as exhilarating on my face as Hunter's touch on my arm. We pass a young couple holding hands and sharing a Styrofoam cup of steaming coffee, and I wonder if they see a couple when they look at us.

"You have an amazing memory," Hunter says, and his voice is so low, at first I think I just imagined he spoke. "I can't believe you remember so many details about school. Man!" He runs a hand through his hair. "I can barely remember the varsity football coach's name, much less Mrs. Allman's class."

"I guess I just have a gift for details," I say. "Probably why m an accountant." We step around an area of sidewalk ped off for construction, and I spot my blue Volvo down street.

"Maybe." He grins. "Or maybe you're just damn smart. I can't believe I didn't know you better in high school, Rory. Or, *shit,* did I?"

He looks so mortified, I start to laugh. "In high school, no, but we were lab partners in seventh grade. Remember Mr. Newman's bio class?"

"Mr. Newman?" He frowns. "Oh, yeah, yeah." He stops and turns to me. "Yeah! I remember now. We dissected the frog together."

"No. That was when Julie Jones was your partner. I was your partner for the earthworm. Remember we had to do the virtual dissection because my parents wouldn't let me cut up a real worm?"

"How do you *remember* this stuff?" He takes my arm to begin walking again, but I pull back. "This is my car."

"Very practical." He nods in approval at my blue Volvo. "I'd expect nothing less."

"Yeah, that's me." Practical, not cool. Not Julie Jones memorable. I start to dig in my purse for my keys, relieved that we're finally here. The more Hunter struggles to remember me, the worse I feel. I should probably be thrilled he confuses me with Julie Jones.

But I'm not. I'm hurt. All these years, I've remembered every little thing about him, gone over and over the minutiae in my mind, and he's never once thought of me.

Not that this should come as any big surprise. Hunter is a nice guy, but none of this means anything to him. I have to stop making a Star Cruiser out of a Tie fighter.

I find my keys, but when I pull them out, Hunter's hand covers mine. My head whips up, and it's like I've been hit with a blaster set on stun. He's staring at me, blue eyes dark and enigmatic. "Thanks for tonight, Rory," he says quietly.

"Oh, um, there's nothing to thank me for." My voice

sounds shaky and high, like it's being broadcast from a com-link.

"I'm glad you came. You reminded me of some things I haven't thought about in a while. Maybe I should have." He looks past me for a moment, but I don't think he's staring at Spaghetti Warehouse on the corner.

The moment seems to drag on forever, and each of my senses shifts into high gear. There's the taste of rum and anticipation on my tongue, the smell of laundry detergent on Hunter's pressed shirt, the feel of his fingers on my skin—touch soft as the cashmere material of my sweater—and the sound of music drifting from the bars and restaurants around us. The notes wrap around one another, mixing and intertwining until they're almost singing.

His hand on my wrist shifts until our fingers lock together, and we're holding hands, fingers intertwined. My pulse jumps. Slowly, he leans into me. His chest presses against my arm, then his knees brush against mine. He's warm, so warm, his heat pulsing into me as his fingers press gently on the back of my neck and he dips his head, brushing his lips against mine.

He's kissing me, and I should close my eyes, but I don't want to. I don't want to miss a moment of this dream. But Hunter's feathery kiss is like a drug, sending my senses reeling, and my eyes close involuntarily. His lips press against mine more firmly, spiraling me into a vortex of heat and rainbow lights and the whoosh of blood in my ears. I melt into Hunter's arms, melt into the kiss.

And then it's over. He pulls away, hands sliding down my back, then releases me.

"Good night, Rory," he says. "Drive carefully."

I blink and stare at him. He steps back, and the sudden distance between us is like a blast from a starship. I fumble for the remote, dangling with the keys from my limp fingers. "Um, okay. You, too."

I don't remember getting in the car or starting it, just glancing in the rearview mirror and seeing Hunter standing on the sidewalk watching me, hands shoved in his pockets. I turn the corner and, once out of Hunter's sight, let out a whoop.

He kissed me. He kissed me. He kissed me! My mind whirls, my heart soars, and . . . I have no idea where I am. I squint at the road signs, finally find one that's familiar, and turn toward home.

He kissed me.

Chapter 6

I pull the car next to the mailbox and stare at my parents' house in surprise. It's Sunday morning and I'm in Evanston at Sunshine and Dan's for brunch, as usual, but I have absolutely no recollection of driving here. I remember getting in my car and backing out of my parking space, but I have no memory of Lake Shore Drive, the elementary school, or passing Allison's parents' house on the corner of the neighborhood next to mine.

Yet here I am, parked in front of a bright purple, two-story colonial. The paint, the approximately five hundred wind chimes swinging from the front porch, the Zen garden, and the van in the drive that looks like it was stolen from the Partridge Family are probably in violation of the deed codes, but the neighborhood association of Rolling Pines gave up on trying to make my family conform to their rules long ago.

I don't conform, either. When I think about my childhood, mainly I remember feeling . . . out of place. My family was different, and that made me an outsider at school. And I was logical, levelheaded, and not prone to passionate outbursts, so that made me the odd one at home.

Me, the odd one.

A red Honda Civic hybrid whizzes past me and pulls behind the van. My sister jumps out before her car even comes to a full stop.

"Hey!" she calls, waving. She's wearing a bright green and pink tie-dyed sari-type skirt with fringe that brushes her ankles, a green hemp sweater that's seen better days, and, despite the cold, beat-up brown faux leather sandals. Her brown hair reaches past her waist, falling alternately in waves and braids, decorated at the ends with multicolored twine. She wears no makeup. She doesn't need to. The seven piercings in Stormy's right eyebrow or the dozen and so in her ears are ornament enough.

"Hey, Stormy," I say, climbing out of my Volvo.

She gives me a warm hug, and I catch the fragrance of jasmine incense on her skin and in her hair. "How have you been, sis? Not working too hard, I hope?"

I give her a wan smile. "I don't think there is such a thing as working *too* hard in the accounting world."

She shakes her head. "When are you going to ask yourself what it's all for? I mean, who are you benefiting here?"

I shrug. "Um, me?"

"No." She gives me a disapproving look, as if I should know the correct answer by now. "You're benefiting the capitalist pig industrialists."

"Industrialists?" I laugh. "Like the robber barons from eighth-grade social studies?"

She nods vehemently. "And that's just what they are, Rory, but they're not after the railroads anymore. Now it's our very souls, our very spirit as an independent nation. They want to make us cookie-cutter versions of one another. A Starbucks on every corner. A Gap in every shopping mall."

"Hey, what's wrong with the Gap?" I tease.

She stares at me like I'm lower than Bantha fodder. "What's *right* with the Gap, Rory? I mean, I don't even know where to begin . . ."

"Then don't." I take hold of her shoulders and give her an affectionate squeeze. "Let's not get into this today, Stormy. Not all of us can live on love. Some of us require good, old-fashioned greenbacks."

With a sigh born of long years of resignation, she nods and links her arm with mine. As one, we turn toward the house.

"I *don't* live on love, you know."

Now it's my turn to sigh because she's going to have to get this one last point in before we can drop it.

"I work, just like you. But Harmony and I try to make this world a better place. We're not just in it for the money."

I try not to roll my eyes. Stormy always says things like this, but I've yet to understand how a shop that sells incense, crystals, and books on Wicca makes the world a better place. Not that I disagree with all Stormy's views. I mean, there's a lot wrong with our world. I just don't feel the need to make an issue out of every injustice.

"Hey, are you two coming?" My stepfather opens the glass storm door and steps outside in stocking feet. "The scrambled tofu and TVP sausage links are getting cold."

"We're coming, Dan!" I say and quicken my step, but I'm not moving fast enough for Stormy.

"Dad!" She releases my arm and rushes up the steps, giving her father a hug that makes it seem as though it's been seven hundred rather than seven days since they last saw each other.

For a moment I watch them embrace. Dan's the only father I've ever known and the man who raised me. I know he loves me, but watching them together, I still feel a twinge of jealousy. When I see him next to Stormy, a little piece of my heart hurts. I wish I'd known my own father. Or at least that my mother knew who he was so she could describe him to me.

Stormy and Dan look so much alike. Both dark-haired and green-eyed, they're lean and sinewy. Anyone who saw them together would know they were father and daughter. But what about my own father? Did he wear glasses like me? Have straight, fine brown hair that crackles with static when the weather turns? Love apples but have a violent allergic reaction to mustard? Would he hug me as fiercely as Dan does Stormy, would he love me that completely?

I watch Dan and Stormy move apart, their movements effortlessly graceful, and wonder if I inherited my clumsiness from my father. I certainly didn't get it from Sunshine. Like Dan and Stormy, she seems to flow when she moves. Always the odd man out, I'm the klutz in the family of the physically and socially nimble.

"And how are you, Roberta?" Dan asks me, coming forward to give me a hug. "Had a good week?"

"The usual," I say, though nothing about it was ordinary in the least. "How about you?"

"The usual." He grins and gives me a hug. It's more reserved than the one he gave Stormy, but he knows I dislike lavish displays of affection.

He holds the door open, and Stormy walks in ahead of us. "I finished up a case Thursday you might be interested in," he says, guiding me with an affectionate hand on my back.

"Oh, the one you mentioned last week?" As I step into

the hallway, the smells of fresh-baked bread, sweet spices, and that indefinable scent that's home envelop me.

"Mmm-hmm." Dan closes the storm door, then the polished wood door behind it. "Pretty interesting outcome if you ask me. I think I told you that the client—"

"Now, Dan, you know the rules. No talking business before dinner. It's bad for the digestion. Hi, sweetheart." My mother steps out of the kitchen, rubbing her hands on a dish towel before wrapping me in her arms. "How are you?"

"Hi, Sunshine."

"Hungry?" Her blue eyes, the lids dabbed with sparkly pink eye shadow, light up hopefully.

"Famished. What are we having? It smells delicious."

"It *is* delicious!" Stormy calls from the kitchen. "Sunshine, what did you use on these tofu eggs? Coriander?"

Sunshine grins. "No, not coriander, but close!" She darts back into the kitchen, and Dan and I exchange a look. It's the same thing every Sunday. Stormy tries to guess the ingredients Sunshine's used in preparing the food, Dan and I talk accounting—my job—or tax law—his job—and cruelty-free, vegan fare is enjoyed by all.

Your typical family get-together, huh? Well, except you probably didn't grow up in a purple house, your family probably doesn't eschew any food that had a face, and you probably call your mother "mom."

My upbringing was a little less conventional. My mother, Sunshine, was a hippie. The first time I told Allison, she said, "Oh, my mom was, too! You should see the clothes she wore!"

But what she really meant is that her mom went through a hippie *stage.* Mitsy Holloway didn't go to Woodstock. She didn't live in Haight-Ashbury. Good old Mitsy didn't mourn the passing of Janis Joplin and Jim Morrison with a zeal most reserve for close friends and relatives.

And Mitsy didn't raise Allison in a commune for the first three years of her life. I was born on October 6, 1972 at the Rainbow Center for Peace and Love in San Francisco, California. My mother had gone to live there a year before and, as free love was the rule, to this day she isn't sure who my father was.

I was born Roberta Joplin Plisowski. Joplin after Janis Joplin, who had died two years and two days before, and Roberta after my grandmother, who died when Sunshine was seven.

Thank the Creator Allison came along in second grade and saved me. When she moved to Evanston, I was eight and Stormy five. Stormy had a speech impediment and couldn't pronounce Roberta correctly. It sounded like she was saying "Wowota," but when Allison heard Stormy, Allie said the pronunciation sounded like "Rory." The name has stuck, though Sunshine still refuses to use it and Dan usually calls me Roberta to humor her.

Sunshine and Stormy bustle into the living room with steaming dishes of food and set them on the table. Brunch is served buffet-style, and we eat sitting cross-legged on the pile of big, colorful pillows. Sunshine's made scrambled eggs from tofu—Dan's favorite—sausage links from TVP, textured vegetable protein; wheat grass smoothies; soy milk; two types of hummus; and freshly baked toast made from unprocessed whole wheat flour. Everything is organic, each item chosen and prepared to inflict the least amount of cruelty and impact on Mother Earth. It's not a bad way to live, and even when I'm not home, I eat vegetarian ninety-nine percent of the time.

I watch everyone fill their plates, then settle in the usual places around the living room. Sunshine turns on some music—it sounds like a waterfall in a rainforest—and for a few moments everyone eats and listens to the croaking frogs on the tape.

The music reminds me of Mr. Newman's seventh-grade biology class, and that makes me think of Hunter. For one glorious marking period, Hunter Chase was my lab partner. Newman's class. Six weeks, thirty days, and 1,650 minutes of sitting next to Hunter Chase. Actually, it was only twenty-nine days and 1,595 minutes because Hunter was absent one day after a football injury. But who's counting?

Hunter wasn't. I put a forkful of scrambled tofu in my mouth and frown. Of the 1,595 minutes we spent together, I think he paid attention to me for about 6.5 of them. He was too busy joking with his buddy Mitch behind him and trying to scare cheerleader Julie Jones with the guts from the animals the class was supposed to be respectfully dissecting.

But he was definitely paying attention to me last night. The skin on my arm where he touched me still tingles. Oh, why can't I feel this way about Tom? Tom is safe. I know Tom likes me, and we've got everything in common. Like me, Tom's a CPA. Like me, Tom went to Northwestern. And like me, Tom scoffs at ESPN, Budweiser, and reality TV. Tom loves *Star Wars,* Robert Jordan's *Wheel of Time* series, and *Star Trek* conventions, especially those where any of the cast from *Star Trek* will be attending.

If Tom weren't such a Wookiee, he'd be perfect for me. But he is a Wookiee, and Hunter Chase, the Ultimate Jedi, is far, far out of my league.

"Dan, honey, you didn't get any wheat grass," Sunshine says, rising gracefully from her cross-legged pose to fetch him a glass from the table.

"Oh, I must have forgot," Dan says, giving me a pained look. He hates wheat grass.

"Well, I'll pour you a glass. It's good for your digestive functions. Do you want some, Roberta?"

"Uh—no thanks, Sunshine. My digestive functions are doing just fine on their own."

"Hmm," Sunshine murmurs her disapproval as she passes me. She hands Dan a glass of thick bright green liquid and sits beside him.

To his credit, Dan pauses for only a moment before taking a sip. Then, instead of the grimace I'd been expecting, he smiles at her. Sunshine smiles back.

A tingle runs up my spine. Look at how much they love each other. When they met, they must have been as different as 'droids and Wookiees, but they made it work. Somehow they made it work. And if Dan Egglehoff, a straitlaced tax attorney from a prominent Chicago family, and Barbara (aka Sunshine) Plisowski, a free love hippie who grew up in a trailer park in Gary, Indiana, can make it work, why can't Hunter and Rory?

After all, opposites attract, right?

"Cumin!" Stormy hollers, holding a forkful of tofu egg in the air. "That's what it is, cumin!"

Sunshine smiles. "You're getting too good at this, Stormy. Now, who's ready for carob cake?"

Later I wander into the kitchen, where Sunshine is standing at the sink washing the last of the dishes.

"Can I help?" I ask, propping a hip on the counter.

She gives me a quick kiss, then hands me a towel. "Want to start drying?"

"Sure." I lift a plate from the rack and rub it dry. Sunshine keeps washing, and for a few moments there's just the sound of spoons clinking and the water sloshing in the sink. I glance at the leftover tofu eggs and wonder what Hunter would think if he were here right now. Would he balk at the thought of wheat grass smoothies? Choke on the carob in his slice of cake? I bet him and his dad had slabs of bacon, heaps of hash browns, and mounds of scrambled eggs at Denny's when he was growing up. He probably wouldn't know what to make of my vegan mother and her weird concoctions.

I lift a glass and rub the towel over it then turn to Sunshine. "Sunshine?"

"Hmm?" She scrubs a pot, tongue between her teeth as she struggles with a recalcitrant spot of grease.

"When you met Dan, did you know right away that he was the one? Everyone says you two were so different, and you still are, but anyone could see how much you guys love each other."

She glances up from the pot and gives me a penetrating look. Though I tried to make the question sound casual, there's no fooling your mom. "Is this about Tom? I didn't know it was that serious."

"No, not really." It's a logical assumption, but the pang of guilt slaps me like the back of the spatula Sunshine's just picked up. I'm still seeing Tom, yet Friday night I was kissing Hunter. Or he was kissing me, but same thing.

Creator! I *cheated* on Tom. Me, Rory Egglehoff, cheated on my boyfriend.

"What's it about then?" she asks, handing me the spatula.

"It's a hypothetical question."

Sunshine grins. "You have this friend?"

"Something like that. You and Dan are such total opposites. He's all serious and you're—"

She raises a plate from the soapy water and eyes me with raised brows.

"You're *you,* " I finish. "So, what if I liked a guy totally different from me? Really social and popular, athletic, and Han Solo–gorgeous. How would we make it work?"

Sunshine stares out the small square window over the sink. "Well, it's not easy. Dan was one of the first people I met when I came to Chicago. I hated Chicago, and I hated him. They both seemed cold and conservative. But he's Margie's cousin, and Margie and I have known each other forever, so Dan and I kept running into each other. And he sort of grew on me, you know? And the more I liked him, the more I liked Chicago, and pretty soon I couldn't imagine living without either one." She sets down a spoon and looks at me. "But it wasn't easy. We compromised. Dan had to give up meat and leather. I had to go to Arnold Schwarzenegger movies and listen to long stories about accounting. But you know what?"

She pulls the plug from the drain and water sluices away. "We're not so different. Underneath it all, we're a lot alike, and when you love someone, none of that matters, anyway. When you love someone, you *want* to do things for them. You want to join their yoga class." She grins because she and Dan recently started going to hatha yoga classes together. "And you even pretend not to know anything about your surprise birthday party."

"Sunshine!" I screech. "How did you find out?"

She shrugs. "I have my methods, but don't worry, I'll be the picture of surprise." She turns back to the sink. "So, will that advice help your *friend?*"

"Yeah, I think so." Maybe there *is* hope for two people as different as Hunter and me. And maybe we're not so different deep down. Deep, deep, *deep* down.

I'm probably making way too much out of one little kiss, but even Allie was excited when I told her about it yesterday. She said I was going as fast as wedding gowns at a Vera Wang sample sale, whatever that means.

"So, tell me more about this Tom," Sunshine says. "Is it getting serious?"

"Hey, look what Stormy found in the basement." The door bangs shut and Stormy and Dan tromp into the kitchen, Stormy holding a glass ball before her.

"Your crystal ball!" Stormy says, beaming.

Dan puts an arm around Sunshine's shoulders. "So Madam Sunshine, tell me my future. Will I get another slab of carob cake today?"

Chapter 7

Sunshine is an artist, but she doesn't like to sell her work. She prefers to give it away to those she loves and sometimes even complete strangers if "the piece calls to them." One of her artistic ventures is creating homemade frames. All around my room are images of me through the years encased in frames decorated with flowers, bamboo, glitter, or whatever struck her fancy at the time. I came up here to search for a sweater I can't find at home and lingered to look at the photos.

No wonder Hunter forgot me. I was so geeky looking. On my desk, there's a picture of me and Allison circa ninth grade and 1986. We've got our arms around each other, our heads together, and the contrasts are stunning. Though probably not even fourteen, Allison is already gorgeous. Her cherry red hair is brushed back from her forehead, falling in glossy waves to her shoulders. Her green eyes seem to take up half her face, and her porcelain skin glows rosy along her high cheekbones.

I look like Yoda next to her. My nondescript brown hair

is straight and limp about my freckled face, my brown eyes look small and squinty under my huge, round glasses, and my mouth gapes wide, gleaming with rows of silver braces. I'm the poster child for geek.

But as different as we were in appearance, Allison and I were surprisingly alike in our interests. I pick up a picture from 1988, where we're both wearing Depeche Mode concert T-shirts, and another Sunshine captured of us lying on my living room floor, deep in discussion, with Kiefer Sutherland in *Lost Boys* on the TV behind us.

I put the pictures down and glance in the large mirror on the wall in front of me, trying to gauge how much I've changed and how much I've stayed the same. I got rid of the braces in tenth grade, so at least my mouth no longer looks like the chrome grill on a car, but my lips look thin and pale as my lipstick came off sometime between the tofu eggs and carob cake. My mud brown, ordinary eyes appear larger without my glasses, but the contacts don't do much else for me. I've pulled my limp hair into a ponytail, which is the hassle-free style I preferred in high school and still wear on weekends and Mondays that come too soon. But there *has* been a change. For Phase One of the Ultimate Jedi Plan, I've been curling my hair in a flirty swirl around my shoulders, tucking the impish curls behind my ears when they get in the way.

I turn from side to side, trying to judge my figure. It's hard in the baggy sweater and loose jeans I'm wearing, but I'd been dressed in Allie's designer skirt and low-cut cashmere sweater Friday when Hunter saw me. All in all, I don't know what Hunter saw that made him want to kiss me. I don't look that different from high school. I'm not gorgeous—I'm not even pretty. I'm just . . . *Rory.* Plain old Rory Egglehoff.

"Rory, did Moonbeam RSVP for Sunshine's party yet?"

Stormy asks, sticking her head through a crack in the door. "I wanted to ask if she'd make her baba ghanoush."

"Oh, yeah." I turn quickly away from the mirror, feeling guilty at having been caught looking. "Moonbeam is coming and bringing Pooh Bear with her."

"Great," Stormy says. "We've heard from almost everyone."

Sunshine's fifty-third birthday is next week, and Dan, Stormy, and I have been planning the party for months. We're putting up a tent in the backyard and renting extra chairs and tables. There's going to be a band, a massive spread of vegan food prepared by one of Stormy's Hare Krishna friends, and at least a hundred guests.

And even though the jig is up since Sunshine knows, she doesn't know that we were able to locate some of her housemates from the commune. She hasn't seen them in years, and I can't wait for the look on her face when her old friends walk in.

Stormy leans against the doorjamb. "Are you okay?"

I straighten the already perfectly aligned picture frames and math contest trophies on my dresser. "Fine. Are we still playing Scrabble?"

Stormy rolls her eyes. "No. Sunshine challenged Dad to Thumb Wars. He lost, so we're playing Yahtzee. Sure you're okay?"

I realize I'm still fussing with the mementos on my dresser and drop my hands. "Yeah. Why?"

She shrugs, causing her waist-length brown hair to fall in waves over one shoulder. "I don't know. You just seem . . ." Her jade green eyes narrow. "Weird. Did something happen at work?"

I chew on my thumbnail, glance in the mirror again, then study Stormy. If you can't trust your sister to be honest, who can you trust?

"No, nothing happened *at* work, but something happened after." I look her right in the eye and lower my voice. "With *Hunter Chase.*"

Stormy arches one brow and sidles inside the room, shutting the door behind her. "The guy from high school?"

"Yep." I fill her in on the details, and when I get to the happy hour Friday night, she gives a squeal of delight.

"So . . . tell me what happened?" Stormy grabs my hand and pulls me down on the floor beside her. We curl our legs under us and sit pretzel-style. "Did he ask for your number?"

"No." Hmm. When I called Allison, she asked me that, too. Why *didn't* Hunter ask for my number? I guess the most likely explanation is that it slipped his mind after three beers and a good night kiss, but it bothers me. Doesn't he plan to call? I start chewing my thumbnail again.

"Did he ask you out?" Stormy prods.

"Sort of," I mumble around my worried nail. Stormy yanks my thumb out of my mouth.

"What do you mean, sort of?"

I grin because her curiosity fuels my own excitement. "We were at this bar with a friend of his."

"Mmm-hmm." Stormy nods vigorously. "And then?"

"And then, he walked me to my car *and* . . . kissed me!"

She clutches both my hands in hers, and the dozen or so silver bracelets on her arms jangle. "He *kissed* you!"

"On the mouth," I add, lest there be any confusion.

"With tongue?"

"No." I roll my eyes toward my poster of Einstein hanging on the far wall. Oh, Albert, give me patience. "It was just a light kiss—but *really* sexy."

"Details! Details!"

"Okay, we're standing next to my car talking, and our

eyes meet, then he leans into me and sort of—" I rub two fingers over my lips. "Brushes his lips over mine. Stormy, it was *so* erotic!"

"And then what?"

"He'd put his hand on the back of my neck, and I felt his fingers tighten and sort of ease into my hair."

Stormy nods more vigorously, eyes wide. "Oh, yummy."

"And then he sort of . . . *drew* me closer against him and pressed his lips against mine." I clasp her hands more tightly. "I swear, I thought I was going to faint. My head was swimming and I couldn't breathe because my chest was so tight. But then, just when I thought I was going to lose it, he broke away. Gently though, and trailing his fingers along my back." I trace a finger over her forearm to illustrate, and she shivers. "He just sort of leaned back and smiled."

"What'd you do?"

I stare at the carpet. "Got in the car and drove away."

Stormy frowns. "Oh."

I shake my head and pick at a loose piece of carpet. "I don't know, Stormy. I was so excited Friday night, but now all I can think is, why did he kiss me?"

"What do you mean *why*? Why *not?* "

"A million reasons." I pull the fragment of carpet loose. Sunshine would kill me if she saw that. "He could have any girl. He's that gorgeous, and I'm just—just—" I meet her gaze. "Stormy, do you think I'm pretty?"

Her expression goes from confusion to astonishment in a nanosecond. She opens her mouth, pauses, then nods assuredly. Nope, Stormy. Too late. Whatever she says now, I know it's not her first thought, that whatever her first impression, she hesitated to say it.

"Rory, you know how I feel about all that materialistic

bullshit Madison Avenue shoves down our throats. It's degrading to women. It objectifies us. It—"

I sigh. "Stormy, it was a simple question. I didn't want a doctoral thesis. I just want your opinion—on me."

"But this relates," Stormy protests, rising to her knees as she warms to her topic. "Hunter kissed you and now you're afraid you won't measure up to the standards set in the latest issue of *Anorexic and Airbrushed Women* magazine."

"Oh, never mind!" I say and climb to my feet. "I knew you wouldn't give me an answer. I know the reason, too."

Stormy stands. "Because it's a demeaning question, and I won't lower myself to answer it." She puts her hands on her hips and we face off.

"No. Because I'm ugly, and you don't believe in lying, but you're too nice to hurt my feelings by telling me the truth."

Stormy's mouth drops open. "That's not true! I don't think you're ugly."

"But you don't think I'm pretty."

Stormy's shoulders droop. "I told you, it's all a bunch of crap conceived by male chauvinists reclining in their leather chairs up in the penthouse of Trump Tower and—"

"Enough already!" I throw out my arms and spin away from her. "I already know the truth anyway. I see it every day when I look in the mirror." I glance around the room for something to do. Suddenly my eyes are burning, and I don't want to start crying in front of her.

Why did I think Stormy would understand—gorgeous-without-even-trying Stormy? She inherited the best features of both Sunshine and Dan, while I'm stuck with the reject genes of a father I don't even know.

To hide my tears, I walk over to the rumpled tie-dyed pillows on my bed and fluff them. "Tell Sunshine and Dan

I'll be down for Yahtzee in a minute," I murmur, plumping a pillow. I reach for another, this one with a spiral design, when I feel Stormy's hand on my shoulder.

"Oh, Rory."

I stare at the pillow, the faded colors blurring.

"I love you, and you're beautiful to me."

"Thanks," I sob. Stormy turns me around and gives me a hug.

"That should be what really matters, but I understand why it's not," she says, her voice soft. She pulls back, holding me by the shoulders. She's being so sweet and so wise, I feel like we've traded places and I'm the younger sister.

"So I'll answer your first question. Truthfully." She stands back and gives me a long look. Very long. What you might call a perusal. I shift, discomfited by her intense stare, wishing my nose wasn't running and I'd worn a less frumpy sweater.

"You're not pretty," she says, giving me the verdict I'd expected. My shoulders slump, and I stare at the floor.

"But," she adds, and I lift my head again. "You have something else going for you. You're interesting."

I narrow my eyes and shoot her a glare. "*Interesting?* What the Dark Side does that mean? That's my standard response when I hate a movie but don't want to say so."

Stormy holds up a hand stained russet with henna tattoos. "Just hold on! That's not how I meant it. What I mean is you're interesting to look at—unusual."

"*Unusual!*" I shout. "Maybe you'd just better stop while you're ahead, *sis*."

Stormy frowns. "Unusual in a *good* way, Rory. Your face isn't what society would call classically pretty, but it draws attention. All the angles and curves and the symmetry. I like looking at it. I like the way it all fits together."

Symmetry? Could that be why Hunter was staring at me so much Friday? Does he find my face symmetrically *interesting?* I can live with that. It's not exactly what I was hoping to hear, but it's not bad.

It could also be a lot of Wookiee shit.

Except Stormy has always been very honest with me. She doesn't mince words or hold hands. She's not mean-spirited, she just believes in telling it like it is. Sunshine raised us that way, and I've always admired how Stormy's adhered to those beliefs, even when it cost her friends or opportunities.

"Thanks, Stormy," I say finally. "Any time you want an analysis of your looks, let me know. I owe you."

Stormy laughs. "That will be never. Looks aren't important. I know it's cliché, but what's inside is what counts. I thought you believed that, too." She climbs on the bed beside me.

"I do." For the most part. "I guess I just wanted some reassurance."

"Wasn't Hunter kissing you enough reassurance?"

I shrug. "I don't know. Maybe it's like you said. Maybe it brought out all new insecurities."

"Well, you can hardly believe that you're some hideous beast. I mean, in the space of a week, you had to choose between two men. Life could be worse."

"What are you talking about?"

She gives me a look that says the answer should be obvious. "Well, after Hunter kissed you, you had to break up with Tom, right? Or had you broken up with the Tomster already?"

"No," I murmur. "I hadn't." I reach for one of the pillows behind me and fluff it.

"So what did he say when you told him it was over? Did it go okay? Did you tell him about Hunter?"

I toss the pillow back and pick up another. "Well . . ."

"Rory, you *did* break up with Tom, didn't you?"

I tell her what I keep telling Allison. "I'm going to."

"When?" She waves her hand dismissively. "Look, you don't have to answer to me about it. You can have as many men as you want—free love and all that—but you should at least be honest about it. It's wrong not to tell Tom about Hunter."

"I know."

"Girls," Sunshine calls from the bottom of the stairs. "Dan is threatening to pull out Uno if you two aren't down here in three minutes."

"We're coming," we call in unison.

"She's in a tiff because I won last time," Dan hollers.

"I am *not* in a tiff. I don't *have* tiffs," Sunshine says as she moves away from the stairs. "That game would bore a four-year-old."

"Hey! What does that say about me?"

Their voices fade, and Stormy and I smile at each other. She's probably thinking something esoteric about the spiritual nature of love, but I feel a tug on my heart. They're still so in love after all these years. I want that so much, it's like temptation personified—a thick slab of chocolate cake set before me; I'm finally being given a fork when, until now, I've only tasted the crumbs. I want more. I want the whole dessert table. And I know who I want to share it with.

Hunter Chase.

Chapter 8

"Why are you hanging on to him?" Allison asks Tuesday evening over drinks at a bar in Lincoln Park. I wanted to talk to her sooner, but Oprah is remodeling Harpo Studios, and Allison's interior design firm is making a bid for the project. Since the proposals are due Friday, Allison had to work practically 24–7. This is actually the first chance we've had to talk for more than two minutes since I told her about Hunter's kiss on Friday.

"I'm not *hanging* on to Tom," I tell her, setting my new favorite drink, rum and Coke, on the table. "I just haven't broken up with him yet."

"Why not? That would have been the primary element in my schematic. Well, dating Tom would never have been part of my conceptual design in the first place, but—"

"He's coming over for a late dinner tonight," I interrupt her. "I'll do it then. It's not like there's any hurry." I twist my drink on the soggy napkin. "It's not like Hunter's beating down my door."

"Hmm." She frowns and dips a finger in her appletini.

"Hmm?" I echo, my heart lurching. "Is that a bad sign? I mean, I thought the girl time/guy time ratio was equivalent to dog years/human years or something."

"It is." She nods but doesn't look at me.

"So, has Hunter gone past the acceptable contact time?"

She laughs. "Jeez, you sound like a human computer program. Acceptable Contact Time," she mimics in a robotic voice.

"Yeah, but that's what we're talking about, right?" I down the rest of my drink and slump in my chair. "I knew it. I just knew it. I blew it Friday night. It's over. The Dark Side wins."

"Jesus Christ, Rory, calm down." Allison reaches across the table and grabs my arm. "We are not to the panic stage yet."

I put my hand over my eyes. "Sorry."

"You need another drink." She signals to the waitress and points to my glass, then, almost as an afterthought, her own. By the time my second rum and Coke arrives, I'm calm again. "You don't have to pretend the situation isn't bad, Allie. I can see all the signs. One: He didn't ask for my number Friday night." I take a long sip of my drink, set my glass on the table, and hold up two fingers. "Two: He didn't call me at work yesterday."

"Yesterday was too soon," Allison interrupts.

"But not today!" I hold up a third finger. "Not today. It would be one thing if he were going to be in the Y and Y offices because then he could stop by and say hi in person, but he *wasn't.* And, as far as I can tell from the three-second peek I got of old Stodgy Stoddard's appointment book, Mr. Yates has no appointments with Dougall Marketing all week." I reach for my drink, but Allison snatches it away.

"Slow down. Are you vying for membership in AA?"

She's right. Even Bacardi won't fix this. I slouch back in my chair again. "I'm doomed."

"Listen to me, Rory. You are *not* doomed," Allison says. "We just need to revisit our original design."

"Oh, what's the point? I feel like—like I got all dressed up for the prom and my date never showed up. I'm a fool."

"No, you're not," Allison says with such conviction that I yearn to believe her. "Pay attention. Hunter *did* show up. *And* he kissed you. That means something."

"But he hasn't called me. *That* means something, too."

"Like I said, we have to take a fresh look at our original concept." She sips her drink, swirling the green liquid after. "My initial impression was that you went from Phase One to Phase Two, Proximity, combining it with Phase Three. From what you said, it sounds like the nostalgia thing was really working for you."

"Uh-huh." I nod, but my head is spinning from the exertion of keeping track of all of Allison's phases. "And now?"

She runs her fingers along the rim of her glass, lifts it, and takes another sip. "I think we're back to Phase Two."

"Phase Two." What was that again? All I really need to know is that two is less than four, and I want four. "Phase Two," I moan, reaching for my drink, and this time Allison doesn't stop me. "But I was almost at Phase Four. So close."

"Maybe. Maybe not. Relationships aren't like accounting, Rory. Everything doesn't line up into neat little columns and tally nicely in the end." She pushes her tousled hair back as if to ram her point home: Life, unlike math, gets tangled. "But there's no reason to panic," Allison says, sounding like one of the *Titanic*'s crew after the last lifeboat has launched. "We have lots of time before Phase Four implementation. The reunion is still almost two weeks away."

"Fine. I won't panic." Much. "What do I have to do to get back to Phase Three?"

"Well, obviously you have to hit Phase Two hard. You have to see Hunter more often, make sure you're fresh in his mind, start him thinking about you, then calling you, then asking you out, and so on. You'll slide right back into Three again."

"Okay, so how do I do that? I just told you, he's not scheduled to be in the office all week."

"Maybe you could go back to that sports bar. Where was it again?"

"Wrigleyville."

"Right. Maybe he'll show up there."

"So I'm supposed to sit around by myself all night, hoping he'll show up? No way—unless you're going to camp out among the Wrigleyville sports junkies with me."

Allison raises a brow. "Uh, no."

"So, then what?"

"I don't know." She glances around the crowded bar, presumably searching for inspiration. "Did he mention anywhere he likes to go? Anything he likes to do? Sports? Restaurants? Concerts coming up?"

"No, no, no." I punctuate each *no* with a shake of my head.

Allison toys with her glass, thinking. In the momentary silence a cell phone chirps, and we both reach for our purses. "It's probably mine," she says and peers at the display screen. "Shit. It's Miranda. Hi, Miranda. What's up?"

I finish my drink while Allison attempts to explain her design, then gives up and says she'll be there in half an hour.

"We better get this fucking job," she mutters, shoving her phone in her purse. "Bryce is going to kill me. This will be the third time I've canceled on him."

"How are things with Bryce?"

She closes her eyes. "Not great right now. Damn it, Rory. I really like him, but we're both just so busy. And this Oprah thing. I have *never* worked so hard."

"What about when you guys did John Cusack's place?"

"Yeah," she agrees. "That was pretty intense, but Miranda is insane on this project. Oprah has become like God to her or something." Allison reaches in her billfold and pulls out a twenty. "Here. I better go."

I nod morosely. "Okay."

"Come on, Rory." Allison circles the table, leans down, and gives me a hug. "It's going to be all right. You'll see."

I nod again, holding back tears.

"Even if you don't end up with Hunter, it's not the end of life as we know it." She grins. "Just as long as you don't end up with Tedious Tom—that *would* be a catastrophic event."

I give her a wan smile because that's what she's expecting.

"Look, I know this isn't your thing, but why don't you come to the gym with me sometime? Maybe some time on the elliptical machine is just the mindless distraction you need."

I snort. "More like a painful, *humiliating* distraction. I don't think so, Allie. But thanks for the offer."

"Well, you know where my gym is. I'll be there tomorrow at six-thirty if you want to join me."

"Six-thirty in the morning!"

"I know. But if I don't get a workout in tomorrow my thighs are going to turn to cottage cheese."

I roll my eyes. "Please. If your thighs are cottage cheese, mine are Jell-O."

"Oh, my God!" Allison screeches in my ear. "I almost forgot to tell you."

I cringe at the high-pitched ringing in my ears. "Can you tell me in sign language? I'm deaf now."

"I talked to Jellie yesterday."

"Jellie Abernathy from high school?"

Allison nods, her hair flying up and down from the force of the movement. "Yes. Guess what? She's getting married and she asked me to be a bridesmaid."

"Great." I open my purse and start rummaging around.

"But that's not the best part," Allison gushes, pushing me over and scrunching beside me in the chair. "The wedding's in New York. She's marrying some Wall Street big shot, and they're doing it—" Here she pauses, almost breathless. *"At the Plaza."*

"What's the Plaza?" I squint up at her.

Allison gapes at me. "The hotel? No, sorry. *The* hotel. I mean, if you get married at the Plaza, you have made it."

"Well, good for Jellie, then," I say.

Allison sighs. "I don't get it, Rory. Why do you hate her so much? She liked you. In high school, she was always saying how smart you were."

"Yeah, like she's going to say something bad about me with you—my best friend—right there."

"Okay." Allison holds up a hand. "I'm not going to go through this with you again. I've asked you over and over if something happened between you two, and you always say no. Obviously you're lying, but if you're not going to tell me, then what am I supposed to do?"

For the thousandth time I consider telling Allison, and for the thousandth time I decide against it. In high school I kept the whole thing from Allie because I didn't want her to have to choose between Jellie and me. Now the incident just seems irrelevant. It would be petty to ruin Allison's excitement about Jellie's society wedding by bringing up something that happened more than fifteen years ago. "Sorry, Allison. She's your friend, and I'm happy for you. You're going to New York."

She beams. "I'm going to New York!" Her green eyes take on a misty sheen. "I'm going to a wedding in the Plaza, and—oh!" She squeals again. Two screams in one night. This is not like Allison. Even in junior high she was not one to giggle and whisper like the other girls.

"Jellie mentioned something about Vera Wang outfitting the entire bridal party. *Vera Wang,* Rory!"

"Very posh," I say, though I have no idea who or what a Vera Wang is. Allison's cell phone chirps again, and she snaps out of her fashion haze.

"Shit. I *really* have to go," she says reading the number on display. "Are you going to be okay?" Her eyes are focused on me again and brimming with concern.

"Fine," I say. "You know me. I always bounce back."

She nods. "Yes, you do. Call me later if things don't go well with Tom, okay?"

"Yeah. Thanks."

"Anytime." She kisses my cheek and, in a blur of silk and designer perfume, breezes out the door. I watch her go, as does most of the male clientele, then I pay the bill and leave, too. The sidewalks in Lincoln Park are crowded, but I welcome the crush of people tonight. I don't want to feel alone. I think about Allison and realize it's been a while since she told me she really liked a guy. She *never* says that, which means Bryce must be kind of special. I hope he recognizes that Allison is worth a little inconvenience and waits out this crazy Oprah job.

I stroll leisurely toward the el, looking in shop windows and stopping for a French vanilla cappuccino. I'm in no rush to get home as all that awaits me is the chore of breaking up with Tom. Not that I expect anything unpleasant. Tom's emotions are buried under layers of Spock-worthy logic and reason. He'll be practical and civilized, if a little geeky and awkward.

Allison and Stormy are right. I should just get it over with. Good-bye, Tom. Hello . . .

No one.

It'll be me, a microwave dinner, and the TGIF television line-up from here on out. My faith in Hunter's interest in me has waned considerably and, with it, any and all positive feelings I might have harbored for the male species. No wedding at the Plaza for me.

And then I stop. I come to a complete halt smack in the middle of the stairs to the el as a vision of Jellie Abernathy in froths of white ruffles and lace slams through my mind.

"Hey, watch out!"

"*Excuse* me!" The angry voices of the commuters forced to stop short behind me barely penetrate my consciousness.

Angelica Abernathy. How I hated her. Correction: How I *hate* her. I hear the train and trudge up the last few steps, boarding in a daze.

Tenth grade. I'd made it through the horror of freshman year and was beginning to get my bearings in high school. I'd held on to most of my old friendships, Allison included, and made a few new ones with other kids who liked math and Isaac Asimov and got excited at science fair time. At the end of the year, my parents had even let me go to the movies with Gerald Hoffer, the boy who had come in third in the district science fair competition. We saw *The Princess Bride*, and we both loved it.

And I had Allison. I was Luke to her Yoda. She showed me how to put on makeup, how to wear the Madonna look without looking like a slut—or at least respectable enough that our parents would let us out of the house—and how to talk to boys on the phone. Like Luke, I lacked confidence and failed spectacularly at most of these tasks, but I tried and, unlike Luke, I didn't give up. So, all in all, it was a perfect summer. It turned out to be one of the last idyllic times in my life, thanks, in part, to Jellie Abernathy.

But, I suppose I can't blame Jellie entirely. It was my obsessive need to belong, my burning desire to be popular, that let her do it. If Luke's love for his father was his weakness, mine was my craving to be popular. And just as the Dark Side exploited Luke's weakness, Jellie Abernathy—a veritable Dark Lord of the Sith herself—exploited mine.

We had Mrs. Morton's English class sixth period, and despite the fact that Mrs. Morton was blunt and critical ("Miss Egglehoff, do you *own* socks that match?" or "Roberta, there *are* other colors besides black"), I loved English that year. The literature we read was actually interesting, *Fahrenheit 451, A Separate Peace, Julius Caesar*—okay, not *Julius Caesar*—and Mrs. Morton's class focused on style analysis. Now, analysis I could understand. Analysis was one area where I excelled.

Unfortunately, Jellie did not. And what was equally unfortunate was that she saw *I* did. The very first time she stopped by my desk before class to talk to me, I should have realized I was being set up, about to be used. Instead, I was so shocked and flattered, I couldn't speak. She must have had a good laugh at my expense, remembering how I stared, mouth agape, astonished eyes blinking behind my enormous glasses.

But I think I can hardly be blamed for my initial reaction. I mean, Jellie was one of the most popular girls at Lincoln if not *the* most popular girl. She was also beautiful. I'm talking drop-dead gorgeous, hit-the-Paris-runways, rich-foreign-men-would-pay-to-look-at-her beautiful. And with her rich lawyer father, her L.A.-imported socialite mother, and their *Gone With the Wind*–style mansion overlooking the lake, Jellie was the closest thing to royalty we had at Lincoln.

So when Angelica Abernathy stopped by my desk in English class one day shortly after we'd begun *Julius Caesar* and complimented me on my sweater—natty, faded black, and shapeless—I almost swallowed the pencil I was chewing before stammering a thank-you. And the next day when I walked into class and she snagged my arm to ask if I could help her with her homework after school, I almost fell over my four eyes to agree.

She invited me to Tara, as I always thought of her house, and I was admitted by a woman who introduced herself as Magda the housekeeper. Awed, I nodded and was escorted through wide hallways, up sweeping staircases, and past huge windows with views of Lake Michigan, to Jellie's bedroom. In contrast to the rest of the house, Jellie's room was a mess. Plates crusted with food, piles of old magazines, and dirty clothes littered the floor. Jellie reclined on an enormous pink-draped canopy bed, but the canopy sagged and the sheets were half off the mattress. Still, when she patted a spot on the unmade bed beside her, I felt like a lowly peasant honored by a royal princess.

I climbed onto the bed, careful not to touch the white satin comforter with my scuffed pleather shoes, and imagined Jellie and I becoming great friends. Finally I was going to be in with the Popular Crowd. No more hearing about their charmed lives secondhand from Allison. I would be part of the Inner Sanctum as well. I would be friends with the queen of Lincoln High School's royal court: Jellie Abernathy.

I was so caught up in my daydreaming that memories of our actual study session are vague. Our assignment was a rhetorical analysis of Mark Antony's funeral speech in *Julius Caesar.* I remember trying to explain to Jellie the difference between logos, ethos, and pathos—and failing miserably—so when Jellie asked if she could just take a look at my paper, I agreed. I was *honored* to give it to her. I practically *forced* her to take it.

I guess when Mrs. Morton accused us of cheating about a week later, I shouldn't have been so surprised. And hurt. Hurt because after our study session, Jellie hadn't so much as acknowledged me with a look, though I'd waved at her in the halls and tried to talk to her in class. I guess it never occurred to me that Jellie would use me to get a good grade on the *Caesar* paper and be so stupid as to copy my paper and turn it in with her name on it.

I stood speechless, staring at the two identical papers, but Jellie was bursting with indignant denials. She raged at Mrs. Morton in a nasal, upper-class voice you'd expect to hear at the ritzy Drake Hotel, not room 227. She stated that, yes, the paper she'd turned in was mine (she would never have convinced Mrs. Morton I'd cheated off her), but it was a misunderstanding. She'd written her own paper but turned mine in accidentally. She said she'd be more than willing to turn her own work in the next day, and Mrs. Morton could drop the whole thing.

I remember staring at Jellie, marveling at her lack of fear when talking to adults. Marveling at her cool confidence, the way she almost made it sound like she was doing Mrs. Morton a favor, the way she subtly threatened Mrs. Morton's with her lawyer father's power. And I remember Mrs. Morton's reaction: how she slowly wilted under Jellie's veiled threats, how she withdrew, one by one, each punishment she'd heaped on us.

Jellie and I started the teacher conference with zeroes on our rhetorical analysis. We ended it with another chance to complete the assignment and no penalty to our six-week grade if we turned the analysis in before the end of the week.

"Jesus Christ, what a bitch!" Jellie sneered when we were outside the room. "Who would have thought the old hag actually *read* our papers. She must have no life."

Jellie's words were a wake-up shower of ice water. "So you didn't *accidentally* turn my paper in?" I mumbled, but I knew the truth all along. I just didn't want to face it.

Jellie rolled her eyes. "You *gave* me your paper to copy. What did you think I would do with it?"

I shrugged. "Use it as a model?" I whispered.

"Yeah, that's a good one." Jellie snorted, her pretty face twisting into something vulgar and ugly. "But no harm done."

I stared at her. Mrs. Morton thought we were cheaters, and we'd almost failed. Worse, my soul was crushed, mashed into tiny pieces as, one by one, all my dreams of popularity were tossed in the recycling bin. Jellie used me. She didn't like me, she didn't want to be my friend. She just wanted to copy my paper.

"What, no thank-you?" Jellie said. The perfect arch of her ash blond eyebrows rose in a thin line. "I saved your ass."

"Wh-what?" I stammered. Did she actually expect me to be *grateful* that she'd plagiarized my work and got me in trouble?

She went around the metal locker bank to hers, a top one in the row a few feet away. "So, what are you doing after school today? Can you help me out with this paper?" she asked, turning the dial on her lock right and then left.

"Can I—can I—"

"Yeah," she said, looking over her shoulder at me. "Can you help me out one more time, Robbie?" Her face was the picture of innocence.

"Rory," I mumbled.

"Come over around five, okay? We can work on my paper together." She pulled out a folder and slammed the locker shut. "Oh,um—yours, too."

I shook my head, still unable to make my mouth work.

Jellie's eyebrows came together, creasing her perfect forehead. "What, do you have *plans* or something?" She sniggered, then looked contrite. Her mouth turned down in a pretty pout. "Don't you *want* to help me?"

I blinked at her transformation. Condescending bitch one moment, helpless princess the next.

"Look, I'll make it worth your while, okay?" she cooed. "The next time I have a party, I'll make sure you're invited."

I stared at her, hating myself because, though I should be insulted, I was beginning to feel honored again, my Coke can dreams recycled into shiny new possibilities. I gave Jellie a nod, feeling sick to my stomach at having sold out so easily. Princess Leia would never have stood for it. Jellie barely waited for my agreement before saying, "So, come over around five, and we'll . . . Oh, no, shit! I forgot it's Friday."

I'd nodded stupidly, agreeing with her that yes, indeed, it was Friday.

"We'll have to do it Sunday or something. I have a date with Hunter tonight."

My heart rammed in my chest. A date with Hunter? "I didn't know you and Hunter were going together."

"There's no *way* I'm canceling on Hunter," Jellie said, brushing her hair back and gloating as though she knew how I pined for him and wanted to rub it in that she had him and I had no chance. "You know what? Let's just make this easy. Just drop the paper by my house sometime this weekend, whenever's convenient for you." She smiled obligingly. "If I'm not home, leave it with Magda."

"Drop—drop—"

Jellie sighed loudly. "Just *drop* it by my house, okay? *Comprendé, mi amiga?*"

Oh, I *comprendé* all right. I *comprendé* in Spanish, English, and geeklish. I was not her *amiga*. I was her lackey. And I was supposed to thank her for the privilege of serving. And, stupid and desperate for acceptance as I was, I might have gone along with it. I might have agreed, written the paper for Jellie, and had my entrée into the Popular World and my chance with Hunter.

But it was Hunter that changed my mind. Jellie's smug grin—the way she seemed to know that I'd give my left pinkie for even a *chance* with Hunter—did her in.

"So, I'll see you."

"No, you won't," I interrupted her. Her eyes narrowed. My knees felt weak, and my breath came short. "I'm not going to write a paper for you, and I'm certainly not going to deliver it to your house. You can write your own paper." The last words were said on a terrified wheeze, but I got them out.

"I see," Jellie said. "Are you sure you want to do that?"

I looked into her eyes and read: If you do this I will personally make sure you stay at the lowest rung of the geek ladder for the rest of your high school career.

And I knew she could do it. I knew even my friendship with Allison would never overcome the wrath and influence of Jellie Abernathy. For a moment, I wavered. Then I remembered the date, and I pictured Jellie and Hunter together tonight.

"I'm sure," I said and walked away, securing for good my rung on the geek ladder.

And now, seventeen years later, I'm exiting the el in Old Town and heading home. Jellie is getting married in high style at the Plaza, and I'm too scared of being alone to dump the biggest nerd this side of the galaxy. I'm still a geek, and she's still a princess. The only difference is that now I've learned to use people, too.

Chapter 9

*"I'm pathetic," I grumble as I push through the re-*volving door of the building housing Y&Y. "I'm a complete coward." If I was any kind of decent person, I'd have ended it with Tom in a good, clean break instead of dragging it out just because I'm afraid to be alone.

I punch the button for the elevator, berate myself for twenty-three floors, then stomp off when the door opens on Y&Y's floor. I'm clomping down the hall toward my office when I hear a long, low whistle behind me. I keep walking. The whistle can't be for me.

"Hey, Roaring Rory, where you been all my life?"

I stumble, but my clumsiness has nothing to do with Allison's strappy sandals. I put my hand out and grasp the wall, catching myself. I force my body to turn around, and my fears are confirmed. Leaning against a door with a lewd leer on his face is the Mynok. Vinnie. Vincent Mancuso, the biggest slime ball in the office. He's so sleazy he makes the sludge at the bottom of the pond on Dagobah look appetizing. He's the type that ranks women on a scale of one to ten.

Not that he's supermodel material. He's short and stocky, with thick black hair everywhere but his balding head. Rumor has it he has a nickname for every woman in the Y&Y office and rates each of us as Too Hot, Why Not, and No Way Not.

I rank as a No Way Not, and my nickname is Remote Rory. So why did he just whistle at me? "What did you call me?"

His leer widens. "Roaring Rory."

"Why?"

"Because"—he steps closer, chest jutting forward—"lately you've looked so hot, you set me on fire. A *roaring* fire." He grins, and I have to fend off a wave of nausea.

His eyes skim over Allison's fitted navy jacket, gaze resting on the spot where it vees between my breasts. Then his eyes slide to the short navy skirt, my naked legs, and the skimpy sandals. "Want to get a cup of coffee?" he says with another leer. "I'm paying."

I stand speechless. Vinnie Mancuso—the office stud—is asking me out. I want to act indignant, but, truth be told, I feel kind of flattered.

But in a bad way. A bad kind of flattered. And that's why I'm going to tell him off—after just one more minute . . .

"Rory! There you are."

"Mr. Yates."

My boss is barreling down the corridor wielding a smile brighter than a lightsaber. "Don't you Mr. Yates, me, Rory Egglehoff. From now on, it's George."

Vinnie raises his eyebrows.

"I just got off the phone with the MacKenzie people. They've been trying to get you all morning. That discrepancy you found on their 8-K saved them a bundle—maybe even a lawsuit."

I shrug. "It was pretty obvious. Anyone would have found it." I'm not being modest. A sharp sophomore accounting major would have seen the error. I haven't done anything brilliant—nothing more than I usually do.

"But *you* are the one who found it, Rory. And before the SEC did, which is the important thing. The client is pleased. And when the client is pleased, I'm pleased. Keep it up." He sweeps his hand toward me, seeming to indicate not just my work but my whole appearance. "I like the changes I see in you. I anticipate great things for your future. Vincent." Yates turns his attention to Vinnie. "I got another call from the EEOC. Another sexual harassment complaint."

"I can explain," Vinnie begins.

"I'm sure you can, but I don't want to hear it this time." Yates starts to walk away, and Vinnie scrambles to catch up.

"But George—"

Yates turns and glares.

"I mean, Mr. Yates, just give me a chance." And the two men disappear around the corner. I stand in the corridor, feeling like I've just been hit by an asteroid. I should be ecstatic. I should be the happiest girl in the galaxy. Vinnie was flirting with me. He may be sleazy, but his dates are always gorgeous.

And Mr. Yates complimented my work. Last week he didn't think I was worthy of lunch with him and Hunter. This week he sees great things in my future. I straighten my shoulders. Why not? Allison always says that people believe what they see. If you look confident, beautiful, and successful, people will see you as confident, beautiful, and successful. And after a while, you'll see it, too. I have a feeling it's taking me longer than most, but maybe I'm finally beginning to believe it.

With new confidence, I stride into my office, set down my briefcase, and perch in my chair. Automatically I reach for the phone to call Allison and tell her about Vinnie. Then I remember that she's going to be at Oprah's studio all day.

Okay, I'm confident, beautiful, and successful, and I've got lots of friends. There's Janet in risk management and that girl who lives in the apartment above me—what was her name, Patricia or Paula or something? And then there's Hunter, or there will be when he falls madly in love with me.

Then there's my family. Sunshine, Dan, and Stormy are always around when I need them, and Tom's not a *bad* guy. Maybe we can come out of this as friends. In fact, I'm going to call him right now. Allison can have Oprah and her interiors. Tom and I will go for drinks after work.

I grab the phone, but the thought of drinks with Tom looks less and less appealing as I dial his extension. Last night he wouldn't stop practicing his Data imitation. Two hours of that is about as much as anyone can tolerate.

I glance at the clock on my desk and, wincing, punch in the numbers. "Hey, Stormy, it's Rory. Did I wake you?"

"Wow! So this is your office?" Stormy says, poking her head in my door Friday at noon.

I jump up from my desk, knocking my knee painfully on the underside. "You're here! Meredith didn't call me." Usually Meredith, Y&Y's receptionist, buzzes us when we have a client or visitor. If it's their first time here, she also escorts them back. I'd been staring at the spreadsheet on my computer, waiting for Meredith's call announcing Stormy.

"I told them I wanted to surprise you."

"Them?" I swallow. Who besides Meredith has seen her? Not that she doesn't look cute. I just wish there was a little more of the midriff-baring orange crop top she's wearing or that her navel ring wasn't visible at the low-slung waist of her camouflage cargo pants. I frown. She could have done without the seven silver loops in her eyebrow, too.

"Yeah," Stormy says, moving into my office. "Meredith and Vinnie. They were up front when I came in."

"Vinnie was up there?"

The last thing I wanted was Vinnie to meet Stormy. I'll never hear the end of it.

Stormy nods. "Yeah. He said his name was Vinnie. Hey, can I sit in your chair? I want to see what it feels like to be a capitalist."

"Sure." She moves closer and I add, "It's leather, though."

"Eeww!" She jumps away as though bitten by a snake. "Why do you have a leather chair?"

"I didn't have a choice. They're standard issue at Y and Y."

"And why are you dressed like that?" Stormy asks, eyeing my shoes and the slim belt cinched around the waist of Allison's slacks with suspicion. "Are you wearing *leather?"*

I sigh. "Stormy, let's not get into this." I avert my eyes. The truth is I do feel bad wearing dead animals. How can I feel otherwise when I'd been indoctrinated as a kid? But I'd long ago made my peace with the fact that sometimes in life compromises are necessary. If leather will get me Hunter, then I guess a few cows will have to be sacrificed.

"But why would you—" Stormy begins.

"So, did Vinnie say anything to you?" I ask, changing the subject. I squint at her, trying to see her as Vinnie might.

Crunchy environmentalist? Sexy hippie? In the outfit she's wearing now, he'll definitely rank her a Too Hot. I dread seeing him later today. He's going to give me that leer he thinks makes him look so sexy and say something completely inappropriate and offensive, like, "Hey, answer me this, okay? That babe with the slamming body said she was your sister. That true? Invite her up again. We'll go out—two for one, you know. Heh-heh-heh."

Just what I need.

"Nothing," Stormy says, sauntering to my bookcase and running her finger along the perfectly aligned, evenly spaced four-inch navy binders. "He just gave me this creepy smile and said hello." She rolls her eyes. "Actually, it was more like 'hel-*loh.*' " She shudders. "Ugh."

"Yeah," I say, then lean over my chair to unlock the desk drawer where I stowed Allison's—I groan mentally—leather purse. The sooner we get out of here, the better. "Vinnie's a real Mynok."

"Really? I thought he looked Italian."

I roll my eyes. "A Mynok is a creature—"

"Stop." She holds up a hand. "No *Star Wars* references. Do you know this Vinnie guy? When I said I was your sister, he acted like he didn't believe it."

"More like he just didn't believe we were related," I mumble, pulling the purse out and sliding the drawer closed.

"Hmm." Stormy perches a hip on my desk, skewing a few files. I resist the temptation to straighten them again. "Well, we may not dress alike, but everyone says we both have Sunshine's cheeks and smile."

"This is the first I've heard of it."

Stormy rolls her eyes. "Are you going to start fishing for compliments again? I thought we finished that last weekend."

A shot of annoyance whizzes through me, but I smile and sling the purse over my shoulder. It's not Stormy's fault that whole if-you-believe-it, it-will-come confidence thing hasn't kicked in yet. It's not her fault I haven't talked to Hunter since last Friday night. No phone call. No office visit. Nada.

"Hey, let's go," I say, trying to sound cheerful. "I brought the revised guest list for Sunshine's party on Sunday, and I thought we could go over it, then shop for party favors after lunch. There's a great Russian vegetarian place on East Adams. Have you been there?"

I head for the door, and Stormy hops off the desk to follow. "Yeah, I think Sunshine took me there one time when we came downtown to shop The Mile."

I frown and turn back to her. "When did you and Sunshine come down to shop? What happened? You hit your heads and forget you hate Marshall Field's and the capitalist pigs who got rich off the rampant materialism plaguing our country?"

"Well," a deep voice drawls. "That's quite a mouthful."

I whip around and gape. Leaning against my doorjamb, not two feet away, is Hunter Chase. And oh, Creator, he looks good. He's wearing a light blue shirt, and it makes his sapphire eyes even more stunningly blue than usual. His spellbinding gaze meets mine, then I watch as it glides away to focus on something behind me. His eyes widen with interest at whatever he sees, and I turn to get a glimpse, too.

Stormy. My pounding heart plummets like a greasy Big Mac into an empty stomach.

Seeing my reaction, Stormy glances at Hunter, then at me, then back to Hunter. "Hi," she says and raises her silver-hooped eyebrow. It's what I like to think of as her coy look.

"Hi." Hunter sticks his hand out, and I step aside, though there's no need. Stormy doesn't shake hands—too establishment.

But instead of a scathing remark about corporate fascism and the subservient symbolism inherent in the ritual of the handshake, my sister reaches out, takes his hand, and squeezes it. Not a handshake but not a brush-off, either. "I'm Stormy."

The mild flirting doesn't really bother me. If I confronted her about it, Stormy would deny any interest in Hunter to the day she died, pleading he wasn't her type. Come on, Hunter is every woman's type. But Stormy does have her standards, bizarre as they might be, and Hunter, with no visible body piercings, tattoos, or hemp clothing, doesn't meet them.

"Hunter Chase," he says as an introduction, since I haven't spoken. "Are you a friend of Rory's?"

Stormy laughs. "No. I'm her sister."

"Really?" Hunter gives me an incredulous look and his gaze sweeps over her again. I can almost see his brain sorting her features and mine into columns labeled *same* and *different.* "She didn't mention a sister to me." He raises a brow, and I shrug.

"I—I guess it never came up."

But he doesn't hear me. He's looking at Stormy again, and now I'm beginning to worry about what he sees. Sure he thinks she's attractive. What red-blooded American man wouldn't? But I saw who Hunter dated in high school, and he'd no more date Stormy than he would a Klingon. His girlfriends looked like Jessica Simpson, and if you got real close to their heads, you could hear the hiss of air escaping.

Okay, so technically I'm not his type then, either, but I already know that, and convincing him otherwise has been hard enough without him knowing about my crunchy, lefter-than-left, throwback to the sixties family.

"Well, now you've met," I trill in a voice I hardly recognize as mine. "I guess we'd better be on our way, Stormy."

"Oh. Sorry." Hunter shifts away from the door. "I didn't mean to hold you up. Going to lunch?"

Stormy and I nod, and I realize that this is the first time I've seen Hunter since last Friday. It also occurs to me that (1) he is not with Mr. Yates, (2) he has stopped by my office, and (3) it is lunchtime.

I grab the doorjamb to steady myself just as Stormy tries to exit. She gives me a questioning look, then turns to Hunter. "Yeah, Rory's taking me to a Russian vegetarian restaurant."

"Sounds . . . interesting," Hunter says, clearly bewildered by the concept.

"Oh, it's not solely vegetarian," I add, and Stormy gives me a weird look. Now, why did I say that?

"Oh, yeah? They have normal stuff, too?"

I stare at him. Oh, Creator! Is it *possible, likely,* statistically *probable* that Hunter was standing here outside my door because he was planning to invite me to lunch with him?

Blast it! Why did I ask Stormy to lunch today? Today, of all days, the day when Hunter decides to make an appearance, to ask me out on a date, possibly to kiss me at some point during this date, and I'm saddled with my *sister.*

Should I invite Hunter to go with us? I study his face as my sister says something about mung bean stew. Hunter's lip curls. Okay, so maybe I won't invite him. Besides, I don't know how chummy I want Hunter to be with my family. Already I'm afraid Stormy's said too much.

"So you're both vegetarians?" Hunter says a moment later, confirming my fears.

Stormy nods. "Oh, yes. Our whole fam—"

"We like to eat healthy," I say over her next confession. I give her a quelling look. Blast it, Stormy, shut up already! She glares right back at me, and I don't blame her. I've never denied my vegetarianism before. I don't preach about it, but I don't hide it, either.

"Right," Hunter says, hedging. I can see his brain working, trying to determine whether this is another one of those girl things, like eating salads, or something more.

"So, I take it you eat meat?" Stormy asks him, and I want to hit her. She's got that judgmental, lecture-coming-on tone in her voice. Oh, Creator, not now. *Please.*

"Oh, yeah." Hunter nods vigorously and grins one of those good ol' boy smiles. I grimace. I know, even before hearing it, that whatever Hunter is about to say next will be wrong.

"I'm a regular meat and potatoes guy. Meat loaf three times a week." The way he says it, I can tell he's joking. Hunter's just trying to be cute, but Stormy won't think him even remotely charming.

"Do you know what happens to that poor . . . *meat loaf* before it makes it to your plate?" she says icily, moving closer to confront him. Uh-oh. Think fast, Rory.

Hunter shrugs. "I couldn't have grown up in Chicago without knowing something about what goes on in slaughterhouses."

Okay, this isn't *so* bad, maybe he'll squeak through, especially if he can work in a reference to *The Jungle.* I inch toward Stormy, hoping to snatch her arm and propel her toward the elevators, down the hall, and as far away from Hunter as physically possible.

I reach out.

"But I don't like to think about that kind of stuff,"

Hunter says, sounding like the broken record Stormy and I and every vegetarian has heard a half a billion times. "It's kind of unappetizing, you know? And abnormal. Humans were meant to eat meat." He grins again, completely oblivious to the fact that he's just insulted us.

"Abnormal?" Stormy shrieks. "Ab—"

My arm whips out, grabbing Stormy and pushing her toward the elevators. Before she can say a word—and I can see from the red tint of her cheeks and the glare in her eyes she's got more than a few words in mind—I sing out, "Well, Hunter, it's been nice seeing you, but we *really* have to go. I only have an hour for lunch, and it's getting late."

Hunter glances at his watch. "Sure, no problem. I was heading out to lunch myself." He glances around and looks a little lost. He really *was* going to ask me to lunch! Joy, like a turbo boost of power, blasts through me.

Now would be the time to ask him to join us. Maybe he'd be willing to try the vegetarian thing for a day.

Beside me, Stormy shakes off my arm, and I catch a glimpse of her in my peripheral vision. She's scowling, back straight, nose high in the air. The picture of self-righteousness.

Hippie self-righteousness.

I give Hunter what I hope is a disappointed look. "Well, have a good lunch, and maybe I'll see you around?" My voice rises on the last word. I hope that didn't sound too pathetically hopeful. Stormy snorts just then, and I know her verdict.

"Yeah," Hunter says, moving away from us, toward Mr. Yates's office. "I'll give you a call sometime."

"Okay. Great," I say. "Please do." Shut up, Rory. "Anytime." Oh, just kill me now!

"Right. Bye." Hunter gives a wave, turns, and heads down the hallway. I sigh. He's never going to call. I've got three strikes against me now. Not only am I a geek, I'm a pathetic, desperate geek, with an abnormal family.

Behind me, one of the freaky family members speaks up. "So you find that ignorant disciple of the mass media attractive?"

I sigh. Right now Russian vegetarian food doesn't sound all that appealing to me, either.

After lunch Stormy and I walk along East Adams Street, glancing in store windows as we pass. I'm checking out my reflection in the mirrors, but she's hunting for a print by Jean-Michel Basquiat. The restaurant is near the Art Institute of Chicago, so there are half a dozen stores catering to the art crowd here. Still, I think she's going to have a hard time finding a shop selling Basquiat. I mean, a graffiti artist living in a cardboard box who died of a heroin overdose? I could be wrong, but I don't think there's a big market for that.

She pauses in front of a window lined with posters of prints by Seurat and Picasso, staples at the museum. While Stormy scrutinizes the artwork, I tug on my blouse.

Thank the Creator I decided to give Hunter one last chance today and put on Allison's come-hither clothes. The black pin-stripe pants have wide legs but are tight at the hips and butt, and the fitted tuxedo-style shirt strains over my small breasts, the ruffles accenting my size 34A chest.

"Hey, girlie, looking good."

I spin around and see the construction workers across the street checking me out. One whistles. "What'cha looking for, sweetheart? I bet I've got it right here." He gropes his crotch.

Beside me, Stormy yells, "Male chauvinists!"

I grab her arm. "Shut up before they get mad."

"You're blue-collar workers! You know what it's like to be exploited. How can you—"

I drag Stormy around the corner.

"I've got your *exploited* right here, girlie," one of the men calls as I pull Stormy away. After a block or so, I release her arm, and we stop to get our bearings. I glance in a shop window and fluff my hair and straighten my blouse. I catch Stormy's eye in the window and stop primping. At the restaurant, I managed to keep our conversation on the Uzbek chickpea spread, Kiev cabbage-apple salad, and the eggplant Orientale, but now she looks ready to *talk*.

"Are you done primping?" she says, moving away from the window. I follow, my cheeks hot with embarrassment at having been caught.

She glances back at me, gives me the once-over. "Very pretentious fashionista. Is that what you were going for? Or did you just want those barbarians to stare at your boobs?" She gives my chest a pointed glance. "Or is it that . . . Neanderthal from high school you're trying to impress?"

"Ouch." I take a step back. "Coming from someone with half her abdomen showing, that's a little harsh, don't you think?"

She shrugs and keeps walking. "I don't know. *I'm* not wearing this to impress anyone. I don't pile on makeup or spray a layer of shellac in my hair."

"Don't you ever give it a rest, Ms. Greenpeace USA?" I stomp up behind her. "I mean, it's like the CD is on repeat track or something.'Save the World' 24–7."

She whirls on me. "You *used* to agree with me."

"I have a conscience like everyone else, but I don't need to push my beliefs on each person I meet. It's embarrassing, Stormy."

She steps forward, and suddenly we're facing off outside CVS Pharmacy. Toe to toe, ugly hemp sandals to Manolo-somethings. Stormy looks like she wants to say something mean and hurtful, then she just sighs and curls her lip at me. "Who *are* you?" She shakes her head in disgust. "I don't even know you anymore."

I snort. "Oh, that's original. Just because I have on a matching outfit and—"

"That is so not it, Rory! Stop trivializing everything I say. I'm your sister, and I'm telling you, you've changed."

I tap my designer shoe and wait. This is a load of Bantha fodder, but I might as well let her get it out of her system.

"You know, I can understand your attraction to that—"

I narrow my eyes, letting her see just what she'll be dealing with if she calls Hunter a Neanderthal again.

"Your high school crush," she finishes lamely. "There's nostalgia, and you always wanted to be part of that crowd. And maybe I'm being a little too hard on him, slightly judgmental."

I raise a brow at her use of the diminutives. A *little* hard on him?

She rolls her eyes. "If you like him and he cares about you, I'll support you one hundred percent. But if you have to do some kind of contortionist act every time he's around because you're afraid he'll think you're *abnormal,* then forget it."

"Contortionist act? What the Dark Side does that mean? You've seen me with him for like five seconds, and I did no acrobatic twisting of any kind!"

"Oh, yeah?" She puts her hands on her hips. "Then what was the we're-vegetarians-for-health-reasons bullshit?"

"That's not what I said. I—"

"Close enough. The point is, you didn't want to admit

you're a vegetarian. And the way you hustled me out of there and didn't even introduce me as your sister. I felt like the ugly stepchild."

"No, that would be me. You're the pretty one, Sunshine and Dan's pride and joy."

"Oh, please." She turns away from me, staring at the pharmacy building before turning back. "Speaking of broken records, buy a new one already."

"That's so easy for you to say, Stormy." My voice rises, and a woman carrying a shopping bag stares at me. "You have no idea what it's like to be me. What it's like not to fit in. You fit in everywhere, and if you don't, you just don't give a shit."

She opens her mouth to protest, but I cut her off. "Well, I do, Stormy. I *do* care. More than I want to admit." My voice is shaky now, and I feel hot tears welling up in my eyes. "Just once I'd like to walk into a room and feel comfortable. Just once I'd like to *belong.*"

"And you're blaming your insecurities on our family? How Freudian."

I glare at her through my unshed tears. "No, I don't blame you guys, but you certainly don't make it any easier. Why can't you and Sunshine and Dan just be normal for once? Just be little sis and mom and dad instead of *Leave It to Beaver* goes liberal, instead of playing judge and jury for every person with a belief that doesn't match yours? We can't even plan a normal birthday party." I pull out the guest list and wave it. "We've got three Rains, two Blossoms, and four, yes *four,* Starbrights coming.

"Our party games are meditation, tarot cards, and chanting. And forget picking up a cake from a bakery. I've tried that Terrific Tofu Chocolate recipe twice, and both times it tasted horrible." I run my hands through my hair. "The last time it came out looking like something that even Jabba the Hutt wouldn't eat, and I almost started crying. Then I thought, why am I stressing? The freaks at the party won't care. It will be all peace and love and bullshit."

Stormy stares at me for a long moment, and I know I've gone too far. I step forward, and the words of apology are on my lips. But she gives me a look so hateful, my throat closes up.

"Sorry we embarrass you, *Roberta.* I had no idea you were so ashamed of me. But don't worry. I won't humiliate you with my presence again."

She turns, and I call out, "Stormy," in a weak, unconvincing voice. But she doesn't turn around, doesn't acknowledge me, doesn't even hurry.

She just slowly walks away.

Chapter 10

I watch until Stormy disappears around the corner, then I turn and walk in the opposite direction. I'm wandering aimlessly, but the next time I look up, I spot a familiar sign and know my path is no accident.

Joe's Collectibles and Antiques. My refuge. My solace. The home of my *Star Wars* glasses.

I'm not a big collector. I can't tolerate clutter or anything that's outlived its usefulness. So I sold most of my *Star Wars* action figures—I kept Han, Luke, and Princess Leia, of course—and auctioned my other toys on eBay. For a good price, I might add. But I do have one collecting weakness: *Star Wars* Burger King glasses.

As a child, there were two things I *had* to do in conjunction with the release of each *Star Wars* movie. The first was to buy the book and read it at least twenty-five times, memorizing every detail.

The second thing was to acquire the collectible glasses sold at Burger King. Of the two tasks I set myself, this was the more difficult. First, it required begging, pleading, cajoling, and wheedling Sunshine into taking me to BK. As a vegan and an anticapitalist, she detested few establishments more than McDonald's and Burger King, and no matter how much I cried, she wouldn't patronize them. Not even for *Star Wars* glasses.

Enter Dan. Wonderful Dan. Dan saved me.

Each week when Burger King released a new *Star Wars* collectible glass, he'd find some errand he *had* to run that necessitated my presence, and mine alone. So, pretending reluctance—didn't want Stormy or Sunshine to suspect our true purpose—I'd trudge to the Partridge Family van, sigh heavily, and climb in. Then, as soon as we were away from the house, I'd positively quiver in my seat all the way to the Forbidden Land. Sunshine wasn't pleased when she saw the inevitable results of these excursions, and she must have known after the third or fourth time what Dan and I were up to, but she was uncharacteristically silent on the subject. She just washed the *Star Wars* glasses and put them in the cabinet, like they had always been part of our dinnerware.

I imagine her attitude would have been vastly different had she known what else Dan and I did at Burger King on those outings.

We ate *meat.*

The first time Dan and I went to Burger King and he returned to the table with a hamburger and French fries, I stared at the food, then watched in horror as he took a huge bite out of his Whopper, juice and ketchup dripping from the corners of his mouth.

"Oh, God," he'd said, closing his eyes in rapture. "This is *so* good." Only it sounded like "Thus os *soh* goh" because his mouth was stuffed full.

"But—but Dan!" I'd protested in a voice that made me sound more like I was three than seven. "That's a dead animal!"

He put the hamburger down, swallowed, and gave me a hard stare. "Roberta, I know what your mother has taught you about eating meat—the harm to the planet and the animal—and, for the most part, I agree with her views." He picked up a fry, bit into it. Enjoying the way he was talking to me as if I were an adult, I picked up a fry and mimicked his action. He nodded approval.

"But I ate meat before I met Sunshine, all my life, in fact. My grandfather worked in the cattle industry, and eating meat is the hardest of my bad habits to break."

I nodded sagely. I understood about bad habits. Sunshine was working to eradicate my nail biting and hair chewing (okay, so I was a strange, neurotic child!).

"I love your mom, Rory. She's the most amazing person I know." His fingers grazed the burger, and I could tell he was itching to take another bite. "But she's not so good at compromise. She's structured her life so she doesn't have to be, but in the real world—in my world—everything's not so black and white. There's not always a clear right and wrong." He nodded to the burger sitting in front of me, still wrapped in its paper covering. "Now, you don't have to eat that. You can throw it away, and we'll pick up some fruit or something else for you on the way home. But—" He glanced around the restaurant stealthily. "If you want to try it—just this once—it's not going to mean you're a bad person. You're free to make your own decision about what you do and don't eat."

With that, he hefted his Whopper again and took a massive bite. I stared at my own small wrapped hamburger, then looked back at Dan. He wasn't watching me, wasn't pressuring me at all. He swallowed his hunk of burger and sipped his pop.

Slowly, I reached down and unwrapped the forbidden feast before me. The beige bun and brown meat looked so innocuous, so insignificant on their thin paper wrapping. Oh, but it smelled like sin. The scents of onions and ketchup and pickles mingled with the unfamiliar but tantalizing aroma of meat to tempt me.

I lifted the burger and took a very small bite. Creator, even now my mouth waters remembering the outlawed taste. Dan had been right: It was so *good.* I swallowed and glanced at Dan. He raised his eyebrows in question.

I smiled. He put a finger to his lips and winked. And that was the day he became my dad.

I've often thought it too bad that Stormy didn't have a similar experience with Dan. Maybe a Whopper would have curbed some of her self-righteousness. Or maybe she's right, and I'm the problem. I'm too indifferent, too willing to compromise. In any case, those glasses were special to me. So much so that I still have them. All twelve of them, four from each film. But because I used them daily, they're no longer in mint condition. Well, the ones featuring Darth Vader and Jabba the Hutt are relatively pristine, but those with Han, Leia, or Luke are marred by chips and cracks, and the pictures have faded almost beyond recognition.

A few years ago, I wandered into Joe's Collectibles with a guy I was seeing who collected *Quantum Leap* memorabilia (don't ask), and I saw that Eddie had two glasses from *ESB* for sale. One featured Lando and Leia, the other Luke and Yoda. At $3.99 each, they were a bargain. But when the new glasses were displayed beside my older ones, the true shabbiness of my originals became horrifyingly apparent. My glasses looked *old.* Luke's nose was rubbed off, and Leia's magenta Bespin outfit had faded to pink. I looked at my other glasses. They, too, were marred with signs of use. Clearly this was unacceptable. A dedicated fan would have flawless collectibles. If I was any kind of true fan, I'd own twelve unblemished glasses.

And so the quest began.

Now I need only two glasses: Luke and Leia from the original film and the Tatooine Desert glass featuring Han and Luke from *Return of the Jedi.* I've been searching for immaculate versions of these glasses the last three years and have everyone I know scouring Chicago, the entire country, in fact, for them. Well, at least I *told* my friends to scour. But I have a feeling no one but me is really on the hunt.

I enter Joe's, and right away Eddie waves at me. Eddie's the owner. I have no idea who Joe is. I asked Eddie once, and he gave me some vague, circuitous answer, so I don't think he knows, either. Probably Eddie's too embarrassed to admit the real reason he picked the name—something lame like it was the name of his pet turtle when he was ten.

"Hey, *Star Wars* chick," he calls from behind a grimy glass counter. The display cases are stacked deep with comic books and sci-fi collectibles. "How's the Force treating you?"

I grin. I love how he calls me *Star Wars* chick, though at thirty-two and the product of a feminist upbringing, I should probably be offended at what Sunshine would label "objectification." Stormy says she is. However, if I'm not mistaken, the last time we were at the video store, some kid called her babe, and I don't remember her jumping all over *him* nearly as much as the bookstore clerk who referred to her as ma'am. So I'll take my one lonely objectification where I can get it, thank you very much.

"Oh, the Dark Side hasn't triumphed yet," I tell Eddie. "Though it's closing in." I lean over the counter to hug him. He smells like tobacco and Lysol, but I don't mind. I probably smell like the beet caviar Stormy and I split at lunch.

"Oh, come on now, space girl. It can't be that bad."

I think about how my sister hates me, my boyfriend is a loser, and I've probably just lost my last chance with the guy I've loved since first grade. "Same old, same old," I tell Eddie.

He glances around the store, stroking his grizzly salt-and-pepper beard. "Well, I wish I could make it better for you and say that I got a lead on one of your glasses, but no such luck. I would have called if I did."

"I know." I lean my elbow on the counter and survey the store with him. It's crowded with rows upon rows of comic books, and in locked display cases against the back wall are action figures, models, and costumes. It's dark and it's dirty, and for some reason, I like it.

"Going to the extravaganza?" Eddie asks.

"Yeah, I'm Princess Leia in the costume show. You?"

"Yep. I'll probably do a booth. Think I'll go as a Klingon. That Chewbacca suit I wore last year was too damn hot."

"You a Klingon? This I have to see."

"I'm glad you stopped by." He heaves his considerable bulk off the counter.

"Really? Why?" I tear my eyes, glazed from the stimulus of too much clutter, back to him.

"Because—" His voice is muffled as he rummages beneath the counter for something wedged under the ancient register. "I thought you might be interested in *these.* " With a triumphant flourish, he holds up three long, slim—I look closer—*toothbrush* boxes?

"I know I ate onions at lunch, but is my breath that bad?" I start to laugh, but the sound chokes in my throat when I spot Chewbacca. "Oh, Creator!" I snatch the box and stare at it, heart banging against my sternum. It's a regular Oral-B toothbrush box, but the outside package depicts Han and Chewbacca with the words *Star Wars* above. The toothbrush is still in its original package, plastic wrap and all. I peer into the carton and see the design on the box's cover is duplicated on the toothbrush's plastic handle.

I snatch the next toothbrush. Luke is on the cover. Eddie hastily hands me the third box, depicting Princess Leia, before I can tear it from him. Studying Leia's outfit, I'm able to date the toothbrushes from *Return of the Jedi*'s release.

"There are six in all," Eddie says, resting his beer belly on the counter again. "You might be interested in that Ewok. What's his name?"

"Wicket W. Warrick." I don't even look up.

"Yeah, but the guy who sold these to me didn't have it. Seems his kid loved the Ewoks and used it."

I nod, unable to speak. The toothbrushes are just too cool. They're cute and stupid and I *must have them.* I glance up at Eddie, trying to hide my eagerness, but it's too late. He's already seen how much I want them, not that I exactly played it cool. "Fifty," he says without blinking. "I checked the books, and that's the going rate."

Without comment, I open my purse and hand him my credit card. The accountant in me screams that fifty dollars is a lot to spend for three toothbrushes I'll never use, but I justify the expense by reminding myself that Eddie is a friend and has always treated me fairly. Besides, the *Star*

Wars–obsessed freak in me hollers, you can't pass up *Star Wars toothbrushes!* I didn't even know they made these!

I leave the store, and suddenly Chicago's pewter skies don't seem quite so dreary. With the generic plastic bag containing the toothbrushes clutched in my hand, I stand motionless outside Eddie's store, stare at the sky, and smile like an idiot.

"Do svidaniya," says a voice behind me, and I whirl to see Hunter grinning down at me. The world tilts, shifts, spins like an asteroid.

"I have no idea what the hell that means, but I figured it fit since you just ate Russian food."

"Hunter," I squeal so loudly my ears ring. "What are you doing here?" Blast it! That came out all wrong. "I mean, um—hi!"

"Don't worry." He holds up a hand then shifts to make room for a guy trying to squeeze past us. Hunter's arm brushes mine, blasting heat through me. "I didn't follow you. I ran into Dave and he had to make a stop here before we head back to the office." He hooks a thumb at the sports memorabilia shop next to Eddie's store. "Dave *says* he has to pick up some trading cards for his nephew's birthday." Hunter narrows his eyes, and I bite my lip when I see the sexy, mischievous glint in them. "Likely story. I think he's buying them for himself." He winks, which puts me automatically at ease, and I grin at him.

"So what are you doing here?" he asks—and I'm back to my prewink stress level.

"Um, me? Nothing." Smooth, Rory. Very sophisticated.

Hunter looks at my bag and raises his eyebrows. Creator! Why does he have to look at me like that? Every time he does it, I swear it's the sexiest thing I've ever seen. It's like the Jedi mind trick or something: One look and I'm all his.

But the frisson of warmth still oozing through me from his touch and nearness fizzles when I follow his glance, lasered on my bag. "Oh, um, this?" I squeak. I cannot let Hunter catch me with *Star Wars* toothbrushes. Why couldn't I like Strawberry Shortcake or the Cabbage Patch Kids? Hunter would probably think that was cute, but a flood of red-hot lava shoots into my face imagining his disturbed expression when he sees a hairy Chewbacca on my toothbrush. "It's nothing." I try to angle the bag behind me, but this only makes him more curious. His brow crinkles. Why does he have to be so adorable?

"Hey, what are you hiding in there?"

Danger, Will Robinson, danger. "Oh, no," I purr. I pull the bag closer, making my movements flirtatious. "This stuff is top secret. Only really cool people—those with a working knowledge of, say . . . the Pythagorean theorem—"

The *Pythagorean theorem*? Where the Dark Side did *that* come from?

"Only those really hip geometry geniuses get a peek in *this* sack," I finish.

"Hey! I'm stylin'." He grins, once again a little boy teasing the girls on the playground. "I've heard of the Pythagorean theorem."

I arch a brow. "Oh, yeah? What is it? Hint: not the hip new club on Rush Street."

Hunter looks hurt. "Well, damn. Can I have another chance?"

"No."

"Come on." He reaches for the bag. "Let me see."

I snort and push the bag farther behind my legs. "Sorry. I could show you, but then I'd have to kill you."

"I'm curious now. What are you hiding in there?"

I need another distraction, but before I can think of one,

Hunter's arm snakes around my waist. I'm so surprised at his closeness and the warmth of his body as it grazes mine, that when he takes hold of the bag, I release it without protest.

For a moment I stand there, paralyzed. Then Hunter opens the bag, and I make a last effort to swipe it away. He cuts to the right and peers inside. "Hey!" With a broad grin, he pulls out the Luke Skywalker toothbrush. "*Star Wars*. I loved this movie when I was a kid. I didn't know they made toothbrushes." He glances up at me, and I smile sheepishly.

He pulls out Han and Chewbacca. "This is cool."

"It is?" Hunter thinks *Star Wars* toothbrushes are cool? Does that mean I'm cool? Whoa. Slow down, Rory. It's one thing to think a movie is cool, to buy it on DVD or pause when channel surfing to catch the last ten minutes. But it is quite another thing to buy toothbrushes depicting characters of said movie.

Hunter's interest in the trilogy is general, fleeting. Mine borders on obsession. I can already picture Hunter telling Dave about the toothbrushes, then making stabbing motions from the shower scene in *Psycho*.

"Where'd you get these?"

"Eddie's," I say.

Hunter glances at the nearby stores and frowns. "Is that around here?"

Blast it! I didn't mean to give that much away. "Um, I meant to say Joe's Collectibles and Antiques." I point at Eddie's store. "Eddie is the owner."

"You know the owner? You must really be into this stuff."

So much for that career as a Rebel spy. I shake my head as nonchalantly as possible. "Not at all." Taking the toothbrushes from his hand, I shove them back in the bag. "*Star*

Wars toothbrushes. *Please.*" I roll my eyes. "These are for a friend."

"Uh-huh." Hunter nods slowly as if he knows he's being duped. "Your nephew isn't having a birthday, too, is he?"

"My neph—" Relief ripples through me like birthday streamers. He's teasing me. "Oh! I get it. No, no. Just a friend who likes *Star Wars.* "

Hunter nods and looks past me. "Boyfriend?"

I shake my head so hard I almost get a concussion. "No. *No.* What would give you that idea?"

"I saw you coming back from lunch with a guy a week or so ago. It looked like you were together."

Tom. Blast it! I'm caught.

"And *Star Wars* movies," Hunter continues, glancing in the window of the sports card store behind us for signs of Dave. "They're kind of a guy thing, so I just assumed—"

"Oh, oh, of course." I cut him off. "Well, actually these *are* for a guy." I hold the bag aloft, and I swear that Hunter's face falls in disappointment. Okay, his expression didn't change or anything, but there was a minuscule turning down at the corner of his lips. I swear there was.

"These are for my friend, ah, Paula. Her son. He loves the new films—*Attack of the Clones* or whatever. He even has a Jar Jar Binks action figure. Ugh! It's a tragedy. I'm trying to turn him on to the originals, they're classics."

Hunter shakes his head and, for a moment I'm certain he's going to say, "Yeah, right. Those toothbrushes are for you, you *Star Wars*–obsessed, abnormal vegetarian mutant, that nerd was your boyfriend, and the kiss I gave you last week? A gesture of pity."

But he doesn't. Instead he says, "Kids today. What's this world coming to?"

"My feelings exactly. I say we lock 'em all up, fill the jail cell with the best American culture has to offer, and don't let them out until they've acquired some taste."

"All right, Madam Führer." He crosses his arms. "Who decides what qualifies for the best of American culture?"

"Duh." I give him a look full of disdain. "*Me,* of course."

He nods. "Of course. What's on the curriculum? *Mein Kampf?* "

"No." I tap a finger to my lips, affecting deep concentration. Hunter's mouth quirks as he tries to hold back a smile. I'm amusing him! It's working. The Ultimate Jedi Plan is working! "For literature," I begin, "they'd read the greats."

"Shakespeare? Dickens? The Brõntes?"

"No one reads them," I scoff. "I'm talking John Grisham, Stephen King, and Michael Crichton."

"John Grisham writes books?" Hunter says with a grin. "I thought he just did movies."

"That's what's so cool about these authors. If you don't want to read the book, you can just watch the movie."

Hunter nods sagely. "The American way. Music?"

"No brainer. Depeche Mode, New Order, and Erasure."

"Erasure?"

"Hmm. Not enough variety? Okay, substitute The Smiths. They're dark and existential."

"You scare me, Rory. If *Dirty Dancing* is on the list of movies, I'll be forced to report you."

"*Dirty Dancing?* Please. *Footloose* was way better."

"Oh, yeah, *Footloose.* Way deeper." By this time we're both starting to crack up. Hunter starts chanting *Sieg heil,* which only makes me laugh harder. And that's when Dave walks up.

"Did I miss something?" he asks, brow wrinkled. "Don't tell me you're pretending to be Nazi commandants again?"

"Damn, you caught us," I say, then almost clap a hand

over my mouth. What's going on today? I'm not usually Miss Witty Comeback.

"Hey, Rory." Dave smiles and gives my arm an affectionate squeeze. "I didn't know you were around. We should have got together for lunch."

"Oh, um—" Ewok shit! Lunch. Stormy. I'd been hoping to maneuver around this topic. I didn't want to remind Hunter about my *abnormal* vegetarian tendencies.

"Next time, okay?" Dave says, and I begin to realize that, though he's big on talking, he's not so big on listening. "And, hey, if you and Hunter are going to be hanging around together so much, the least you could do is introduce me to one of your girlfriends."

The air chokes in my throat, and I feel an attack of hyperventilation coming on. I glance at Hunter to see how he'll respond to Dave's assumption that we're *together.*

But Hunter looks nonplussed. "Hey, what about Allison Holloway, Rory? Is she still single?"

"Uh-huh," I stammer. Didn't Hunter *hear* what Dave just said? Didn't he understand the implication?

Hunter looks at Dave. "She'd be perfect for you. We'll all have to go out sometime." He turns back to me, but all I can manage is a nod.

Dave glances at his watch. "You can tell me about her in the car, bro. We have to get moving if we're going to make it to Ashley, Smith, and Davidovich on time."

"Yeah, okay. Good seeing you again, Rory," Hunter says. "I hope the kid likes the toothbrushes."

I have no idea what he's talking about but, like an imbecile, I keep nodding.

"Don't be a stranger, Rory," Dave calls and heads toward a mammoth black SUV. It looks like something Darth Vader would drive.

Hunter gives me a last grin. "Hey, I'll give you a call, okay?"

I nod. "Great," I say weakly, but I don't think he hears because he's halfway to the Vadermobile.

He's going to call me. He's going to call me.

The guys climb in, Dave starts the engine, and they pull away, Hunter giving me a quick wave out the window.

He's going to call me!

Then I frown. Wait a parsec. He still doesn't have my number.

Chapter 11

The next morning as I dash out the door in my old running shoes, I spot the blaster from Tom's Data costume on the coffee table. Annoyed, I stash it in my gym bag to drop off at Tom's later, then stomp down the hall to the elevator.

But I'm not really mad at Tom. I'm mad at me. I didn't break up with him last night. On the el I have time to think of a hundred reasons why—I was tired, he was late, I was on the Web, searching for a place nearby that sells recycled paper plates to use at Sunshine's party, and he was wearing his *Star Trek: The Next Generation* Data costume. The extravaganza is only a week away, so he was in full Data mode—stilted movement, halting speech, and everything.

How do you break up with a guy wearing a Data costume? He looked so goofy, I couldn't decide if I felt sorry for him or wanted to burst out laughing. That made it pretty easy to shuttle him out the door before he got any ideas about staying the night. But not before he convinced me to try on my Princess Leia costume so we could greet the pizza delivery guy in character—but that's another story.

Mad isn't even the right word for what I feel. I'm disgusted. I want to break up with Tom. I should break up with Tom. And yet I don't break up with Tom.

I haven't seen Allison in forever, so here I am at six forty-five Saturday morning on the way to her gym. I'm exhausted, but I couldn't sleep anyway, thinking about Stormy's accusations and my dilemma with Tom. My eyelids droop, as heavy from lack of sleep as my mind is full of questions.

"You sure about this, Rory?" Allison asks when she spots me. I'm so tired and distracted that I almost slam into one of the StairMasters. She pauses her stair climbing and gives me a concerned look. "Are you okay?"

"Just tired," I mumble. "Late night."

"Oh, no!" She hops off the machine, and a peroxide-bottle blond with boobs straining her tight chartreuse sports bra leaps forward.

"Hey, is this machine free?" she squeaks. "People are waiting."

Allison gives her a withering look and, no surprise, it works. The blond steps back. "But, uh, take your time."

With a thin smile, Allison says, "No, it's all yours," and sweeps her eyes over the blond's thighs with a look that says, "You need it more than I do, honey."

Neither of them need it. With her red hair pulled into a high, straight ponytail on top of her head, a healthy glow on her face, and outfitted in cropped gray running shorts and a matching tank, Allison looks like she should be on the cover of a fitness magazine. Popular Crowd all the way. No bimbo would dare usurp her territory.

Now I am another story. Withering looks have never worked for me, and since I'm wearing baggy yellow sweatpants and an ancient Debbie Gibson concert T that hangs to my knees, no one looks at me twice. Except Allison.

She puts her hand on my shoulder. "Sweetie, are you okay? I've been so busy I forgot to ask how it went when you broke up with Tom. Was it bad?"

I bite my thumbnail. "Uh, sort of."

"Do you want to talk about it?" She gestures to the juice bar in the corner. I do. Even more, I'd like to crawl back into bed and moan.

"No, I'm okay. Where were you heading next?" Please don't say the treadmill. Please don't say the treadmill.

"The treadmill."

Blast it. "Great." I try to sound bright and enthusiastic, but it's a blasted challenge when I haven't slept, am surrounded by hard bodies strutting to the blaring music adding to the pounding in my head, and the sun has yet to make an appearance.

We walk to the dreaded treadmills, Allison's hand still on my arm. The alien machines grin maliciously at me. It's like they know I'm coordination-impaired. Whenever I try to use a treadmill, I end up tripping and skidding off in a flailing heap of arms, legs, and wounded pride.

Allison steps up to a machine, and I take the open one beside her. She begins confidently inputting data, while I stare in confusion at the display.

"Tell me what happened, Rory." I haven't punched any numbers, so she adds, "Do you remember how to get started?"

"Uh, yeah," I lie. "Just give me a minute."

Allison nods and increases her speed, pumping her arms as she finds her stride. "Did you let it slip about Hunter? Was Tom mad that you cheated, if you want to call it that, on him?" She gives me a sideways glance.

"No, it wasn't like that," I say, still studying the torture apparatus. "Things didn't—" I stare at the alien buttons and flashing lights. "Things didn't go exactly as planned."

From the corner of my eye, I see Allison break her rhythm, then find it again. "You *did* end it with him, didn't you?"

I punch a button on the contraption, becoming increasingly interested in the readout.

"Rory?"

I glance at the machine, then her. "No, okay! I didn't! I couldn't . . ."

She jabs a finger at her machine, and it whines to a stop. Grabbing hold of the display panel to steady herself, she eyes me with pity. "You're never going to do it, are you?" she accuses.

I stare at her in stupefaction. She's never looked at me like this before, like I'm as pitiful as a flea on Chewbacca's ass. "Yes, I am. But Tom was late and I was looking for recycled paper plates, and then he was wearing the Data costume and I was Princess Leia and—well, *you* try breaking up with Data, Allison."

She puts her hands on her hips and shakes her head so that her long tail of hair swishes across her back and shoulders. Her lip curls as if to say, "You are pathetic." And I *feel* pathetic.

"I don't understand why you do things like this," she finally says, and the censure in her voice slices through me. "What are you so afraid of?"

"Nothing. I just—you were talking about Jellie that night and then I started thinking I wouldn't have a date—"

Allison's snort interrupts me. "So basically you're just using Tom until someone better comes along."

I open my mouth to protest, but I have nothing to say.

She's right. Allison shakes her head again. "I really don't respect you right now, Rory."

"Allison!" I want to grab her arm and shake her, beg her not to lose respect for me, not to look at me with such contempt. Instead I clench my hands on the machine's handrail. "Don't say that. I'm *going* to break up with him. I'll—I'll do it tonight." As long as he's not wearing that Data costume.

Allison steps off her machine. "I don't care if you never do, not if you're only doing it for me. You need to do it for you. For your own sense of self-respect, not to mention that it's the right thing to do." She steps forward, gripping the rail near my hand and staring hard into my face. "You have a once in a lifetime chance to be with a man you've always dreamed about, and you're jeopardizing it for a los—someone you don't even like. Why?" She squints at me as if trying to see inside, to see what vital cog or dial has sprung loose.

I open my mouth to reply, but I can see in Allison's face that she thinks she's got it all figured it out. "Are you so afraid of being alone, of having no one, that you'll cling to anyone to avoid it?"

I clutch the rails tighter. She knows me so well, sees right through me.

"Maybe it's time you took a hard look at your life. A hard look at Roberta Egglehoff, and decide who she is and who she wants to be."

And then my oldest, dearest, best friend turns her back on me and walks away. And now I really feel alone.

I forgot how much I hate gyms. I do *not* belong at Chicago Hard Bodies. The place is packed with people, so the lines for the machines are endless, and no one seems to notice.

They're all chatting with one another like this is some kind of dance club rather than a torture chamber.

I've searched the whole club now, but I can't find Allison anywhere. I tug up the yellow sweatpants and, gathering my stringy hair into a ponytail, pretend all the models and fashion plates don't intimidate me. Trying to look like I belong, I make my way across the first floor. Most of the weight machines are down here as well as the StairMasters, but she's not hiding behind any of them. I glance at the second floor, housing the remaining cardio machines, and frown. I'll look one more time, and then I'm out of here.

With heavy steps—heavy because of my reluctance but also because I seem to be the only woman present weighing more than 105 pounds—I start upstairs. I mount the last step, stumble sideways to avoid a gaggle of skinny, giggling girls, and promptly bump into something big and sweaty. "Oh! I'm so—" I spin around, the apology barely out of my mouth, and choke.

It's Hunter. But it's not.

At least this isn't any Hunter I'm used to seeing. This guy is *built.* This guy is *ripped.* This guy is all of those words Allison is always using to describe the men she dates. Creator! If I'd had any idea the man looked like this under his clothes, I'd have found a way to see him undressed a lot sooner.

"Rory!" he says when he finally gets a look at my face. "What are you doing here?"

"I—I—" All that comes to mind are the words, "Take me now."

"I didn't know you were a member." Hunter smiles down at me. "Maybe I should come more often." His gaze is warm, and I feel my skin heat where his eyes skim over me. A light sheen of sweat glistens on his tan face, a few drops beading along his upper lip. I stare at the tiny droplets and wonder what he'd do if I reached up on tiptoes and licked the moisture away. The thought shocks me so completely, I take a step back, and only then do I realize Hunter's been holding on to me, steadying me after our near collision.

I glance down at the hand he's wrapped around my bare upper arm and inhale at the sharp jolt of desire that rips through me. His bronze skin and heavily corded muscles contrast sharply with my pale, thin arms. I feel like a porcelain Victorian lady. Like a graceful, dainty creature instead of an awkward geek.

"You okay?" Hunter asks, leaning down to look in my eyes.

"What?" Snap out of it, 'droid brain! "Oh, I'm fine. Great. I'm here with Allison."

He glances around. "She's a member? Where is she?"

"She had to go, and I stayed because—" Think. Think. Think. "Because I'm doing research for our project."

"Project?"

"Yeah." I lower my voice. "You know, our plan to brainwash—I mean, reeducate—America's youth."

He laughs. "Oh, yeah?"

"Mmm-hmm. Scoping it out as a possible reeducation center."

"Concentration camp, you mean."

I shrug. "You say tomato . . ."

He starts laughing, and I'm so relived I almost collapse with relief and joy. I can't believe he actually bought that.

"So I guess part of this plan is to whip America's youth into shape."

"What?" I gasp, putting a hand to my heart. "No way! I figure if we put the kids in fitness clubs we have a two-for-one. Blast them with The Cure while simultaneously showing *Melrose Place* on all twenty mounted TVs."

Hunter groans—but he's still smiling! "And if the kids aren't receptive?"

I gesture to the StairMaster. "Built-in torture chamber."

He throws his head back and laughs. I bask in the warmth of his approval, and heat at the sight of his chest. My basking turns quickly to ogling as I stare shamelessly at his tight white tank top. Hunter's sweaty, and if this were a wet T-shirt contest, he'd be the winner.

What is *wrong* with me? I don't ogle men.

Maybe I'm stuck in Alternate Rory Universe. Hunter's laughter is dying down, and when he looks at me with those gorgeous sapphire eyes, I drag my searing gaze away. The gym feels like a sauna. I swallow to hydrate my parched throat.

"Thirsty? Did you bring any water with you?" He glances at my hands, empty except for the as yet unused towel Biff or Buff shoved at me when I walked in the door. Hunter holds up an enormous blue bottle. "Here, have a sip of mine."

It's one of those neon-colored power drinks, which tastes like Wookiee spit unless you've sweated out half your body's weight in water, but I'm not about to refuse the offer. Accepting the bottle, I take a small sip, wincing at the sour taste even as I tremble at the sweet knowledge that my lips are now precisely where Hunter's have been.

I swear, in Real Rory Universe, I would fall over laughing at the romanticized fuzz poofing into my brain, but right now I can't seem to turn the marshmallow fluff machine off.

I swallow the Wookiee spit and hand the bottle back to Hunter. "Better?" he asks. I nod, though I feel exactly the same, like my brain is a toasted marshmallow.

"Hey, the smoothie bar here is pretty good. How about something with a little power to give you a boost?"

Oh, Creator, yes! But I can't agree too readily or he'll think I don't want to work out—true as that may be—so I say, "Oh, no! You don't have to do that. I don't want to interrupt your workout."

He shrugs, the muscles of his shoulders rippling deliciously. "I was just about done anyway, only the treadmill left." He gestures to the dreaded machines, whirring and vibrating behind us. "What were you going to do?"

Rip that tight shirt off your body and shamelessly rub myself all over you. I flush. "Um, I was going to do the—the—" I point hopelessly at the machines behind us as all nonsexual thoughts desert me. "That, too."

"Well, hey, two right next to each other just opened up. Let's grab them. We can earn that smoothie."

I turn around and see a lithe brunette, shimmering with perspiration, stepping daintily off a treadmill. The one next to her is empty, and, unbelievably—for the *second time in one day*—no one is waiting.

Maybe because it's practically second nature for me to run headlong into situations I know can only end like Mark Hamill's post–*Star Wars* movie career—badly—or maybe because the reward of a smoothie with Hunter at the end of this humiliation (assuming he's still willing to be seen with me) is almost worth the ignominy of Hunter seeing me on a treadmill, I follow him.

Predictably, it's worse than the last Mark Hamill film.

I jab the big green start pad and prepare to walk, jog, and run my way into Hunter's heart, but the machine doesn't groan into gear. I frown at the screen, and it flashes back at me.

TIME? TIME? TIME?

Beside me, Hunter taps one button and begins a brisk walk. Hmm. I look back at my machine.

TIME? TIME? TIME?

Insistent little machine, isn't it? I press start again, this time more forcefully, but the readout doesn't change.

TIME? TIME? TIME?

I grit my teeth. I'm actually a reasonably intelligent person. I scored 1300 on my SATs—perfect 800 on the math section, thank you very much. I graduated at the top of my class—summa cum blasting laude—from Northwestern. I make over 70K a year, and I earn it. How many people do you know who can calculate the value of a client's investment, taking into consideration at least five interest rate changes?

In their head.

So I should be able to program a blasted treadmill. But all these evil machines are different! I study the screen on this one and decide it must want to know how long I intend to torture myself on it. I don't know how much time Hunter put in, but I decide twenty minutes is a relatively safe bet. If he goes longer, I'll just add more.

I tap in 20:00 and, after scrolling my finger above the keypad for a moment, press enter. Taking a deep breath, I prepare to begin my workout, when the machine flashes WEIGHT?

Huh? What the Dark Side is *this?*

WEIGHT? WEIGHT? WEIGHT?

Not only is the machine insistent, it's rude. Why the Dark Side does it need to know my weight?

"Doing okay, Rory?" Hunter asks. I jump and whip my head to look at him. He's increasing his speed to a jog.

"Great. I'll be running in a jiffy."

He laughs. "A jiffy. I haven't heard that in a while. You crack me up."

Great. Wait until he sees me run on this thing.

WEIGHT? WEIGHT? WEIGHT?

If I can ever get it going.

I type in 125. I have no idea if this is accurate, but it sounds good. It's what I put on paperwork, and no one has challenged me yet, so even if it's a bald-faced lie, which I'm pretty sure it is, I can at least *pass* for 125.

Okay, here we go. I press enter—now more than ready to impress Hunter with my twenty-minute, 125-pound workout—when the Creator-damned machine flashes INCLINE?

Incline? I don't want an incline. How do you say no?

INCLINE? INCLINE? INCLINE?

What *is* this thing? The space shuttle? We're not at NASA. Just blasting *start* already!

"Sure you're okay, Rory?" Hunter asks. "Want me to help you with that?"

"No!" I say, forcing a cheery tone. "I'm ready now." I jab my finger at the keyboard and hit enter, but when I move my hand away, I see my mistake. In my hurry, I have pressed 8.

The machine whirrs to a start, and my heart pounds in rhythm with my feet. Blast it! I'm going to have to work out with a level eight incline for the next twenty minutes. I don't think I can even maintain a flat level one.

Momentarily I consider hitting stop and starting this whole thing over, but then Hunter will ask if I need help again, and probably insist on giving it, and I'll feel like an even bigger dork than I already do.

The machine grinds and begins to tilt upward, and I have to work a little harder to keep up, though my speed is still easy walking. After about fifteen seconds at the new incline, I decide it's not so bad. I can handle this. Hunter is now running at a comfortable pace beside me, so I increase my speed and start to jog.

When I glance at him, he grins. Searing warmth, which has nothing whatsoever to do with the sweat popping out on my forehead from the workout, blasts through me.

"Looking good, Rory," Hunter says. "You've got a great stride."

"Really?" I say, breathless. My legs are starting to ache from running uphill. "No one's ever told me that before."

The machine grunts and wheezes and the incline increases again. I have to grab the handrails to keep from stumbling because I'm jogging at a forty-five-degree angle now.

"Hey, you're really challenging yourself," Hunter says. "I'm going to have to work to keep up." He hits a button on his control panel, and the incline on his machine increases as well.

Men! Why do they have to be so competitive? Now, even if I knew how to downshift the incline on this stupid contraption, I can't or I risk losing our "contest."

Not that I care. Not that I'm trying to compete against Hunter. But I don't want him to think I'm a loser or a weakling. I increase my speed by a few tenths of a point, and now I'm running.

The machine screeches again, and this time I stumble when the platform beneath me inches upward. I clutch the handrails for dear life as the ground beneath me shifts to what has to be a ninety-degree angle. I'm practically running vertically here.

I glance at the numbers on the display screen and want to cry. I've only been running for five minutes. Oh, Creator! Fifteen more to go, and I'm already panting, the sweat dribbling down my temples. I am never going to make it fifteen more minutes.

My legs feel heavy and tight—I probably should have

stretched before getting on this thing—and I grasp the rails tighter to keep my balance. Please, Creator, don't let the incline tilt any further.

"Doesn't this feel *great?* " Hunter calls out. "Gotta love it when those endorphins kick in."

Endorphins? All I feel is pain. Ewok shit! The machine lets out a shriek, and once again my world shifts.

The incline creeps steadily perpendicular, and I clutch at the handrails in desperation. My breath is wheezing in and out, my calves are on fire, and I still have twelve endless minutes to go.

"Bet you're feeling the burn now, Rory," I hear Hunter say. I don't dare glance at him, afraid I'll lose my precarious balance. I don't even *want* to look him. He's running at a brisk pace and doesn't even sound winded.

Creator! He really *likes* this. I, on the other hand, am struggling just to stay upright.

And then I'm not. Not upright that is. Something happens: (1) I either accidentally release my vise grip on the handrails, (2) I stumble, or (3) some force beyond me (but obviously allied with the Dark Side) gives me a hard punch in the chest. Then I'm flying backward off the treadmill.

For a moment I feel like I'm in a fantastic dream. I'm airborne with the lights of the gym streaking by me, and an old New Order song supplying the in-flight soundtrack. Then I land with a hard thud, and the dream implodes like a supernova in reverse. My head whacks into something solid, but not overly hard, and my tailbone slams into the polished gym floor. I groan and lie completely still until the world stops spinning. When I open my eyes a half a dozen light-years later, I'm staring at the gym's ceiling.

I blink. The ceiling tiles have water damage. They're brown in spots and should probably be replaced.

"Shit, Rory! Are you all right?" A gorgeous male face cuts in front of the tile's swirly brown patterns.

I mumble something that's supposed to be reassuring, but Hunter doesn't look appeased.

"Oh, fuck, Rory." He bends down and peers at me more closely, then raises his head and calls out, "Somebody do something! She's bleeding."

Who's bleeding? If someone is bleeding, I need to get out of here because the sight of blood makes me nauseous.

"Ma'am, are you all right?" A black man wearing a shirt with the words "Chicago Hard Bodies" blazing across his pectoral muscles bends over me. "Don't move, okay? We're going to call for an ambulance."

An ambulance? Blood? What is *going on?* Then the generator kicks on, the power is restored, and the lights in my brain flicker. I start to sit up. "No."

Hunter lays a hand on my shoulder. "Just lie still, Rory."

"No." I struggle against his grip and manage to prop myself up on my elbows. "I'm okay. I don't need an ambulance."

The black man eyes me skeptically. "Miss, you took quite a fall. I think it would be better if you wait for the paramedics to come and check you out."

"No, really." I can feel the heat of embarrassment painting my cheeks. "I just had the wind knocked out of me. I'm fine." And then to prove it, I sit up and force a fake, driver's-license-photo smile.

"Rory, you're bleeding."

"Where?" I climb to my knees then lurch unsteadily to my feet. I wobble but refuse to grasp any of the machines for support. I *cannot* allow them to call that ambulance. If people find out, I'll never hear the end of the jokes and ribbing.

Hey, Rory, hear about State Farm's new insurance coverage? Home, auto, and *gym.* Ha, ha, ha.

Hey, Rory, lucky for you "uncoordinated" doesn't count as a preexisting medical condition.

And the doctors at the hospital, what are they going to write in their charts?

Patient Status: Stable.

Cause of Injury: Acute clumsiness.

Prognosis: Mortification for life.

Hunter catches my elbow and steadies me, though I'm still pretending I don't need any help. "Your elbows are bleeding," he says, and points to the garish red smear on my Debbie Gibson T-shirt. I glance at my elbow and see a raw scrape marring the skin. Tiny drops of blood bead the red welt. My head swims.

"Oh, that's nothing," I say, my voice too bright, like the sixties and seventies psychedelic colors Sunshine painted the living room when I was five. Some of those groovy designs are swirling before my eyes now, and I close them briefly to ward off what I imagine an acid trip feels like.

"Johnny, you still want that ambulance?" a voice calls from the first floor. The black trainer looks at me, and I shake my head and flash my DMV smile.

"I'm fine. Just embarrassed."

Johnny nods and hollers back, "No, she's okay." Then he turns to the crowd of people gathered at a safe but nosy distance. "Okay, folks." He claps his hands. "Show's over. Get back to your workouts or I'm going to have to cut your calories!"

There's a smattering of chuckles, and the club's members filter away. Machines begin to whir, New Order cranks up on the sound system, and hard bodies once again begin to churn out sweat.

I glance at Hunter. "Um, I think I'll just head home now.

I've probably had enough of a workout for one day." I laugh at my lame observation and start to walk away.

He doesn't stop me. Half of me is relieved. I can leave quietly, bear my shame alone, and know for certain that any chance I might have had with Hunter is officially null and void. The other half of me desperately wants to look back at him, to stop and plead that he give me just one more chance. But even I'm not *that* pathetic.

Right? My steps falter. Right. I push on and make it to the stairs. I haven't started crying yet, but the tears smart behind my eyelids when Hunter puts his hand on my shoulder.

"Hey, where you going?" he says softly.

I turn to look at him, and I can tell by the way his face falls in sympathy that he sees my unshed tears.

"Let's go get that smoothie," he says and wraps a big, warm arm around my waist. "Better yet." He pulls me securely against him. "Let's get a *drink*."

Chapter 12

Hunter's serious about the alcohol, so we go to a café by the lake, sit outdoors, and sip mimosas. Hunter swears the pizza here is great and insists on ordering a large of the specialty, which is thankfully vegetarian. I swear up and down that I'm not hungry, but when the pizza comes, Chicago-style and all doughy, warm, and dripping with cheese, pesto, and basil, I scarf half of it down. After the morning I've had, the pizza tastes better than sex.

Well, sex with Tom. Not Hunter. I wet my lips as he bites into another slice of pizza, using his tongue to catch a string of dangling cheese. What does a girl have to do to be that piece of cheese? But when I almost say it aloud, I know I have definitely had one too many mimosas.

"Feeling better?" Hunter asks after swallowing.

"Hmm? Oh, uh, yes." I rub my scraped elbow. "The mimosas helped."

"I had a feeling they might."

Actually, I had just about forgotten the incident at the gym. Being with Hunter has that sort of mind-numbing effect on me—like a cup of hot cocoa with just enough rum to make a girl tingle.

"So, tell me the deal with your sister," Hunter says, effectively stifling the tingle with this shower of iced Gatorade.

I choke on a sip of champagne and OJ. "Who?"

"Your sister." He flashes a grin. "You know, a female sibling sharing half of one's gene pool. Or at least I think it's half. I never paid much attention in bio."

"Too busy flirting with Julie Jones," I say and immediately wish I'd kept my mouth shut. Blast those mimosas!

Hunter's grin widens, his white teeth gleaming. "Is that jealousy I hear, Miss Egglehoff?"

I roll my eyes. "No." Arrogant, stuck-up, scruffy-looking nerf-herder. Okay, not scruffy-looking. "Don't be ridiculous, Hunter." I toss my hair back, a gesture that probably doesn't produce the desired sex-kitten effect as my scraggly locks are secured with a clip at the back of my neck. "That was eight—um . . . a long time ago."

"Uh-huh." He reaches across the table and takes my busy hand, nervously folding and refolding the corner of the damp paper napkin under my mimosa. "Did you have a crush on me in seventh grade, Rory?"

Ooh, he can be so arrogant at times! The way he's smiling, I know he's doing this just to goad me, to tease me. But the joke hits a little too close to home.

I think about making a defiant gesture—tearing my hand out of his or something equally dramatic. But I don't. Instead I give him a withering glance and snort out a "No."

Hey, it's not a lie. I had a crush on him *every* year, not just seventh grade.

"Are you sure?"

His thumb caresses the skin between my thumb and first finger, and I shiver. "Yeah."

"Yeah?" He caresses my palm, sliding his thumb over the soft inner skin, then begins tracing slow, lazy circles. "What about now?" His gaze is locked with mine, and I'm floating in zero gravity. I shake my head, the movements so sluggish they feel like slow motion.

"That's too bad."

I open my mouth, and my voice comes out as a whisper. "Why?"

"Because I have a crush on you."

My hands begins to tremble in his. "Y-you have a—"

His thumb strokes the inside of my wrist, where my pulse beats a rapid march against his skin. He raises a brow. "Are you sure you don't have even a *small* crush on me?" His voice is low and so incredibly erotic.

"Mmm-hmm," I murmur because it seems some sort of reply is expected.

His sapphire eyes widen slightly, and his thumb suspends its languid movements. "So, yes?" he says softly.

"Yes."

He raises a cocky eyebrow. Blast it!

"I mean, *no*. Oh, I don't know!" With Chewbacca-strength will, I pull my hand out of his. "You're—you're confusing me. And—and—" I grasp at something, anything, to turn the topic. "I thought we were talking about my sister."

Ewok shit! Why'd I have to bring that up again? I'm more confused than a cheerleader trying to decipher the new tax code. Still, the topic of Stormy is ten thousand parsecs better than discussing my feelings, past or present, for Hunter. Especially *with* Hunter!

He looks reluctant to change the subject, so I press forward. "Stormy is definitely one of a kind."

Hunter nods, and my stomach rolls. Just thinking about Stormy makes me feel ill. I can't believe the venom I spewed at her yesterday. She was out of line, but I wish I hadn't said all I did about our family. Sunshine's party is tomorrow, and I'll make it up to Stormy then. I'll make sure everything is perfect and that Sunshine, Stormy, Dan, the Hare Krishnas, and the rest of the eccentric guests have a great time.

Across from me, Hunter sits back and looks thoughtful. "You and Stormy don't seem very much alike. She strikes me as a free-spirit type, while you're—" He gestures vaguely, his hand jerking toward the azure blue waters of Lake Michigan behind him.

"Mundane and predictable?" Resentment bubbles up in me. I haven't felt it this strongly since I was a senior and found out the guy I'd been dating was only using me to get close to Stormy. Is there anyone who's not ga-ga over Stormy? And now she's beguiled Hunter, too.

He shoots me a scowl. "No. That wasn't what I was going to say at all."

"Okay, then what were you going to say? Conventional? Conformist?" I cross my arms.

"Maybe."

I raise my brows in triumph.

"So what? Why are those put-downs?" He leans both elbows on the table and looks me in the eye. "What's wrong with being predictable? It means people can count on you. What's wrong with being conventional? It shows you've outgrown all that alternative Nirvana/Kurt Cobain shit everyone conformed to when we were kids." He runs a hand through his dark, wavy hair. "In college I got so sick of people going on and on about all their angst. I was like: You're sitting in a coffee shop at two in the afternoon. You slept until noon. You don't have to go to work, and your parents are paying all the bills for your apartment and your top-notch education. What the hell do you have to be unhappy about?"

I blink in surprise. His usual easygoing expression is gone, and his features are tense and animated. I'd never have guessed Hunter could be so intense, that I'd see his eyes darken to cobalt with passion. It's hard to imagine Hunter Chase—Mr. Preppy—sitting in some campus coffeehouse studying with a bunch of slackers. But I like the image. I like seeing these steep sides and sharp angles, aspects of Hunter I hadn't known were there.

I can't help but smile. "I know what you mean about college," I tell him, warming to our topic. "It's so ironic. All these privileged yuppie kids trying so hard to be different—"

"And they're all exactly alike," Hunter finishes for me, and we both smile. We have more in common than I think either of us expected. I remember having the same feelings toward the coffeehouse slackers at Northwestern. Only I felt guilty for harboring those feelings, like I was a traitor to my family and my upbringing. If Stormy had been sitting in those cafés surrounded by angst-ridden wannabe philosophers, she would have been foremost among the anguished.

But lately all the activism and the save-the-world conspiracy-theory mumbo jumbo in my family has really grated on me. I love Sunshine and I love Stormy (though she's not my favorite person at the moment), but once in a while it's nice to have a conversation that doesn't end with an über-liberal rant about some multimedia corporation's plot to take over the world.

Allison has always been the person I count on to get my jokes and, in turn, make me laugh. It's fun reminiscing with her about high school and a relief to have a rant-free, nonpolitical conversation. Now I'm sharing the same experience with Hunter. I can't remember the last time I laughed or smiled this much. Even now when I glance at Hunter, I can't suppress another giggle, seeing him grin at me over his champagne glass. With a pang of shame, I realize just how much I judged Hunter unfairly in the past—considered him just a pretty face. And isn't that superficial judgment crap what I always hated about the Popular Crowd? That they judged me based on my appearance, not who I was. And here I've been doing the same all along.

Unfortunately, this new realization is not necessarily positive. I feel like Princess Leia in *Star Wars* when she escaped a half-dozen Stormtroopers on the Death Star by jumping into the even more dangerous trash compactor. My assumption that Hunter lacked intellectual skills never made me like him any less, but the more I see the intelligence behind his handsome face, the more I like him. *Really* like him. I'm in trouble now. The trash compactor has started its compression, and my feelings for Hunter are becoming more than just a crush or a high school sophomore's shallow version of love.

The walls are closing in, and it scares me. I could get hurt here.

I finish the last few drops of my mimosa, resisting the urge to signal the waitress to bring more liquid courage. With my empty glass, I gesture to the Chicago skyline in the distance. "I wonder how many of those oh-so-alternative college kids are sitting in offices in those buildings today. Running companies all week long, then going home to their suburban cookie-cutter two-stories and two-point-four kids. How many do you think have *sold out,* as they'd say?"

"Most," Hunter says, with an acknowledging nod. "But not all. Look at your sister."

And we're back to Stormy again. Well, let's see how interested Hunter is when he hears about the *real* Stormy.

"Stormy didn't go to college. She tried taking a few classes at the community college, but she 'couldn't get into it.' Now she works in retail, a place called Harmony's Harbor."

The waitress stops by to ask if we need anything else, and Hunter shakes his head, his eyes never leaving mine.

"A sailing store?" Hunter asks when the waitress leaves.

I laugh. "No. It's a New Age place, complete with crystals and incense, candles, and books on Wicca."

"Wicker?"

"No! *Wicca*. White—good—witchcraft. Harmony, the store's owner, is a coven leader."

Hunter gapes at me. "*Coven* leader? There are covens of witches in Chicago?"

"Yep." I nod. "All over the country. They have campouts on weekends and meet weekly to practice magic and do spells and stuff."

"Jesus!" Hunter sits back and stares at me. "Do they sacrifice animals?"

"No. Nothing like that. They only do magic for good. They believe that any evil you do comes back to you threefold. Stormy's not a Wiccan—she doesn't believe in organized religion, even Wicca—but she goes to the campouts sometimes, and she'd never be a part of anything that harms animals."

"Oh, right." Hunter nods to the waitress, and she sets down the check. She's placed it midway between us, rubbing it in that she can tell we're not a couple. But before

I've even glanced at the small black folder looming in the space between us, Hunter slides it next to his napkin then under his forearm. "Your sister's a vegetarian, right? Animal rights activist, too, I bet."

"All of the above." I frown. What happened to his vegetarians-are-abnormal attitude? I keep waiting for him to ask me how I deal with such a weirdo, but he doesn't appear to judge her at all.

"What about you? Do you eat meat?"

I pause. I've successfully avoided the issue so far, but now that he's asked me straight out, I don't know what to say. Should I tell him the truth? He doesn't seem turned off by anything I've said about Stormy so far, but maybe that's a false front and inside he's thinking, "What a sideshow freak." Should I risk him thinking the same of me, or do I out-and-out lie?

"Not around my family," I say. Something inside me rebels against this falsehood, not just because it's a lie, but because it's an invention. Vegetarianism is a big part of my family, a big part of *me*. I grew up believing in the sanctity of all life, and I still believe in most of what I was taught. But it seems like every time I get around Hunter, I show him less and less of the real Rory, rounding my edges out with fabrications and inventions.

"Man, what do your parents think of all this?" Hunter asks. "Your sister not going to college, working for a witch. Are they completely freaked out?"

"Um . . ." I glance at the waters of Lake Michigan and wish I could jump in. How to tell Hunter about my family? Or how to tell him *something* but not turn him completely off me. A weird sister is one thing, but I'm sure he wouldn't understand my parents.

"Well, actually my mom and stepdad are pretty much okay with it. They're kind of . . ."

Radical? Extreme? Freaky?

"Liberal," I say. "My mom—that sounds so weird to me, Stormy and I call her Sunshine usually—was a flower child. You know, San Francisco during the sixties."

"Wow." Hunter is staring at me in rapt fascination. "So, she was into the whole peace and free-love thing?"

Free love? Try commune, Hunter. But I am *not* going to tell him I was born in a commune. I'm sure he already thinks I'm a total mutant.

"Did she go to Woodstock?"

"Oh, yeah." I roll my eyes. Get Sunshine started on Woodstock and you'll be trapped in Sunshine's Trip Down Memory Lane for hours. "The highlight of her life. Have I ever told you my middle name?"

"Nuh-uh." He grins like a little kid who's been promised the scoop on a whopper of a secret.

"It's Joplin." I meet his laughing eyes. "As in Janis. Oh, and Stormy? Her name is Stormy Baez Egglehoff. Isn't that awful? I think I got off easy with Joplin."

Hunter laughs. "Yeah, you're probably right. Jeez. I feel so boring. The only names preppier than Hunter are Blane and Muffie, and my middle name is even more unoriginal—Zachary."

I know, I almost say, but, thank the Creator, I don't.

"So what about your stepdad? Don't tell me. He sells blood wholesale to Chicago's vampire community."

"Very funny, but no. My parents' marriage is proof that opposites attract. He's a tax attorney."

Hunter shakes his head. "Of course. What else would he be?" He grins and I do, too. Maybe my family isn't as freaky as I'd thought. Maybe Hunter will think they're cool, not abnormal.

"I would never have guessed that your family was so unusual," he says, and I feel my grin slide and melt away. "Looking at you, I'd guess your folks were white bread, enriched flour all the way."

I swallow and look at the table. "Oh."

"I mean that in a good way, Rory," Hunter says and reaches over to squeeze my hand. "Jesus, you're sensitive."

"Sorry." I look up at him and force a smile. "It's just people always tag me as conventional or predictable, and it's not meant as a compliment."

"Anyone who thinks you're predictable or boring doesn't know you," he says. "And they've definitely never worked out with you."

I grin halfheartedly. He's being polite, but from experience I know that no matter what I tell him, I can't win. People's reactions are pretty much the same: They see me either as a freak or a bore.

"I'd give anything to have a family like yours."

I look up in surprise. His gaze is directed behind me, and his eyes are clouded and unreadable. "It sounds like your parents were really, I don't know, *accepting?* " He glances at me, then looks away again.

I can't argue with that observation. No matter what the offense, I've always been able to count on Sunshine and Dan listening and helping with open minds. Nothing was taboo with them. Sex, drugs, and rock and roll were our nightly dinner table topics.

Hunter frowns. "I think my dad would have flipped if I'd ever done anything to make people talk. And my grandparents." His mouth twists in disgust. "The country club set all the way."

"But—but you had everything. You were homecoming king, captain of the football team. Voted Most Popular, Most Handsome, Most Athletic. Even teachers fell over their grade books to ingratiate themselves to you."

"Is that how you saw it? All I saw was the pressure I was under. Every day I was afraid I'd fail."

"You were afraid? I lived in terror from September to June. Do you have any idea what it's like to walk down the hall and pray no one sticks their foot out to trip you? Pray that no one smacks a 'Kick Me' sticky note on your back? Pray that your one friend at lunch isn't absent so you won't have to sit alone—*again.*"

"Yeah, but at least it ended when you got home. At least you were safe there. Your parents cared about you, accepted you, loved you. I had to be perfect at school and at home." He puts a hand over his eyes and massages the bridge of his nose.

"Not many people know this, but when my mom left, my dad had a complete breakdown. He had to go to an in-patient psychiatric hospital for three months, and my grandparents came to stay with me." He moves his hand and his eyes meet mine. He looks so weary. So vulnerable.

"I remember asking my grandmother over and over again what was wrong with my dad, whether he was ever coming home. I'd just lost my mom, and then my dad disappeared, too. But every time I tried to talk to either of my grandparents, they hushed me, told me it wasn't a topic for discussion. That the best way to help my dad was to stay out of trouble and make good grades. To be the perfect, trouble-free son." He sits back, the chair creaking at the violence of the action. My heart is sliced clean through. Oh, Hunter. I had no idea.

I think back to sixth grade and try to remember Hunter,

remember what he'd been like after his mother took off and he came back to school. I know I'd felt horrible for him and wished I knew what to say or do to make him feel better. But now that I think about it, I also remember that this feeling didn't last long. Hunter just hadn't seemed to *need* anyone to buoy him. He'd come back to school a little quieter but, other than that, perfectly fine.

That poor little boy.

"And so I became the perfect son," Hunter goes on. His voice is level, almost emotionless. He's buried the hurt and pain so they won't affect him. "Even when my dad came home and my grandparents left, we never talked about where he'd been or about my mom. Before my mom left things weren't great, but I remember my dad laughing and joking. He loved to go hunting and fishing and hiking. After she left, it was like he went mute or something. He never spoke, never acknowledged me. Half the time I came home to an empty house, and I never knew when my dad would be home. When he did come in, he didn't even say hi, just went straight to bed or turned on the TV without a word. It was like I didn't exist." He runs a hand through his hair and shuts his eyes, the submerged pain flaring in them again. I watch his struggle to master his emotions, tightening my fingers into a fist. I want so badly to touch him, to comfort him, even in that small way.

"I was fucking twelve years old and alone in the world. The only time my dad paid any attention to me was when I played sports. He never missed one of my games. So I became the stereotypical all-American sports hero. If my dad wanted a quarterback who dated the head cheerleader and was crowned homecoming king, that was what I'd be."

I finally reach across the table and put my hand on his

arm, a weak gesture, but I don't know what else to do. To my relief, he grasps my hand in his. I stare into his eyes. He's right. I may have been tormented at school, but I always had a place to go home to, parents that loved me, a safe harbor in the storm of adolescence. "Hunter, I am so sorry. I wish I'd known—"

Shaking his head, he says, "No one did. And I don't want your pity." He gives my hand a squeeze. "I just want you to understand why I say that a weird family who loves you is better than a privileged family who ignores you. Why when I call you predictable and reliable, I mean that as a compliment. Nothing was ever certain in my life. I couldn't rely on anyone. I couldn't trust anyone to be there for me. My grandparents were always 'overcommitted,' my dad was 'too busy.' "

"But what about your friends?" I ask, leaning forward. "You had so many friends. Couldn't you lean on them?"

He snorts. "Please. None of the guys I hung out with or the girls I dated in high school, or college even, cared about me, wanted to know who *I* was as a person. It was all about appearances. Who you ate lunch with, who you dated, that was all that mattered, not who you were. The first time I realized everyone doesn't use their . . . *friends* to gain popularity or be part of the in crowd, I was a senior at Michigan and interning at McCann-Erickson. My project manager didn't give a shit who my friends were or that I'd pledged DEKE. At the end of the day, all the big boys wanted to know was how many hours I put in and how much money my design would bring in.

"In high school, people used to talk about Allison, wonder why she hung out with a . . . someone like you."

I bite my lip. He'd been about to say "geek," I'm sure, but he hadn't.

"But I understood. You're a real person, Rory. Allison was probably the smartest one among us to grab on to you."

I stare down at the table, fighting the tears burning behind my eyes. It wasn't just Allison who'd been lucky with our friendship. Over the years, we'd laughed and cried, shared everything from cappuccinos to deep secrets. She'd given me more support, more advice, more love than anyone else. And now we weren't even talking.

Across the table, Hunter shifts and I glance up. "I don't know why I'm so sentimental all of a sudden," he says. "Maybe it's this stupid reunion coming up. Are you going?"

I was. I'd reserved my spot last night, and if I'd needed more incentive to make a good impression on Hunter, that was it. But I never dreamed we'd be sitting by the lake, sharing some of the most intimate experiences of our lives. And now he's brought up the reunion. This is the moment I've been waiting for. The insecure teenager in me wants to play it cool. Say, "Oh, I think I heard something about that" and wave my hand distractedly.

But the woman I am now, a woman on the edge of confidence, successful at her job, respected and valued by her coworkers, dares to hope. I'm starting to believe Hunter Chase might actually be interested in Rory Egglehoff. The *real* Rory.

I wet my lips, rally my courage, and say, "I RSVP'd last night. I'd sort of been looking forward to it." I give him a shy smile, my heart racing. I feel like I'm fifteen again, standing on my porch, waiting for Gerald Hoffer to give me my first kiss good night.

"So you're going?" Hunter asks.

"I'd like to go . . ." Blood rushes to my head, and I look down, trying to hide my vulnerability. I feel dizzy. Please. Please. Please. "Are *you* going?"

"I was thinking about it," he says. "But I don't want to go alone. I thought—" He shrugs.

My head jerks up, and our eyes meet.

"I thought maybe if you were going, we could go together."

Oh, Creator! Oh, *Lord!* Oh, whatever divine force is responsible for this, thank you, thank you, thank you! "I'd *love* to. I was hoping you'd—" I break off, clenching my hands together under the table. Don't blow it now, Rory. Don't scare him off by revealing too much. "I mean, I'd like that. It sounds fun."

Hunter gives me a wide smile. "Great. It's a date."

I almost melt into a huge warm puddle of mush. A date! A date!

"Shit." Hunter's looking at his watch. "I have to get going."

"Oh! I'm sorry. I didn't mean to make you late."

"You didn't," Hunter says. "I'm glad we ran into each other this morning." He pulls out a twenty and a ten from his wallet and sticks them in the black folder with the check. "In fact, you want to do something tomorrow? I know it's short notice, but—"

"Yes!" I practically scream. Calm *down,* Rory. "I mean, sure."

Dan's taking Sunshine to the Morton Arboretum tomorrow for her birthday. Sunshine's been dying to see the wildlife refuge and the thirty thousand different tree specimens. They're supposed to have a late lunch at the Ginkgo Tea Room and come home around seven. While they're out, Stormy and I are supposed to set up for the party, but we'll be done by twelve or one at the latest.

"I'm free all afternoon," I tell him. Is this also a date? Are Hunter and I *dating* now?

His face clouds over. "I need to meet with Dave and some of the guys to go over an account in the afternoon. I was thinking maybe we could hang out in the morning. Do brunch again or go to Navy Pier? I know it's Sunday, so maybe you have family stuff. Church or"—he grins—"a coven meeting?"

"No, I'm playing hooky. I've already mastered this week's topic: Bat's Breath, Not Just for Potions Anymore."

Hunter laughs, his eyes warming with genuine amusement. Yes! We *must* be dating. I mean, brunch and Navy Pier? Those seem sort of datelike.

"No vampires or werewolves, either, but—" I pause. Am I really going to give up a chance to see Hunter to decorate for a party?

Am I really going to blow off my mother's birthday for a guy? For a date that might not be a date, but certainly isn't anything more? Sunshine has done so much for me over the years. What better way than a wonderful party to show her how much she means to me? What kind of daughter would I be—what kind of *person*—if I chose a boy over my mother?

"No family stuff," I say, amazed that the voice I hear is mine. I must be mistaken. I wouldn't say that, I'm not that shallow, not so desperate for Hunter that I've lost sight of my principles. "What time do you want to get together?"

Blast it! Where is this coming from? Who is this person speaking?

Hunter smiles at me, and everything—the party, Allison, my family—fade to insignificance. "Give me your address, and I'll pick you up at ten."

I hastily scrawl my street and apartment number on a napkin. He takes it, stands, and I follow suit. In the restaurant's parking lot, I say a jaunty good-bye and turn toward my car, but before I take two steps, Hunter catches my wrist, just below the scrape on my arm.

"See you tomorrow, Rory," he murmurs and leans in to kiss my cheek. His lips are smooth and warm, and he smells like soap and the clean breeze off Lake Michigan. I close my eyes to capture this moment, to commit it to memory and keep it in my heart always.

On the way home, my head still full of Hunter, I call Dan to tell him I won't be able to help Stormy decorate. I lie and say an emergency came up at Y&Y and I have to go in. In fact, I tell him, that's where I'm heading right now.

The rest of the way home, my face burns. I tell myself it's from the warmth of Hunter's parting kiss, but deep down I know the truth. Shame is hotter than passion any day.

Chapter 13

*Despite the injuries my fitness-challenged body sus*tained at the gym, I don't crawl into bed for a few hours of much-needed recovery time when I get home. Hunter is coming over tomorrow and I'm full of nervous energy, so I do the logical thing—clean my apartment. With the focus of a Jedi Knight and the velocity of the Millennium Falcon zipping through the galaxy at light speed, I scrub, scour, and swab every corner and crevice (even the baseboards!).

Three hours later, when I plop on the couch and flip on the TV, hoping to catch an episode of *Star Trek: The Next Generation,* I still haven't washed away the guilt I feel over not helping Stormy tomorrow.

TNG isn't on. Perfect. I've got access to two hundred channels, and *TNG* isn't on even one of them. Five stations are playing reruns of *Full House,* but I don't think that's going to help. I need Whoopi Goldberg and her words of wisdom—dispensed with synthetic alcohol and dry wit in *The Enterprise*'s Ten-Forward. A rerun of *Buffy the Vampire Slayer* flashes on the screen, so I settle for that instead.

Buffy is not as wise as Guinan, Whoopi's *TNG* character, but she'll do. So while Buffy and Angel work out their dating dilemmas—arguably a bit more complicated than mine—I obsess about Sunday with Hunter versus Sunday with Sunshine and the gang.

I am a dreadful person for neglecting my family. I should make up with Stormy, not blow her off. Surely she'd excuse me for delaying our reconciliation if she knew the reason.

I sigh. No, she wouldn't. She'd never put a man before her friends or family. I'm a bad, bad person.

Buffy is just about to kick the butt of a nasty night crawler when the phone rings. I jump at the noise, sending my bowl of popcorn airborne. So much for my thorough vacuum job. Now I'll have to haul out the monster Oreck again, and won't Mrs. Wobowski below me just love hearing that at quarter to nine in the evening.

Swearing and gathering as much stray popcorn as I can, I glance at the caller ID. Then I swear again because the number on the screen is Tom's cell.

Blast it! I'd blissfully forgotten about Tom for the past oh, sixteen or twenty-four hours, and I'm not ready to be reminded. I may *never* be ready to be reminded. The phone rings for the third time, and I glare at it. Maybe this is it. Maybe I need to quit procrastinating, pick up the phone, and just get it over with.

I drop the loose kernels of popcorn clutched in my fists and grab the receiver before the answering machine can pick up. "Hello?" I say, not bothering to keep the annoyance from my voice.

"Rory? Where are you?"

I frown. Isn't that obvious? "You're calling *me,* Tom. Clearly I'm at home." A sense of determination settles over me.

"Oh-kay," he says, drawing the word out. "I guess the question is why. I thought we had plans."

Eek! I shoot a look at the clock on the DVD player, but I already know the verdict: Saturday night, 8:43 P.M. Plans with Tom. In all the excitement of the morning, anything that wasn't Hunter-related fell into the far reaches of my galaxy. I'd completely forgotten Tom and our date.

I can't believe I've done this. It's so out of character. I *never* forget dates and appointments. It's so irresponsible, so careless, so *not* Rory Egglehoff. Spacing out like this, more than standing Tom up, concerns me.

"Rory? Are you there? What happened?" Tom asks. "I thought we were meeting at the movies to catch the sneak preview of *Alien Superheroes*. I charged the tickets on Fandango like a week ago, and it's starting in fifteen minutes. There's no way you can make it now."

"Oh, Tom, I'm so sorry." Feeling like my world is spinning out of control, I fumble for an excuse. Would he accept temporary amnesia due to treadmill head injury? Hmm. Maybe more explanation required for that one than I want to give.

"Something . . . came up and I—I couldn't get away. I just got home." I am a really bad liar. *Why* am I lying to Tom anyway? Why not just tell him I don't want to see him anymore?

"So, why didn't you come straight to the theater?" Tom asks, and now he sounds annoyed.

"Um—"

"I thought you wanted to see this flick. You sounded excited when we talked about it."

Yeah, that's because I'd been dreaming about Hunter at the time.

Hunter. Gorgeous, sweet, funny Hunter, who wants to

take me out tomorrow. And who—Creator willing—would never use the word "flick."

Okay, I really need to dump Tom. I don't like doing it over the phone, but I suppose now is as good a time as any. "Look, Tom," I begin. "We need to talk."

"Yeah, we do," he interrupts, voice full of uncharacteristic authority. "I don't think it's right that every time we get together, we do your things—hang out at your place or watch a movie you rented."

My jaw drops. "Those are *my* things? I've been trying to get you to take me out to dinner for a month, but every time you come over, you order pizza instead. *Pepperoni* pizza!" I shout accusingly. "I would love to go out for once!"

"Well then why aren't you here?" Tom shouts back, and I flinch back into the couch cushions. I've never heard Tom sound this upset. "Isn't this *going out?*"

Okay, I can see I'm not going to win this battle. Time to send the Tie fighters back to base and deploy the Star Destroyers. "Look, Tom, I just got really . . . busy and forgot. It won't happen again. In fact, I don't think we should—"

But he's not listening. "Fine, babe, I forgive you. But I still think there needs to be more compromise in our relationship. Next time if you can't make it, call me so I can ask Grant or Stan if they want to go."

As far as I'm concerned, he can go to the movies with Grant and Stan every night from now until the end of the millennium.

"And if I'm going to have to suffer through your high school reunion, I don't think it's too much to ask for you to be in the costume show at the Creatures and Features Extravaganza next weekend. Grant said he called you, and you told him you still weren't sure."

"I know. I don't think it's going to happen, Tom," I say. "In fact, I don't think any of this is going to happen."

"Why not?" Tom asks, sounding a little concerned now. "What's wrong?"

"Tom—" For some reason my voice sounds thin and breathy. The words are on the tip of my tongue: *I don't want to see you anymore.* But I don't say them. Doubts, like the extraterrestrial parasites who burrowed into the crew in *Alien,* slither into my brain. Ssss.

Hunter seemed interested in me today, but maybe it was just morbid curiosity, a voyeuristic peek at the weird and wacky.

Ssss.

Surely he'd want his girlfriend—or wife—to be white bread through and through.

What if Hunter changes his mind about the reunion?

Ssss.

What if we go out tomorrow, he sees what a nerd I really am, and decides he wouldn't be caught dead with me?

Ssss.

What if he runs into someone from my family and—

Blast it! What am I thinking? Tom's steady, reliable—my blaster shield, my alien predator antidote. He may not be the best boyfriend, but he's a good friend. He deserves better than this.

"Tom, you're right," I say suddenly. "There does need to be more compromise, and I do appreciate you going to the reunion with me."

"Huh?" Tom's clearly not expecting this easy capitulation.

"Tell Grant I'll be in the costume show."

"You will?"

"Yeah, and I'm sorry about tonight. I'll make it up to you, I promise."

"Yeah?"

I can hear the excitement in his voice. Yuck. Not like that Tom. He doesn't deserve *that* much. "Hey, you better get going or you'll miss the opening credits of the movie. I'll talk to you on Monday, okay? We can grab lunch and work out the details for the costumes we're wearing at the extravaganza."

"Okay. Sounds good, babe. See you Monday, then." He clicks off, and I hit the button on my own phone. What the Dark Side did I just do? Did I just reserve a big chunk of next weekend for Chicago's biggest dorkfest?

I stare at the scattered popcorn surrounding me. My sister hates me. My best friend isn't talking to me. Oh, and I have, not one, but two dates to my high school reunion.

I rub my temple. It feels like my mind, not the popcorn, just burst and scattered all over the floor.

Twenty-seven, twenty-eight, twenty-nine, and thir—

The intercom buzzer startles me, and I stop pacing and swing to face it.

He's here. For about three seconds I contemplate running and hiding under the bed—well, that or just not answering. Then I take a deep, cleansing breath, sucking in air scented with Sparkling Citrus, an ozone-depleting room freshener, and wobble the five steps to the door.

I unlock the deadbolts, turn the knob, pull the door open, and feel my heart lurch into my throat.

He is standing in the hallway. *He* is smiling at me. *He* is holding—oh, Han Solo with a cherry on top!—*tulips!*

I gasp and make a grab for the flowers. "Hunter!" I hold

the perfect pink buds to my nose. "I can't believe you got me flowers!" Then I thrust them away, feeling my cheeks heat. "These are for me, right?"

He grins. "Yeah. I passed a flower place on my way over. Think of them as a get-well present."

I feel my face flush hotter as I remember my embarrassing swan dive from the treadmill yesterday, but Hunter doesn't seem to notice. "I forgot how much I like Old Town. It feels a lot more like a real neighborhood than Streeterville. How do you like it here?" He looks up and down the building hallway, and I realize I haven't yet invited him in.

"Oh, come in!" I jump out of the doorway. "I didn't mean to make you stand outside."

"Thanks." He steps inside, I close the door, and for a moment we both stand awkwardly in front of it. I'm holding my breath and looking frantically about, trying to gauge how my apartment must look to Hunter. Allison did the decorating, so I know it's not tacky or ugly or anything, but I wonder if he'll approve of what Allie and I refer to as "conservative funky." Conservative because Allison complained she couldn't tear me away from Ethan Allan and color schemes centered on navy or beige, and funky because Allie insisted on adding her own "touches," including a retro lamp with a psychedelic base, forties-style lime-green kitchen appliances, and an Andy Warhol print in the corner.

I was skeptical at first, but the eclectic mix has grown on me. But most people look somewhat bewildered when they first walk in.

To my surprise, Hunter doesn't even blink. "Cool apartment," he says.

"Thanks. Allison helped me decorate." Just saying her name aloud causes my chest to tighten. I miss her so much. I miss not being able to share what's happening with me and Hunter. All my dreams are coming true, and the one person who's been there with me all the way doesn't know, and probably doesn't even care.

My heart feels like it's been cut clean through with a lightsaber, and I try to imagine what Allison's doing right now. Sunday mornings she likes to get the paper, go to a café, and catch up on world events—or at least those in the style section—but lately she's been putting in so many hours at work on the Oprah project, she's probably spending Sunday morning catching up on her sleep. I wonder if her firm got the project. Maybe Allison is munching on gourmet caviar pizza with Oprah and Steadman at Spago right this moment.

Well, whatever she's doing, I tell myself, she's not thinking about me, that's for sure. I haven't heard a peep from her since our argument at the gym yesterday morning—not a phone call, not an e-mail, not even a telepathic message.

Allison and I don't argue often, but when we do we always get over it quickly. I think this is the first time one of our fights has lasted more than twenty-four hours. One of us always calls the other, we both apologize and insist on taking the blame, then we veg on the couch with a pint of chocolate caramel swirl ice cream and *Pretty in Pink,* if it's her turn to choose the DVD, *The Empire Strikes Back,* if it's mine.

"She's really good." Hunter moves into my living room, running a hand over the navy chenille throw on the back of my beige couch. "I should get Allison to come over and redo my place."

"Yeah," I say quietly, still clutching the tulips. "You should." And if she didn't hate my guts, I'd call her right now and suggest it.

He looks at me questioningly, as though wondering why I don't offer to act as go-between, but before I'm forced to invent a lie, his eyes flick to the glass display case in the dining room. Oh, Bantha shit! The *Star Wars* collectibles.

In my haste to eradicate every last speck of dust last night, I neglected to look at the big picture. I forgot about my dark secret, and now it's too late. Hunter is already moving toward the cherry and glass case housing my *Star Wars* collectible glasses, a few prized action figures, and the three toothbrushes. The toothbrushes I *claimed* were for someone or other's son but which are now sitting, quite conspicuously, front and center on the middle shelf of the case.

"Hey, what's all this?" Hunter asks.

"Oh, nothing," I say casually. My mind races for a way to distract him. "Can I get you anything? A drink? I've got water or coffee, and I picked up some bagels this morning . . ."

"Nah," he says, moving inexorably closer to the case. I restrain the urge to jump in front of him, heading him off at the pass, so to speak.

"Oh, um, are you sure?" I move alongside him, trying discreetly to block his view. "I don't mind toasting one of the bagels."

"I thought we'd get lunch at Navy Pier." He snaps a glance at me, then his attention is back on the case. He's right in front of it now. "Riva is good."

In the glass reflection, I see my mouth drop open. *Riva?* I've heard people talking about it at work but never eaten there. According to Janet in risk management, who wouldn't be seen anywhere not outlandishly trendy or exorbitantly expensive, Riva is excellent. She ate there a few months ago and couldn't stop raving about the porcini mushroom rigatoni because "It was *sinfully* fabulous, darling."

And now Hunter is taking me there for lunch? After months of pizza and Chinese take-out with Tom, I'm not used to this kind of extravagance. I glance down at my khaki slacks and navy sweater set, wondering if I should change. I glance at Hunter. He's wearing khakis and a blue Oxford shirt with the sleeves rolled to his elbows. Guys have it so easy—casual and dressy at the same time. Hunter's still staring at my neatly arranged *Star Wars* glasses, and I wonder if I should just forget the whole thing. He's never going to want to go out with me after he gets a good look in the display case.

"Cool," Hunter breathes.

Huh? I frown and peer at the shelves just in case there's something I missed.

"I remember these glasses. I used to drink out of Darth Vader all the time."

"Really?" A pinprick of light pierces the black hole sucking me in.

"Yeah." He reaches for the handle of the case, then looks at me. "Can I open it?"

He wants to open the case? I don't believe this. He really must think my glasses are cool.

"Rory?" Hunter's looking at me expectantly.

"Oh, um, yeah." I reach over and unlatch the case for him. He takes out the Darth Vader glass and peers at it, a silly, half smile on his face.

"How'd you manage to hold on to this? I think I broke mine after a week."

I bite my lip. The defining moment. "That's not my

original," I murmur. He raises a brow and looks at the glass again, inspecting it. "I—I sort of collect them." I can feel my face burning, and I keep my eyes downcast. There's no way he's going to think collecting *Star Wars* junk is cool. Any minute now he'll burst out laughing or utter some polite but inane comment and make his escape.

"Yeah? How much is all this worth?"

I peek at him, not quite believing what I'm hearing. Why isn't he rolling on the floor, wracked by fits of laughter. "Not that much," I stammer. "Fifty dollars if the set was complete, but I'm still missing two."

"Which ones?"

"Luke and Leia from the first movie and the Tatooine Desert with Han and Luke."

"The *what* desert?"

"Tatooine—never mind." Blast it! I close my eyes in mortification. Time to come clean. He'll definitely tuck tail and run. "I guess I'm sort of a *Star Wars* freak. I know it's dorky."

"Dorky? It's cool."

I almost fall back against the glass door. "It is?" This can't be happening. I bite the inside of my cheek just to make sure I'm really awake.

"Yeah. *Star Wars* is one of the best movies ever made."

Oh, Force. Oh, Master Yoda. Please, *please* don't let this be a dream.

"It's not as good as *Rambo* or *Terminator,* " Hunter continues, "but it's up there."

"*Rambo* or *The Terminator?* " I shout before I can stop myself. "You're saying that two men who can barely speak the English language are better actors than Harrison Ford? *Please!*"

ecurity still lurks in the periphery, waiting to swal-
: up.

xt time you buy *Star Wars* toothbrushes or some-
else you think is stupid, just admit it," Hunter says.
ght think it's lame, but there's nothing I hate worse
a liar."

He raises a brow, and I immedia
Double blast it, Rory! Why can't you k
for once! This is Hunter Chase, and h
cool. So what if he's a little misgui
chance, you can enlighten him. In no t
error of his ways and have forg
Schwarzenegger and Stallone.

"I hate to break this to you, Princess Lei
with a grin, "but Sylvester Stallone or A
zenegger could kick Harrison Ford's ass with
behind their backs."

I snort, but inside I feel my indignati
Hunter called me Princess Leia. *Me,* Princess L
a halfhearted attempt to summon my earlier a
that's supposed to endear them to me? Harriso
sensitivity, charisma, the ability to articulate
labic words—there's simply *no* comparison." I
know. I'm shutting up. I just had to make that o
point . . .

"You feel pretty strongly about this, don't
princess?" Hunter's grin widens. "I admire a girl
knows what she likes." He reaches out and squeeze
arm, and I'm suddenly aware of how close we're stand
how good he smells, and of the tulips—the unexpected
he brought me—in my arms.

"Especially when what she likes is pretty damn cool."

I can't help myself, I grin like a bad caricature of Jar Ja
Binks. Hunter squeezes my arm again. "Rory, I like you, so
stop feeling like you have to impress me or something. Just
be yourself."

A shaft of pure sunlight floods into my soul.

Hunter glances at the case with the glasses again and I
tense, my anxiety reminding me that the black hole doubt

Chapter 14

When I was a little girl, one of my favorite games was Princess Leia Saves the Galaxy. I'd sit on our stairs to the second floor, holding a spatula in each hand, and pretend I was piloting the Millennium Falcon. In the game, Han Solo was wounded, and it was up to me to defeat the Empire and save the Rebel Alliance. Mostly the game involved me making spacecraft noises and rocking side to side, but sometimes I wanted another player, and then I'd recruit Stormy. Her job was performing the role of the wounded Han Solo, the voice of Luke Skywalker in his nearby X-wing fighter, and, when the Falcon was hit by an Imperial blast, she'd play Chewbacca and repair the damage.

This wasn't Stormy's favorite game. Okay, she hated it. I think her very first demonstration was directed toward me. She argued that she was being discriminated against because "I always have to be the boys, and you always get to be the princess girl." Then she held up one of Sunshine's old protest signs with a peace symbol on it. "It's not fair,

Rory!" She started marching in a circle, chanting, "I won't play! I won't play!"

She was six.

So after that I pretty much played Princess Leia Saves the Galaxy by myself. When Allison and I became friends, I tried once or twice to get her to play, but she always wanted to bring her Barbies into the game, and that just ruined everything. So it was just me and the spatula controls. I loved pretending I was zooming around the universe at light speed. Han Solo watch out. The *Falcon* may have made the Kessel Run in less than twelve parsecs when he was the pilot, but if I were in control, I bet we'd have made it in eleven.

Now I know the truth. If I were the universe's last hope against Darth Vader and his minions, the Rebels were doomed. I'd be retching in the spaceship's version of the ladies' room before Chewie could say "Rrrwfr."

The realization that all the piloting practice on the stairs in my parents' house was for nothing comes on what should be an enjoyable sightseeing tour of Chicago by water. But as the *Seadog* speedboat races past the blur of what I think is Buckingham Fountain, Riva's gourmet porcini mushroom rigatoni sloshes in my belly, threatening to form a tidal wave if I don't get off this boat in the next three parsecs. Over the Led Zepplin song blaring on the stereo system, the captain announces we're turning back to Navy Pier. I close my eyes in relief, but then he cranks up the music and the turbo-charged engines, and we swing sharply around. I groan as the mound of food in my stomach lurches. Suddenly helping Stormy decorate for Sunshine's party tonight doesn't seem so unappetizing.

"Hey, there's the Yacht Club and Grant Park again!" Hunter yells over the roar.

"Mmm-hmm." I nod my head, keeping my lips clamped shut to prevent a flood of food from spewing forth. I can't remember the last time I felt so ill. In heart or body.

"Look at that baby go." Hunter points to a towering white yacht. "One day I'm going to have one of those and sail it through the Great Lakes." He turns, sapphire eyes shining with excitement. "Wouldn't you love to do that, Rory? Take two weeks and just explore. Pure freedom. Go anywhere you want, just you and the wind and the water. God, I'd love to do something like that."

His enthusiasm is contagious, and I can't help but grin, though my stomach churns even as my lips curve into a smile. I would love to explore the Great Lakes with Hunter. I'd love to do just about anything short of highway robbery with Hunter—and maybe that, too.

Hunter gives me a bright smile then looks back at the water. He's smiling now, but all I can think is how he said he hates liars, and I feel like the biggest liar this side of the universe. My chest tightens remembering all my lies: falsehoods about my family, my vegetarianism, Allison. Lies about me, Rory Egglehoff, and who I am. Once again, I'm being sucked into that deep, dark black hole. Every time I think I've escaped, I realize I've only fallen deeper.

"I've got a bad feeling about this." A main character says it in each of the *Star Wars* films, and it never fails that their fears are realized at the worst possible moment. Is that what I'm setting myself up for? Have I irrevocably altered my karma so that I'm now destined to spend the rest of this life and the next trying to atone for all my perjuries? Because there's no way I'll get away with these deceptions; I am not one of Fortune's favored. Allison: yes. Jellie Abernathy: definitely. Stormy: wouldn't lie in the first place . . .

But I am in deep Ewok shit here. And fibs about being a

vegetarian or a *Star Wars* freak aren't going to be my undoing. By far, the biggest, the worst lie of all is Tom. Hunter registers off the dial on every boyfriendly-type interest indicator. The problem is, I already have a boyfriend. Oh, and the even bigger issue? When Hunter—who hates liars above all else—asked about Tom, what did I do? That's right. *I lied.*

As if Hunter can somehow sense my inner turmoil, he takes my hand and squeezes it in his warm, strong grip. I try to give him a smile, but my stomach is in knots. I'll never survive the humiliation of Hunter witnessing me heaving my half-digested, expensive Riva lunch over the *Seadog*'s side. What have I gotten myself into? What the Dark Side am I going to do?

The Ferris wheel at Navy Pier draws closer, and the insane captain of the *Seadog*, a man obviously in league with the Empire, finally begins to slow his instrument of the Dark Side. The rigatoni's violent roiling in my stomach settles to a tolerable churning, and I'm able to at least appear steady on my feet as we exit.

"God, wasn't that invigorating?" Hunter says, taking my hand again as we stroll down Dock Street toward the Pier's main attractions. "Hey, do you want to give the Ferris wheel another shot?"

The contents of my stomach roll in violent objection. "Ah, no. I think I'll sit this one out."

He consults his watch, and I stare at his thick, masculine wrist, covered with curly dark hair. Creator, he is so sexy.

"—is that okay?" Hunter asks, and I realize he's been speaking.

"Oh, um, sorry." I push my tangled, wind-whipped hair out of my eyes. "What did you say?"

"You're bored with me already, huh?"

"What! No!" I shake my head so vigorously, the hair falls back in my eyes. "Not at all. Don't be ridiculous. You're—you're—"

He leans over and takes my chin between thumb and forefinger. "What?" he murmurs. "What am I, Rory?" His lips brush my skin just at the corner of my mouth.

"You're—" He caresses my lower lip with his thumb. "Hard to resist," I whisper.

"Really? Let's test that." Then right there in the middle of the sidewalk, in broad daylight, and in front of dozens of tourists, Hunter kisses me. Okay, this is better than party decorations any day.

It's a gentle kiss. His lips caress mine, pressing just enough so that I know he means it, so that I feel a tingle all the way to my toes, and so that I know he'd like to take this just a teeny bit further. His mouth, his lips are telling me—oh so subtly and very sexily—that if we were alone, he might do more than just kiss me senseless.

The blood pounds in my head. I feel dizzy, wonderful, terrified. Suddenly I'm overcome with doubts. He's an excellent kisser. I'm halfway to orgasm just from the brief brush of his mouth on mine, but what does he think of me? Do I turn him on? Does he like the feel of my mouth against his? *Am I even kissing him back?*

Blast it! I forgot to kiss him back. I sort of pitch forward, intent on kissing him fervently and passionately in return, showing him that I am as sexy and adept at this lovemaking stuff as he, but he's already pulling away.

Dark Side take it! I want to scream, but then, to my surprise, instead of sneering at my pitiful response, he nuzzles his lips against my neck and murmurs, "When can I see you again, princess?"

A shiver runs from the spot where he brushes persuasive

lips over the tip of my earlobe to the juncture of my thighs, where I'm exceedingly aware of the feel of his leg pressing against mine. I don't even try to suppress my quivers, and I hear his faint chuckle next to my ear. The deep sound rumbles through me like thunder on a velvet night or the primed engine of the *Millennium Falcon*.

"Tonight?" he asks, pulling away so that I can see his brilliant blue eyes. "I have to meet Dave in an hour, so I've got to take you home. But I don't want today to end. How about dinner tonight?"

I find myself nodding without even considering what all of this means. Hunter wants to see me again. Hunter wants to spend more time with me. Hunter thinks I'm wonderful. Hunter—oh, Force—Hunter wants *me*.

A wave of alarm crashes through me, and dread mixed with arousal flood me in equal measure. The Force knows I want him, too, but am I ready for this? Is it right to sleep with him when I'm still technically seeing Tom? Tom and I don't have a formal commitment, but when you're sleeping with someone, exclusivity is pretty much expected. So, if I sleep with Hunter, what does that mean? Do we have any future? We're supposed to go to the reunion together, but is there any more than that between us? And how can I miss Sunshine's party for something that could turn out to be so fleeting?

Agh! Question overload. Head at risk level ten for explosion.

"What do you say, princess?" He tucks a stray piece of hair behind my ear, and though I know my hair is thin and straight and scraggly, he makes me feel like the girl on the Pantene commercial. "Dinner at my place? You bring the wine. I'll cook."

Oh, I love it when he calls me princess. And he's going

to cook? Did Han ever cook for Leia? This is definitely an uncharted galaxy.

This is a *forbidden* galaxy. I cannot go. I have to go to Sunshine's party—even if I'll probably never have this chance with Hunter again. Even if it means closing the book on my lifelong dream.

But, dream or no dream, the party is tonight, and there is absolutely no way I can miss that. Not to mention, if I go to Hunter's—not that I would even *consider* skipping my mother's birthday, though if I asked her she'd probably tell me that realizing my dreams is vastly more important than attending some silly party—anyway, if I go to Hunter's, I know what's going to happen.

A fizzy shiver of anticipation bubbles through me.

"How's seven?" he asks.

"Seven sounds perfect," I hear myself say, and he kisses my nose in agreement.

I spend the rest of Sunday afternoon in the Victoria's Secret dressing room trying on hose and garter belts, bustiers and corsets, finally settling on a matching golden lace panty and bra set, then going merrily on my way. Okay, maybe *merrily* is not quite the word I'm looking for. Maybe guilt-ridden and scared out of my wits is more appropriate. I've decided to call Dan and Stormy before I leave for Hunter's and tell them something unavoidable has come up at work. I promise to come later. And I will. I'll just stop by Hunter's first . . .

When I get home, I rush to my room, shed my clothes, and pull on the Victoria's Secret underwear. Oh, Creator. I don't know about this. I looked much better in the dim dressing room.

I'm so busy obsessing about my body—how my stomach

is too fat and my butt saggy and my boobs too small—that I don't even glance at the caller ID when the phone rings. Welcoming a distraction from the unforgiving mirror and my lame attempts to make my droopy butt appear firmer and higher, I drop my derrière and pick up the phone.

"Hello?" I turn to the side and study my reflection as I suck in my tummy. Blast it. Is it too late for sit-ups to make a difference?

"Rory?"

I jump at the voice on the other line and immediately swivel away from the mirror. "Yeah?" I can't believe she's finally calling me.

"It's Allison." There's a pause.

"Hey," I say.

"Hey," she answers. "I, um, just wanted to call to say hi. You know, see how you were doing."

"Oh, I'm fine." I pull a robe over my new underwear, feeling vulnerable in the slinky lace and satin, and sink to the floor. "How are you?"

"Okay. I—I kind of thought you'd be at work. I tried you there but got your voice mail."

I frown at the floor, digging my callused feet into the carpet. "It's Sunday," I say. "Why did you think I'd be at work?"

"That's what Stormy said."

I bolt up, my heart racing. "You talked to Stormy?"

"Yeah. I swung by your parents' because I thought you'd be doing stuff for the party. I—I sort of wanted to talk to you." She breaks off for a moment as I digest this latest bit of info. Allison actually stopped by my house?

"You drove to Evanston just to talk to me?"

"Stupid, huh?" Her sharp laugh is self-deprecating. "You weren't even there. Stormy and some of her scary friends were chanting and spreading leaves and twigs everywhere."

"Like from outside?"

"I know, and I guess I had a what-the-hell-is-this look on my face because Stormy said it was part of the nature theme. Next time you see her, tell her I have two words for her: artificial foliage."

"Okay," I say, not sure if I'm more flabbergasted that Allison went to so much effort to see me or freaked out that Stormy is moving the backyard into the living room. "Okay," I repeat.

Allison doesn't respond, and I know she's waiting for me to explain why, after months of planning this party, I wasn't there to help on the day that really matters. Why I obviously lied to my family and said I was working when I wasn't. Why I've morphed into some awkward, half-articulate mutant who can't even tell my best friend I'm glad she called.

"So, um, did you RSVP for the reunion?" Allison asks. My head spins at the sudden change in subject. The reunion can't be the reason she drove out to see me. Can it?

"Yeah," I finally respond. No point in lying. "I called Friday night."

"Me, too."

Silence.

"Are you still going?" I venture into the void, not certain I want to know the answer. Right now it feels like life would be a whole lot less complicated if Allison *didn't* go to the reunion.

"Of course. Are *you?*"

"Sure. Why wouldn't I?"

"I didn't mean to imply that you weren't going to go. I was just wondering. I mean, asking." She heaves a sigh.

"Look, Rory, I'm not good at this shit, okay? I just wanted to call and check in and say that if you want to go to the reunion together, I'd love to be your 'date.' You know, if you need one."

"I don't. I have one." Bantha fodder, I have *two*.

"Okay, then."

There's another long pause. "Aren't you going with Bryce?"

"We broke up," Allison says, and her voice breaks.

"Oh, Allie. What happened?"

She sniffs. "Last night he told me he didn't want to see me anymore. That—that—" She blows her nose loudly. "That he'd found someone else. He said he wasn't looking, but I was just so busy all the time." Her voice chokes off.

"Good riddance! The guy's a complete idiot to dump you."

She laughs on a sob. "Thanks, Rory. But I'm not so sure. I really blew it this time. I think maybe Bryce was The One."

"You do?" In all the time I've known Allison, she's never said a man was The One. Not even when she was engaged to Tad.

"I'm just so *hurt*," Allison says and begins to cry harder. I start to sweat. What should I say? Allison breaking down like this terrifies me. It's like our roles have been reversed. Suddenly I've got the date and she's just been dumped. I cry on *her* shoulder, not the other way around.

"Hey," she mumbles, "do you want to come over tonight? You can stop me from eating this entire pint of Ben & Jerry's."

The blood freezes in my veins. "Um—"

"I know you've got your mom's party, but maybe after?" Her voice is shaky, pleading. "Or I could stop by the party . . ."

I take a deep breath. I've never heard her sound so vulnerable. "Allison," I begin, hating myself already, "if this were any other night—any other time—I'd be there in a parsec. But I can't tonight." I pause, holding my breath for her response. She's silent. "Allison?"

"Okay," she says, her voice flat. "I know how important this party is, how hard you've worked on it."

The bile in my gut rises into my throat.

"I guess I'll just see you at the reunion then."

"Will you be okay?" I ask. "I can call you later tonight—"

"I'll be fine," she snaps. "There's a message from Jellie on my voice mail. I think I'll give her a call back."

"But, Allie, all she'll talk about is the wedding. Won't that upset you even more?"

"Maybe. But at least she's not too busy to talk to me."

"Allison! You know that's not true."

"Whatever. Do me a favor and bring the clothes I loaned you," she says, voice clipped and short. Business-like.

My throat closes up in reaction to the acid eating away at the lining. Is this it then? The real end of our friendship? "Okay," I whisper.

"Take care, Rory."

"You, too," I say, but she's already hung up.

I replace the receiver and want to bang my head against the towers of a Trade Federation battleship. Those towers are spiky enough to take out a few brain cells. Maybe if I lose a handful, I won't be such an idiot. Maybe I won't be such an insensitive bitch. How could I do this to Allison? She really needed a friend tonight. She really needed *me*. And I know that no matter who or what she had going on in her life, if our situations were reversed, she'd be there for me. Is Hunter really that important to me? More important than Allison's friendship?

But it's more than just Hunter now. I don't want to do

anything to jeopardize my chances of going to the reunion with him. I want to walk in that ballroom on Hunter's arm, looking gorgeous and feeling confident and *popular.* Tom's newfound interest, Vinnie's flirting, the whistles from men on the street have gone to my head. I don't want it to end. I like being the one everyone is looking at, the one everyone envies.

I put my head between my knees. What is this? Fifth grade? Na-na-na-na boo-boo. I got a better boy than you do. Ugh!

I stand up and crane my neck to see my alarm clock. It's almost five, and I need to start getting ready for my date with Hunter. I pad to my closet, still holding my old blue terry-cloth robe closed. I rummage around and, in less than three milli-parsecs, decide I have nothing to wear. The corduroy khaki skirt, white Oxford, and baby blue sweater vest seem far too prim and proper, and jeans are just too casual.

My gaze falls on a pair of slim low-rise pants with a skimpy black top hanging beside it. The top is tight and almost sheer with asymmetrical white designs strategically placed. Beneath the outfit, still in the Marshall Field's bag, are a pair of sexy, strappy black heels. I frown. It's one of the outfits Allison loaned me. One that I have to return.

She must really hate me now. But I deserve her hate. I deserve worse. This is like a breakup. You pile all of the little things the guy has left or forgotten or you've borrowed in a box or shopping bag and make an exchange. You get back your tampons, toothbrush, and three old barrettes. He gets back his razor, deodorant, and Klingon ears. You keep the "Darth Vader Lives" T-shirt you slept in one night and "forgot" to return. He doesn't ask about it, though you know he's royally pissed, and you both go your separate ways.

Is that what I want to happen with Allison and me? I have the urge to snatch the phone up, call her back, and ask if she's eaten all the cookie dough from the ice cream yet and if she's still willing to share. I could invite her to Sunshine's party. That would cheer her up. That would be the right thing to do.

Maybe if we sat down among the peace and love crowd, we could work this out. She could pour out her hurt over Bryce, and when she's feeling better, I could tell her about my success with Hunter.

But to do the "right" thing, I'd have to cancel my once-in-a-lifetime date with Hunter, and a date with Hunter isn't necessarily the "wrong" thing. I can see Allison tomorrow. I can wish Sunshine happy birthday for the next thirty years, but I may never have another chance with Hunter.

And I guess that's what it comes down to. I'm so afraid of losing Hunter, losing my dream of being the popular girl, that I'm letting my selfishness triumph.

If I were Princess Leia, I'd never let the Dark Side win. I'd fight for the forces of good to the bitterest end. I look at the phone, then Allison's outfit, then the clock. Five-twenty.

Hanging the outfit on the closet door, I drop my robe. When I'm dressed, I stand in front of the mirror. I look great, not at all like a servant of the Dark Side. But the truth is, I'm no Princess Leia.

Chapter 15

"Your directions were great," I tell Hunter as he ushers me into his apartment, a large one-bedroom in Streeterville.

After nodding appreciatively at the view of Lake Michigan, visible through his large window, I scan the rest of the room, taking in the comfortable, male atmosphere. There's a large, forest green couch and a worn maple coffee table with matching lamps and entertainment center. The TV squatting inside the mammoth Temple to Entertainment is huge—flat screen *and* big screen. The volume is low, but I recognize a few of the Bulls players running and tossing a basketball on screen. I count at least seven remotes, three as big as my forearm, displayed in places of honor on the coffee table, and can't help but smile. Complete control of the TV, stereo, and DVD player. Every man's dream, and every bachelor's reality.

"What are we having?" I crane my neck to try and get a peek down the dark hallway, where the bedroom must be. "It smells wonderful."

"*You* smell wonderful," Hunter says, surprising me by leaning in for a quick kiss. "You *look* wonderful, too. In fact, 'wonderful' isn't quite the word I'm looking for." He lowers his voice, and the room temperature rises. I can feel the intensity of his gaze.

You'd think I'd be getting used to the male response to the new Rory. But Tom and Vinnie's attentions are easy to ignore, and I can always pretend to be offended. But what do I do now that I *want* to encourage the attention? If this were the movies, I'd throw some witty, flirtatious rejoinder back at Hunter. I'd smile, arch a curved brow, and whisper sexily, "Oh, yeah, what *is* the perfect word?" And if I wasn't scared half out of my mind and blushing furiously from Hunter's compliment, I'd say it, too. Instead, I barely manage "Oh, um, ah."

Hunter doesn't seem to notice that I've turned into Chewbacca with a speech disorder and takes my hand, leading me to the couch. I sit daintily on the edge, then almost tumble back as the plush cushion collapses under me. Hunter squeezes my hand, then releases it. "Can I get you a drink?"

"Sure." The couch seems to have a gravitational force all its own, and I'm struggling with all I've got not to topple over, legs splayed in the air, butt sinking between the abyss of the cushions. I'm struggling even harder so Hunter won't notice my difficulties. "Water would be fine." The couch cushions suck at me, and my hold gives another fraction of an inch.

"Now don't go crazy on me, princess," Hunter says with a wink. "If I put a splash of lime in it, are you going to start dancing on the table?"

My face flames hotter. "No. I just—"

"Rory, I'm kidding. One water coming up, but just in case you're interested, I've got wine and beer, too."

I nod, then in a last-ditch effort to drop the one-syllable, grunting Chewbacca impression, I add, "Maybe with dinner."

Creator, I could use a glass of wine right now. The couch sinks lower. I could use a *bottle*. Would it be too weird if I told Hunter I'd changed my mind? Would that make me seem indecisive or—

"You got it," Hunter says, "but I hope you're not expecting dinner to be anything gourmet." Hunter heads into the kitchen. As soon as he's out of sight, I haul myself out of the quicksand couch and glare at the big, green beast. Scooting into the middle, I find a more solid spot and perch on the edge. "Stupid couch," I mutter.

"What was that?" Hunter slides open two panels on the bar separating the kitchen and living room. "I didn't hear you."

"Oh, nothing." Just talking to your couch. Creator, why do I always have to act like such a Klingon when I get nervous? No social graces.

Hunter sets a glass of water on the bar. "One water. And one beer." I hear the pop of a beer can and then the fizz as he pours it into a glass. A man drinking beer out of a glass. No, correction: a *bachelor* drinking beer out of a glass. This has to be a concession to my presence.

Either that or he's gay.

I watch Hunter take a swig of beer, admiring the muscles of his neck, which are visible beneath the open buttons of his light blue shirt. Creator, please don't let him be gay.

He sets the beer on the bar, and suddenly I realize that his next step will be to bring me the water, sit down on the couch beside me, and then, knowing the sucking power of this big green baby, we'll be pulled together and on top of each other in no time.

Yes! my starved libido shouts.

But Hunter doesn't bring me the water. I hear him in the kitchen, moving things around, while my water sits on the counter looking forlorn. There's sort of a crash and Hunter swears.

"Is everything okay?"

"Fine. Why?" he practically growls.

"No reason." I extract myself from the couch and go to the counter. He's lifting a large silver bowl from the floor. Wow. He's really trying hard. All this for me?

I'm suddenly very thirsty. I down the water just as Hunter looks up. "Thirsty?"

I smile. "A little."

He shakes his head. "What am I going to do with you, princess? Sure you don't want a glass of wine?"

Yes! Thankfully, enough of my sanity remains, and I decline. I'm so keyed up that wine—actually, a food substance of any kind—would wreak havoc on the acrobatic flips my stomach performs every time Hunter calls me princess.

Hunter is facing the stove, seeming to study the timer. While his back is to me, I do a personal inventory. My throat is clogged with a lump of guilt over Allison and Sunshine, and the rest of me is so charged I could be plugged into an electrical outlet. My hands are sweaty, my heart pounds, and I feel a sticky sheen of sweat threatening to stain the armpits of the blouse. Stuttering, sweating, and smelling like Wookiee. At this rate, I'll be dead of heart failure before dessert.

I take a deep breath, hoping to ward off an attack of hyperventilation. Just in case, though, I peer into Hunter's kitchen, hoping to locate where he might store paper bags. Maybe I could sneak one into the bathroom—

"Hey, I'm just going to check on this," Hunter says, startling me. He opens the oven door, bends over, and looks inside. He's blocking my view of dinner, something Italian I assume from the rich tomato smell, but the view of his rear end is completely unobstructed.

"Hmm. A few more minutes," he says, voice muffled from inside the oven.

"Delicious." I murmur, still staring at his butt.

He straightens. "Huh?"

Looking quickly away, I stammer, "I mean it smells delicious." What is *wrong* with me today? I never ogle men's butts. Sunshine would *kill* me. How many times has she harped about men treating women as objects?

I should be ashamed of myself. And I would be . . . except he has such a round, tight ass. Oh, Creator, I feel my breath catching again.

Hunter picks up his beer, then sets it down again. "Are you okay? You look pale."

"I'm fine," I wheeze.

Get control. Get control. You are calm, you are confident, you are . . . Princess Leia. Right. Princess Leia. What would she do? How would she act?

Well, she sure as the Dark Side wouldn't hyperventilate in front of Han—or any other man.

"So," I say to Hunter in my best sexy but confident Princess Leia Organa voice. "I didn't know you could cook."

Hunter gives me a sheepish grin. "I can't. Not really." He picks up his beer and walks around the kitchen wall to stand beside me at the bar. He sets his beer next to my water and rests his arm beside mine. His closeness tantalizes and terrifies me at the same time. Sixty-seven percent of me desperately wants him to kiss me. But thirty-one percent is plagued by fears that I'll disappoint him—that I'll be a crappy lover, that I'll mess everything up somehow.

Then there's the other two percent. It doesn't know what the Dark Side to think.

"If we both end up with food poisoning, I take full responsibility," Hunter says.

"I thought you wanted to cook." I glance at him then back down at our arms. We're almost touching.

"I did." Hunter settles on one of the two bar stools at the counter and looks up at me. "Truth is—" He gets that sheepish look again. "I've been feeling sort of like a fraud."

I grasp the bar for support. "You have?" *He's* been feeling like a fraud? Doesn't he know that *I'm* the one who's the fraud? Oh, Ewok shit. Maybe he does.

What if he met Tom at Y&Y and Tom told him we were together? Maybe Hunter's planning some elaborate way to get back at me and—

"Yeah. You know, I took you to Riva and on the *Seadog* and I guess I've been trying to show off a little, but that stuff isn't really me."

My anxiety shifts from shouting red to blaring neon orange. "It's not?"

"No." He leans his elbow on the bar. "I'm more of a hamburger and pizza guy. Give me a bowl of popcorn, a cold Sam Adams, and a Bulls game on TV"—he gestures at the muted screen—"and I'm a happy man. All that other stuff was just for show."

I stare at him, flabbergasted, not sure I understand what he's saying. I mean, I understand the words, but I must be misinterpreting the meaning behind them. Is Hunter telling me that he's been showing off for me? Is he saying that he was trying to—to—

I swallow. *Impress* me? "But—but *why?*"

Tom, the dork, trying to impress the new attractive, confident Rory I can understand. And Vinnie—well, he goes for anything in heels. But Hunter . . .

Hunter could have anyone.

"What do you mean, why?" Hunter reaches over and takes my hand. "I like you, Rory."

"You keep saying that." I'm not trying to be dense or force him to stroke my ego; I just can't believe what I'm hearing.

"Yeah. I'm still waiting for you to believe it." He pulls me closer until I'm standing between his knees, my hips brushing against his thighs. "You're funny, smart, attractive . . ." He brushes a piece of my hair away from my face and leaves his hand there. His touch is light as he runs three fingers over my cheeks and down to my lips. "Sexy as hell in this outfit."

I feel his other hand on the small of my back, and with gentle pressure, he pulls me to him. I wish I could say that this time I'm ready, that this time there's no hesitation on my part and I kiss him back right away, but I wouldn't be Rory Egglehoff if my life were that easy.

I *do* hesitate, and it's just enough for Hunter to glance up at me just when I'm leaning down to him, and his nose collides with my forehead. Hard.

"Oh, blast it! I am so sorry." I jump back and then, losing my balance in Allison's heels, flail helplessly, waving my arms about like crepe paper tied to a fan. I'm just about to fall flat on my ass when Hunter grabs my arm and saves me.

"Whoa! Princess, calm down. I'm fine."

"But your nose!" Oh, I *knew* I'd mess this up. I reach out and touch his nose. "Is it okay?"

He rubs it gingerly. "Nothing's broken. I've permanently lost my sense of smell, but who needs it anyway?"

I laugh, and he grins back at me, and this time *I* lean in to kiss *him*. This kiss is much more natural. My heart still pounds. I'm still tense as a Klingon before battle. But I'm no longer panicking. I'm actually starting to enjoy the kiss.

And when he presses his lips more firmly against mine, a subtle cue to deepen the kiss, heat shoots through my body like an explosion. Forget Allison. Forget Sunshine. Now there's only Hunter.

He takes the lead—which is probably for the best, since I can't seem to think—and before long I'm pressed against him like a Mynok on the *Millennium Falcon*. We're both breathing hard, and Hunter's hands are caressing my back and hips, moving slowly but inexorably lower.

He moves to kiss my neck, and I angle my head to the right, giving him unrestricted access. Creator, the way his mouth moves over my skin is what fine silk sheets on bare flesh must feel like. And when his lips move to my earlobe and he nibbles gently, I gasp.

"God, you smell good," he murmurs, working his way down the column of my throat.

"I do?" I whisper and inhale experimentally. I frown. I don't smell the drugstore perfume I put on, but something sort of unpleasant. Something acrid and . . . burning.

"Hunter!" I jerk out of his arms. "Something's burning!"

"Shit!" He jumps off the bar stool, toppling it over, and runs into the kitchen just as the smoke alarm starts to go off. I run after him.

"Shit!" Hunter yells again over the screeching alarm. He yanks open the oven door, and a plume of black smoke billows out. We both cough and wave frantically, but the smoke only thickens and the alarm seems to screech louder.

"Where's the smoke alarm?" I shout. "I'll wave a towel in front of it."

"In the hall, right outside my bedroom," he hollers back. I grab one of the towels dangling from the handle of the oven and shuffle/run—I'm wearing heels, remember—toward the siren. I wave the towel under it but the scream continues, so I finally just rip open the base and disconnect the battery. For a moment, the silence is so loud I can't hear anything, then Hunter yells, "Fuck! Oh, fucking A!"

"What's wrong?" I shuffle/run back to the kitchen in time to see Hunter dancing around and fumbling to turn on the faucet. I do it for him, and he immediately sticks his hand under the cold water. There are bright red welts on his thumb and first finger. I take his hand and stare at the angry marks. "Hunter, what happened?"

"Fucked up as usual," he growls. I release his hand, and he sticks it back under the water. "Forgot the most important piece of culinary equipment."

I frown. "What's that?"

"Oven mitt." He grins, and all I can do is shake my head. The man has third-degree burns on his hand, and he's smiling at me. Is this guy a Jedi or what?

While Hunter applies ointment, salve, ice, and other assorted remedies to his wound, I extract the charred remains of dinner from the oven. "What is—I mean, what *was* this?" I toss the food and scorched cookie sheet in the sink.

"Pizza," Hunter says, frowning at it. "Gourmet meats and fancy vegetables."

I blink, wondering for a moment why he'd put meat on the pizza, then remember I'd lied about being a vegetarian.

Still, the fact that he made such an effort, bought gourmet toppings and everything, touches me. "Oh, Hunter. I'm so sorry." I stare at the ruined mess. "If it's any consolation, it smelled good when I got here."

He shakes his head ruefully. "Nothing to be sorry about. Just another example of me trying to show off and having it bite me in the ass."

"No." I put my hand on his arm. "No, it was sweet of you to make it for me. Really, really sweet."

"Yeah, well it's not sweet now, just burned beyond all recognition."

"Not at all. Look, there's a green pepper." I pick up a black glob.

He frowns. "That was a slice of zucchini."

"Oh." I bite my lip. "I guess it shrunk."

He laughs. "Just a little. Hey, Rory, let's just drop all this get-to-know-you, impress-you shit, okay?"

"Um, okay." Like that is ever going to happen. What am I supposed to say? Oh, Hunter, I know you think vegetarians are abnormal, but since we're not impressing each other anymore, you should know that I'm a vegetarian. And a *Star Wars* freak. Oh, and have I mentioned my boyfriend Tom?

"Let's just be honest with each other," Hunter says. "I'll start." He leans a hip against the counter and crosses his arms over his chest. "I don't cook. I get delivery or eat out six of seven nights. And I don't eat at places like Riva. Usually I head to Pizzeria Uno or Subway."

His "revelations" calm me somewhat, and I grin. "The Subway people know my order by heart, and my idea of cooking dinner is throwing a Lean Cuisine into the microwave. You don't have to try to impress me, Hunter. I already like you. I—I've liked you for years."

"Yeah," he says. "I get that. I just don't get why." His sapphire eyes are questioning when he looks up at me, and I see that he's being completely honest. He really doesn't know why I like him. And now I'm confused. This man has to have women coming on to him daily. The real question is why he likes *me*.

"I guess it's just that we're so different," Hunter says when I don't answer right away. "You're so smart and articulate. You know about shit—like the Pythagorean theorem and stuff I barely remember."

"But you're smart, too, Hunter," I protest. "I've seen you talking to Yates. He thinks you're God's gift to Y and Y."

Hunter waves this compliment away. "I'm good with people, Rory. I can schmooze them. That's my job. It has nothing to do with being intelligent. It's all an act." He sighs and rolls his neck, appearing incredibly weary and adult. For once the boyishness is gone from his features, and he looks all of his thirty-two years.

"Sometimes I feel like I'm in high school again. Trying to show off. Trying to impress everyone, and inside wondering who the hell I really am."

Lately I've been wondering a lot about who I am, too. But I don't say that. Instead I say, "Well, that's an act *I* could never pull off. I can barely speak my own name when I meet someone new."

"I don't know why not. Hell, Rory, you'd be the life of the party if you just tried a little harder. I could listen to you talk about your family for hours. Your mom sounds so cool, and your sister is a trip."

"Yeah," I say, but I don't take it as the compliment Hunter intended. Instead I feel like even more of a freak. Like my family is a sideshow or something. And then guilt crashes down on me—guilt for ditching them and even more guilt for being ashamed of them.

"Anyway." He takes my hand in his good one. "For whatever reason, we both like each other, so we can stop playing games now, right?"

"Right." I nod my agreement. I do want Hunter to stop playing games, be himself around me, though if his worst infraction is taking me out to a nice restaurant, he doesn't know what embarrassment is. I, on the other hand, seem to have become the expert on the art of deception. But if I'd been the *real* Rory from the beginning—vegetarian, freaky family, *Star Wars* super fan—we wouldn't be standing here right now. He wouldn't have given me a second glance.

"Okay, so if I promise to cook for you another time, is it okay if I order us a pizza?"

"Sure," I say, and my heart sinks a little. Not that I expect him to fix us another dinner, but another take-out pizza from Domino's is so Tom. I hope I'm not wrong about Hunter. What if he's really a Wookiee in disguise?

Hunter grabs the phone and pulls a flyer off the fridge. "I usually order from Gino's East. Sound good to you?"

I raise my eyebrows. "Gino's? That's better than okay. I mean, it's the best pizza in Chicago."

"Don't tell Dave that. He swears by Malnati's. Tell you what. I'm too hungry to wait for delivery. You call them, tell them 'Hunter's usual,' and I'll go pick it up."

"Wait. I'll go with you."

"No way. Just hang here. Ruining dinner was my fault. I'm not going to drag you around the city." He grabs his keys from the coffee table.

"It's no big deal, Hunter."

He holds up a hand, keys dangling from his fingers. "Just hang out and relax. I'll be back in twenty minutes."

"Twenty minutes? It'll take them longer than that to cook it."

Hunter grins. "Not if you say it's 'Hunter's usual.' Dougall did some work for them last year, and I got to know the owners. Trust me, that pizza will be ready before I get there."

"Okay."

He kisses my cheek and heads for the door. "See you in a minute."

The door slams and I stare at the phone, the flyer in my hand, and the charred remains of Hunter's pizza in the sink. Three minutes ago we were kissing, and now I'm here alone, wondering what happened. My head is still spinning.

Finally I call Gino's, making sure to mention Hunter's name, which does get an immediate response and an assurance that the pizza will be ready pronto. Smiling, I hang up the phone and start cleaning up. I know it's a bad idea, but I imagine myself doing this nightly. Hunter cooking dinner, me cleaning up. Hunter coming in with the last of our dishes, then wrapping his arms around my waist, kissing my neck.

I spot Hunter's beer and take a long swig. Yuck. I hate beer, but the taste didn't bother me when I tasted it on Hunter's mouth. I shiver. Where the Dark Side is that wine?

Chapter 16

"Like the pizza?" Hunter asks, leaning back to rest his broad shoulders against the coffee table. We're both camped out on the floor, and our spoils are spread between us. I eye the greasy pizza box, the liter of Pepsi, the roll of paper towels, and the half-empty bottle of merlot, and smile. The conversation was as good as the meal and, now on my second (well, the second Hunter knows about) glass of wine, I feel a pleasant buzz.

"Great choice on the wine," I answer and take another sip. "I don't usually like red, but this is good."

"Dave gave it to me," Hunter says, his eyes watching the path of the glass to my mouth. I feel a flare of warmth in my belly that has nothing to do with the alcohol. I take another sip.

"His family owns a small winery in Napa Valley. He used to play in the vineyards and stomp around in vats full of grapes."

"Dave?" I laugh at the image of big, macho Dave up to his purple knees in grape mush. "We should introduce him to Allison. She's always going to wine tastings and reading *Wine Spectator.*" The mention of Allison twists at my heart. Is she home right now, drinking a bottle of wine, drowning her misery all alone?

The guilt lasts only a moment. Another sip of wine, a glance at Hunter's admiring gaze, and I'm pleasantly numb and tingly again.

"Dave and Allison. I've been thinking about getting those two together, too. You know, Dave's last girlfriend was a real piece of work."

I lean forward, interested. "What do you mean?"

"She came off as this great girl, really into Dave, you know? And he really fell for her, too." Hunter scowls. "Then it turns out the whole time they were dating, she already had a boyfriend. She was using Dave to get back at the other guy because he'd cheated on her."

My head spins and I feel as though I've been hit in the head with a two-by-four. Hunter sets his wineglass on the coffee table and starts to clear the mountain of leftovers between us. When he lifts my plate, he frowns. "Was the pizza okay? It looks like you picked off all the hamburger."

I flush and try to avoid his eyes. "Oh, um, I guess I'm still kind of full from lunch."

"Yeah, right."

My heart stops, and I take a quick breath. Blast it, he knows! He knows all my lies—Tom, the vegetarian thing. I should have just eaten the damn dead cow and been done with it.

"I know what's really going on here."

"You do?" The two-by-four hits again, and the room spins wildly.

"Yep. You're still queasy from the *Seadog.*"

I have no idea what he's talking about. Did I black out

and miss some discussion about Jacques Cousteau's last find?

"Yeah. You tried to hide it, but you looked green on the speedboat ride this afternoon. Not a big sailor, are you?"

A tidal wave of relief spills over me. "No, not really," I whisper, not just because I'm still recovering from the all-encompassing fear that Hunter had figured me out, but because he's very close to me now. He's hunkered down, plate in one hand, the other reaching out for me.

He places three fingers under my chin and notches it up. "Just need to get your sea legs, princess," he murmurs and leans in to kiss me.

Mmmm. His mouth tastes like rich merlot, and I immediately forget about vegetarians and *Seadogs*, focusing instead on fusing my lips with his, pushing my fingers through his thick hair, and running my hands over his broad shoulders.

A moment later the plate falls to the floor, and Hunter and I both jump as soggy pizza crust and greasy hamburger pieces bounce onto the carpet.

"Shit. Give me one minute." He rises and takes our plates and the pizza boxes to the kitchen.

"So, what were we talking about?" I say cheerfully when Hunter comes back into the living room.

"Dave." He lifts my wineglass from the floor and sets it on the coffee table next to his. "Come sit here." He pats the cushions behind him. "You can try to beat all of Dave's deep dark secrets out of me." He settles on the couch, loose and casual, and my mouth goes dry. The way his legs stretch out in front of him, the way he's thrown his arm so casually across the back, the way his smile is inviting and wicked all at the same time make me dizzy with attraction.

"I gotta warn you, though," he says, roguish glint in his eye. "I hold up well under torture."

Now would be the time for me to give a saucy flip of my hair and say something sexy. It would be a lot slicker than standing robotically, jerking rigidly to the couch, and sitting all prim and proper on the edge of the cushion beside him. But I have to hand it to Hunter. He's a Jedi in the true sense of the word. If he notices my discomfort, he doesn't comment.

"Yeah, Dave's a good guy." He picks up the wine bottle and gestures to my half-empty glass. I shake my head stiffly.

"He's also really good at what he does." He tops off his glass. "I'm lucky to be working with him."

Picking up his wineglass, Hunter looks at me, and I realize it's my turn to say something. My mind is completely blank, but I finally manage, "How long have you and Dave worked together?"

Hunter fills me in on his relationship with Dave—where they met, how long they've known each other, past accounts they handled—all the while making no move to pounce on me. By the time we're talking about the end of Hunter's basketball career, when he popped a knee playing for the University of Michigan, I'm snuggled up next to him, on my third (well, the third Hunter knows about) and, I swear, *last* glass of wine, and he's leisurely stroking my hair.

I love the feel of his hands in my hair. I've always loved that feeling. I used to bring Sunshine my hairbrush in the evenings before bed and beg her to brush my hair. I didn't care about bedtime stories, I just wanted to feel the warmth and security of her touch.

I'm getting that same feeling right now with Hunter.

There's no push for us to start making out, no not-so-subtle hints that it's time to move to the next step, none of those junior high dating moves. We're just sitting and talking, getting to know each other. And for the first time in a long time, *I* actually want more. I want this to go further.

"So what about your friends," Hunter drawls, his voice a low murmur in my ears. "Besides Allison, who do you hang out with?"

"Um . . ." The first name that pops into my head is Tom, but a nanosecond later, I blast it into deep space. There is no way I am going to let thoughts of Tom ruin this time with Hunter.

My next thought is of Janet in risk management and Meredith, the receptionist at Y&Y. Sometimes we go for drinks after work or shopping on our lunch breaks. But they're more acquaintances than friends. Then there's my old college friends and roommates, now scattered about the country, but we still keep in touch via e-mail. I tell Hunter about a few of them and mention the Y&Y crew, too, careful not to bring up Tom's name, and ending with, "Sometimes I wish I had more friends, but I really don't have time."

"I know what you mean," Hunter says. "We finished a huge deal with a major player a few weeks ago, and I was working ninety-hour weeks to get everything done. When I finally emerged from the dungeon, I didn't even recognize the names of the movies playing." His fingers tug on the ends of my hair, then move lower to trace the nape of my neck.

"Oh, now that isn't right," I say with a shiver. "No matter how busy I get, I always have time for the movies."

Hunter grins, "Oh, yeah. I forgot you've got a thing for sci-fi films."

"It's not a *thing.*"

He raises a brow. "You have *Star Wars* collectible glasses."

"So?" I cross my arms. Hunter grins and shakes his head.

"Come on, Rory. Just admit you have a thing for *Star Wars.*"

Admit I have a *Star Wars* thing. No, correction: a *Star Wars obsession.* I take a deep breath. I feel so close to Hunter right now. I really think he likes me. Maybe he'd think my fixation with all things intergalactic was cute or quirky.

"There's a little more to the *Star Wars* thing than you think, Hunter," I begin. My insides are trembling, and I have to clutch my hands together to keep from digging my stubby nails into the couch cushion.

Hunter waves a hand. "I know, you've got all that memorabilia. I told you, I think your collectibles are cool."

My knuckles start to ache as I tighten my grip. Does he really mean it? *Star Wars is* pretty cool. And my obsession does sort of make me unique. Some people think sci-fi junkies are geeks, but I've always thought my passion gives me character.

A burst of hope rises in me. This could be the start of a real relationship. If I tell him about *Star Wars,* I can work up to revealing the truth about a few other things. I could even consider inviting him to meet my family. "Hunter," I begin, my throat dry as the Tatooine desert. "About those *Star Wars* glasses. My collection is a *little* more than just a thing for sci-fi movies."

"Yeah, you should have someone look at them."

"I have, and—"

But he's not listening. "You know, I gotta admit, I've been half afraid you were going to tell me that in your spare time you dress up like Mr. Spock and go to those creepy Buck Rogers conventions."

"Star Trek," I squeeze out as my windpipe fills with sand.

"Oh, right," Hunter says. He runs a hand through his hair, and my neck feels chilled without the warmth of his touch. "God, I was at a marketing conference once in St. Louis and half of the convention hall was us, and the other half was space aliens. Those sci-fi junkies are weird, Rory. Talk about a freak show. They were actually speaking in made-up alien languages." He chuckles. I try to smile, but I'm tightening up.

"I guess it takes all kinds, huh?" Hunter runs his hand up my arm and looks to me for concurrence. For a long moment, I say nothing. I can still tell him. Take a chance and see what happens, if he likes me enough to get past my freak-show side. If he still likes me when he meets the *real* Rory. The real Rory would be jumping up and down in staunch defense of my fellow science fiction lovers, trying to convince Hunter that convention-goers are fun not freaky. The *real* Rory would defend my passions to the bitter end, not caring what Stormy or Allison or anyone else thought of me. I'd shout, "I do go to those conventions. I have a Counselor Troi costume in my closet, and I'm Princess Leia in the Creatures and Features Extravaganza costume show next week."

It occurs to me that I am one of the "kinds" Hunter is referring to. The "kind" he wouldn't want to be with.

On the other hand, the new and improved Rory thinks costume shows and conventions are kind of silly. The whole time I'm there I feel like I'm dressed up for Halloween, only I've messed up and it's not October 31 but March 31. I do, if I'm honest, kind of feel like a dork at the conventions. I could give them up if Hunter thinks they're stupid.

Wait a parsec! Give up my love, my passion, my whole

reason for being? But the seconds are ticking by, and I still haven't defended it. I can't have changed that much. I mean, I am who I am, right? I'm a *Star Wars* fanatic. If Hunter doesn't like it, too bad.

Straightening my shoulders, though they're pretty stiff already, I glance at Hunter, into those sapphire blue eyes, at those perfect lips, and those perfect teeth, and that thick, gorgeous, perfect hair, and I say, "Yeah, those people are such dorks. I might collect toothbrushes, but at least I'm not a dweeb."

Hunter laughs and tops off my wineglass, finishing the bottle. I take a sip—okay, a gulp—and try to get back into the mood. This is just a small glitch, Rory. It's not a big deal. I don't need to go to sci-fi conventions. In fact, the extravaganza Saturday will be the last one. Besides, when the time is right, I'm going to tell Hunter all my dirty secrets. When I'm sure he really likes me, when I'm sure he really wants to be with me.

Because one thing I know for sure is that I want to be with him. And right now, with the wine in my blood and the feel of him pressed against me, and the smell of his cologne, I want very much to kiss him. So, drawing on every last ounce of confidence—and some I've borrowed from my mentor, Princess Leia—I turn to Hunter and brush a kiss against the corner of his lips. I feel his mouth curve into a smile under mine, and his hand pauses momentarily in its caress of my hair. Other than that he doesn't move.

I lean back, look at his face, and he raises an eyebrow. A challenge? Okay, the real Roberta would be running for the door right now, but this Roberta has the backing of Princess Leia. So I raise an eyebrow, matching his challenge, and lean forward to kiss him again.

This time I'm not quite so tentative, and after a moment of gently exploring his lips—all the while freaking out because *I am making out with Hunter Chase!*—I run the tip of my tongue along his mouth.

He groans—exactly the response I'd been hoping for—and pulls me tight against him, finally returning the kiss fully. I don't know how long we stay melded against each other, but pretty soon the black hole couch has its way, and we're sucked down until I'm sprawled on top of him. I open the first few buttons of his shirt and start kissing that hollow at the base of his throat while his hands explore my back. I can feel his fingers move up and down my spine in long, languorous strokes, and I shiver with each one. He, in turn, chuckles and strokes even more boldly.

Things are progressing nicely—Hunter's unfastening the clasp of my bra, and I've got his shirt raked down his shoulders—when, looking at his tan, muscled chest, it once again strikes me that I am about to be intimate with Hunter Chase. *Me and Hunter Chase.* I don't think, even in my wildest imaginings, I ever believed this day would come. I mean, I wanted it to come, but somewhere deep inside I always felt I'd be stuck with gangly geeks. I never believed I'd be running my hands over a man who actually has six-pack abs.

And maybe you don't deserve to.

Where did that come from? Hunter flips the clasp on my bra, and I push the thought away. Now is not the time for self-introspective psychobabble. I just want to enjoy being with Hunter, having his lips on me, his mouth on my neck, his hands sliding up my rib cage to—oh, Creator . . .

It's not you he's kissing.

Blast it! Where the Dark Side are these thoughts coming from? They're ruining the mood.

"Are you okay, Rory?" Hunter asks, his hand pausing in mid-caress of my breast.

"Yes, yes, I'm fine." Don't stop now, Hunter. "I'm great." I give him a reassuring grin and reach for the Final Frontier: the button on his pants.

Once I unfasten that, there's no going back. We are on our way to distant galaxies and orgasms yet unknown. Although from what he's been doing so far, there's not too much guesswork about how this night is going to end. The real question is not will there be an orgasm, but how many?

What about Tom?

"Blast it!" I jerk up, and Hunter's heavy-lidded eyes widen with concern.

"Rory, what's wrong? If we're moving too fast—" He pulls his hands from under my top, but I grab them just as they reach my waist.

"No, no, it's not that." The words come out in a flood. "It's just—just a, um, muscle cramp." I gesture to my left leg, pinned at an awkward angle against the couch. I move it, make a show of awkwardly flexing it in the confined space, and say, "All fine. Now, where was I?" I lean forward and kiss his jaw, then trace a path to his neck. It's a heady feeling to have the opportunity, the *right* to kiss Hunter like this. To have him *want* me to kiss him like this.

I run my lips lightly over the stubble on Hunter's chin, thoughts of Tom almost banished to the far reaches of space, when Hunter murmurs, "What does 'blast it' mean?"

"Huh?" I glance up at him.

"You said, 'blast it.' What does that mean? Is it like 'damn it' or 'shit' or 'oh, fuck' or—"

"Okay, Hunter. I get the idea." I laugh, but it sounds

tinny. Even in moments of intimacy, my geekiness comes out. Hunter's still looking at me, half smile on his lips, so I answer, "Yeah, I guess it's sort of like that. You know, some people say 'fudge' or 'oh, fooey.' I say, 'blast it.' "

"It's cute. You're cute." His hands reach under my top again. "I usually just go for the gold. 'Damn,' 'shit,' 'fuck' . . ." On the last word, he presses his mouth against my breast, and I can feel his warm lips through the shirt's thin material. My breath catches, and I don't think it's any coincidence that Hunter's last word was "fuck."

I close my eyes and tilt my head back, holding on to Hunter's shoulders because my head is spinning. Creator, his mouth is so hot. And his lips. . . .

You blew off Allie and Sunshine for this.

Shut up. Shut up. I try to focus on Hunter's mouth again.

You are so shallow. He doesn't want you. He doesn't even know you.

Shut up!

If he knew what a dork you really are . . .

"Fuck!" I jerk back and roll off the couch, pulling my top down as I do so. Hunter blinks in confusion, his impossibly blue eyes staring up at me.

"I'm sorry. I didn't mean to upset you. I thought—"

I hold up a hand, silencing him. "It's not you, Hunter. You didn't do anything." I search the floor for my discarded sandals, slip them on, all the while avoiding his gaze. "I just can't do this right now. I just—" I glance around for my purse, find it, and snatch it up. "I'm not who you think I am." I press my fingers to my temples. "I'm a fake and a fraud and a . . . a . . . *liar.* " I dart a glance at him, judging his reaction.

He frowns, but I can see from the hazy look on his face,

he's not really getting what I'm trying to say. He starts to speak, and I cut him off. "I'm sorry. All I wanted was for you to like me."

"I *do* like you." Hunter starts to get up, and I practically run for the door. "I think you're incredible."

I yank it open and turn back to him. "You have no idea how much I wish that were true." I slam the door closed with a final thud.

Chapter 17

*The next day at work, I hide in my office. I'm terri-*fied I'll see Hunter and want to avoid Tom as well. Tom comes by midmorning, but I hear his voice down the hall and jump under my desk before he reaches my office.

"Rory?" It sounds like he's standing in my doorway, and I can picture him glancing around the room. "Hey, babe, are you in here?" There's a pause, then "Hey," he says to someone walking by. "Have you seen Rory?"

"No. I was looking for her, too." It's Vinnie. I crouch lower. Get back to your cesspool and leave me alone!

"We have some unfinished business—if you know what I mean." Vinnie's slimy voice slides over me, and I curl my lip in disgust.

"Not really," Tom says. Creator, he's so clueless. "Should we hang in here and wait for her?"

"Wait around for a chick?" Vinnie says. "Not my style."

"Maybe we could check the bathroom," Tom suggests.

"Good idea. We might even need to go in and have a look around," Vinnie says, voice trailing away. Eew!

Great. If Tom and Vinnie aren't sued for sexual harassment first, the next time I look they'll be rounding up a posse and distributing an all points bulletin. I'm going to have to hide under this desk forever, or at least until everyone goes home.

I don't get it. A month ago I would have given my Princess Leia action figure—okay, not Princess Leia, but definitely Luke Skywalker—to have Tom's full attention. And Vinnie—sleazy as he is—has given me an ego boost with his flirting. Of course, now that I don't want them, they want me. And the one person I do want, I've lost forever.

The phone rings, and I feel like screaming, "Leave me alone!" But I'm expecting a call from a client, so I have to answer it. I just hope it's not Tom or Hunter. I snort. As if Hunter would ever want to talk to me again. Holding on to a leg of the desk for support, I lean back, reach one arm up, and drag the phone under the desk.

"Roberta Egglehoff," I murmur, cupping the receiver so my voice doesn't carry.

"Roberta? Is that you?" It's Dan.

I jerk upright, banging my head on the bottom of the desk and clamping down on my tongue. "Oh, hi, Dan. What's up?" My vision is blurred by shooting supernovas of light and pain.

"Just thought I'd give you a call. Make sure everything is okay. What happened to you last night?"

I squeeze my eyes shut. Guilt crashes down on me. I still can't believe I skipped Sunshine's party—the one we planned for months—to eat pizza with a guy. "I'm fine," I say. "Tell Sunshine I'm sorry. Things are crazy around here, and I lost track of time."

"I know how it is," Dan says. "I'll be living at the office from now until April fifteen. Your mother hates tax time."

"So she reminds us each and every year."

Dan laughs. "Yeah, well, I miss her too when I have to put in long hours. And we both missed you yesterday. You know, I called your office last night."

My heart thuds in my chest. "Really? Oh, I must have been at the copier or in the restroom."

"I left a message on your voice mail."

"You did?" Blast! I knew there was something I forgot to do this morning. "I—I didn't get it."

"I left about three or four. One each time I called."

I swallow. He knows. "Oh, um, I don't know what happened," I stutter. "I'll make it up to Sunshine next weekend. I promise." It's lame. How can I possibly make it up?

"I really wish you'd been there yesterday," Dan says, echoing my thoughts. "Sunshine was pretty upset. I don't like seeing her like that. She lives for you girls."

"I know. I'm sorry," I whisper.

"Stormy told us what happened between you two and that you girls hadn't talked since. You really shouldn't leave things like that, Roberta. She's your sister, and she loves you."

What is this? Guilt Trips R Us? "I know, I know. I really wasn't trying to avoid her. I just had to . . . work." It sounds less convincing every time I say it. And Dan is no fool. He sees right through me. Besides just being with Hunter, another benefit of skipping the party is that it gave me an out from dealing with the stuff between Stormy and me. I just wanted to float in weightless, careless space a little longer in the knowledge that Hunter wanted to be with me before having to drop back to earth. Before Allison challenged me about Tom again, or Stormy accused me of selling out.

But I've lost Hunter now, so I might as well suck it up. "I'll send Stormy an e-mail and apologize," I tell Dan. "Sunday we'll have a bonding fest and make it all better."

"An e-mail, Roberta?" Dan's disappointed tone contrasts sharply with the light one I'd been trying to affect. "This is your sister. Don't you think you should see her in person? And you know your friend Allison stopped by last night, too."

"*Allison* was at Sunshine's party? *Why?*"

Dan is silent for a long moment, then he says, "I suppose because she loves Sunshine and wanted to celebrate with us." There's no mistaking the accusation in his voice. "Allison seemed pretty upset, but she wouldn't give us any details. I think she really came to talk to you."

And I wasn't there.

The space under the desk no longer feels safe and hidden. Instead, I feel like the darkness is closing in on me. Outside, Dan probes with a flashlight, highlighting each and every one of my faults.

It's always been a bad habit of mine, but when I get defensive, I get angry. "What is this, Dan?" I hiss into the phone, still conscious of the search party combing the halls and cubicles of Y&Y. "Why are you hounding me?"

"Hounding you?" He sounds confused. "I'm not hounding you. I just wanted you to know—"

"Know what? That I'm treating everyone like Ewok shit? That I'm a bad daughter, a bad friend, and a horrible sister? Why do you even care about Allison? I mean, I can understand where you're coming from with Stormy. She is your daughter. I know it's only natural for you to take her side. You always did."

There's a gasp on the other end of the line, and I immediately regret the words. I wish I had that time machine from the movie *Galaxy Quest.* Tim Allen used it to go five minutes back in time so he and the rest of the starship crew could save the day. If only I could go back in time . . .

Unfortunately, I think it would take more than five minutes to salvage all I've screwed up.

"Rory, you know that's not true. I've always treated you and Stormy the same. I love both of you equally."

It's the truth. There never was any favoritism. And yet I'd been jealous at times. Jealous that she had a father and I didn't. And then, of course, I'd feel horribly guilty at my feelings. Dan was wonderful. Dan loved me. Dan was as much my father as Stormy's. Only he wasn't my *real* father. He wasn't my dad. I didn't know who my dad was. I never would.

"Dan, I'm sorry. I don't know where that came from. You've been the best father a daughter could have. Please, I'm sorry."

"Look, honey, I know it was hard for you growing up, not knowing who your dad was."

"No, really. I didn't think about it all that much," I say, and it's mostly true. I didn't think of my real dad often, but questions about him always niggled at the back of my mind. "I had you, Dan, and I wouldn't want any other dad."

"I'm glad to hear that, but it wouldn't be normal if you didn't at least wonder about your biological father, and Sunshine and I always tried to be very open with you about that. For your mother's part, she's always felt horrible about this. More than anything, I think she wishes she could tell you who he was, something about him."

"Yeah."

Sunshine's never said this to me, but the regret I saw in her eyes whenever I asked her about my real dad taught me long ago to curb my curiosity. "I wish Sunshine wouldn't feel bad. I'm okay. It's just sometimes . . ." I pause, not sure I want to say this to Dan but needing to say it to someone. "Sometimes I feel like I don't fit in with our family. Like I'm the misfit, and I don't belong. I felt like that all through school, too, but that was to be expected since I was pretty much a nerd."

"Roberta, that's not true. You were smart, curious, hard-working. We are so proud of you."

I smile. "Thanks, Dan. I know you were, but those qualities didn't make me popular. And then I'd come home and feel like I was a freak there, too. Why couldn't I get excited about organic gardening? Why didn't I want to make crystal jewelry and chant to the moon? Why was I the only one who voted in favor of Disneyland for summer vacation over six weeks of harassing whalers with Greenpeace?"

"Hey, now, I was coerced into that!"

"I know. You're not like Stormy and Sunshine, either, but you're always at ease with them. You're always comfortable. Why aren't I?"

There's a long pause, and then Dan says quietly, "I don't know, Rory. I wish you didn't feel that way. I wish I could change that for you, but I think it's something only you can do. You're searching for answers, thinking maybe your dad holds some of them for you. But even if you met him, you wouldn't find what you wanted. Whoever he is, he's just a guy like the rest of us. He doesn't hold any secret insights into who you are. Only you know that."

I sigh. "Yeah, I know. I've got to figure it out for myself and all that Bantha fodder."

"It's not Bantha fodder, Rory. I'm not a psychologist, but

ask yourself why it's so important for you to fit in. Why not just be Rory? Why not just love Rory? We do."

Tears well up in my eyes, and since my tissues are out of reach on the top of my desk, I wipe the wetness away with the sleeve of my red jacket. "Thanks, Dan. I love you, too."

"Then I'll see you Sunday, right? Sunshine will make us do all those crazy bonding activities and maybe that will help."

"Yeah." I sniffle. "I'll see you Sunday."

I put the phone down and huddle under the desk in silence.

A long time later I emerge, blinking at the bright fluorescent lights overhead. I sit in my Y&Y-issue leather chair and stare at the spreadsheets scattered before me. Today the numbers are just a jumble of lines and circles. They have no meaning, no significance.

But what does? Allison. I glance at my phone. I should call her, ask how she's doing, apologize for blowing her off last night.

Stormy. We haven't spoken for three days, and that's never happened before. Usually, after an argument we make up within the hour. Four hours, tops.

Hunter. I groan and put my head down on the pile of paperwork. I can feel my cheeks heat just thinking about last night. How could I have run out like that, without even an explanation? The man cooks me dinner—well, buys me dinner—serves me wine, tries to get to know me, and then I run out of his apartment like I've got half the Imperial army on my tail. He's never going to speak to me again.

The reunion is Saturday and, unless I want to face Hunter, Allison and—the cosmos help me—Jellie Abernathy alone, Tom is my only prospective date. Same old Roberta Egglehoff. Outsider. Outcast. Wookiee dater.

I shake my head, causing some of the spreadsheets under my face to whisk to the floor. Dan's right. Why do I care so much whether I'm popular or not? Isn't the whole idea of popularity, of fitting in, being "one of the crowd," all in the mind, anyway? I mean, I have friends and family who love me, so I'm popular with them—well, not right now, but I'm going to fix that. *They* think I fit in. So why don't I feel that way?

"Uh, Rory?"

I jolt upright and see Tom standing in my door. "Are you okay? Should I come back at another time?"

I sigh, watching Tom shift awkwardly. I'm not dressed in Allison's Ultimate Jedi Clothes today, but I've gotten used to being glamorous. This morning I pulled out a flirty red skirt I bought on a whim, but was never brave enough to wear, with a sleeveless silk blouse and red jacket. I look attractive without being too sexy, but Tom's still looking at me like I'm the newest Play Station model. I try to muster some interest in him. There must be *something* about Tom I'm attracted to.

I stare long and hard. Nope. Nothing. The more I look, the more repulsed I feel. "Hi, Tom. Come in. What's up?" This is good, I tell myself. This is very good. Now's my chance to break up. If I do it here in the office, we can keep it civilized and professional. It will be more like terminating a business partnership than a relationship.

"Just wanted to see how your weekend went. How's your family?"

I want to grab Tom by the shoulders and shake him, he's trying so hard. But it's too late. "They're good."

"Did you see them yesterday?"

I'm instantly suspicious. Does he know I was out with Hunter yesterday? "Why do you ask?"

"No reason." He shrugs and steps inside the door. His eyes rake over me, lingering on my chest. I feel like pulling my jacket tight over my silk blouse.

"Wasn't yesterday the big party?"

Tom remembered the party? He never remembers anything about me. That makes two direct hits, when normally Tom is way off the mark. In fact, he doesn't even know there *is* a mark.

"So, how was it?" He moves closer to my desk, surreptitiously peering over the top to check me out—probably hoping I'm wearing a micro-miniskirt. I resist the urge to reach for a bottle of Lysol and coat myself in it.

"Fine. Sunshine loved it." Or so I heard.

He nods and an awkward silence, thick as the mists on Dagobah, hovers between us.

"So, Tom—"

"Are we—?"

We both chuckle nervously, and Tom says, "Go ahead."

"No, you go ahead," I say automatically and then want to kick myself. Just spit it out: I don't want to be with you anymore, Tom.

I peer at him, still standing self-consciously in front of my desk. He looks sort of ill and has finally stopped checking me out. Now he's shifting from foot to foot and tugging at his Tasmanian Devil tie. Maybe he's nervous because he wants to break up with me? I feel a surge of relief. Maybe I won't have to do this after all.

Either that or he has to go to the bathroom.

"I just wanted to check that we're still going to the extravaganza together Saturday. I got the tickets."

My heart drops into my stomach. Blast it! I'd completely forgotten about the extravaganza. How can I say no now? Tom's bought the tickets. And if I don't go, he won't just be out fifty dollars, he'll be reamed by his friends since they're counting on me to play Princess Leia in the costume show.

I stare at Tom. He's got a hopeful baby Ewok look in his eyes. How can I say no to that? I've treated everyone I love like Wookiee crap. Maybe this is the one thing I can do right. And maybe Tom will be the one person in the galaxy who doesn't despise me.

But, Creator, a whole Saturday trapped at the extravaganza in a Princess Leia costume. Normally, I'd love it, but now the thought of Hunter finding out I'd spent Saturday with Tom and a gaggle of Trekkies makes me shudder.

Hunter. Saturday. The reunion.

I close my eyes. "Tom, I just don't think I can go. I've got too much going on."

Tom glares at me. "Like what?" he bites out.

"My high school reunion is that night."

"We already talked about this. Your reunion won't interfere with the extravaganza." Tom frowns. "The costume show will be over by five."

My heart sinks again, sliding into my lower intestines. "Oh," I say. "Good point."

"Besides, you have to go. You're Princess Leia."

"Right. I'm Princess Leia."

"So, here's the plan," Tom says. "I pick you up for the extravaganza, we go and have an awesome time, then we can stop back at your place and change for the reunion. I'll bring a tie with me."

I stare at him, desperately searching for a way out. Just tell him, Rory. Just tell him you don't want to go to the reunion, the extravaganza, or anywhere else with him ever again. Courage. Use the Force.

I open my mouth to drop the meteor, but then an

image races across my mind: me walking into the reunion alone.

I can hear the whispers, see the pity on my classmates' faces, feel Allie's angry eyes boring into my back. After the way I brushed her off last night, she'll probably be glad I'm alone.

And Hunter. Hunter won't show any emotion. He'll nod coldly and turn away. It will be like I never existed. Was never part of his life.

I'm not thrilled about being outed for the Wookiee dater that I am, but can I make it through the reunion alone? Can I make it through at all? Somehow staying home seems even more cowardly. If I don't go, then everyone will know they won, they got the better of poor, unpopular Icky Egglehoff.

I look at Tom again, eyes so hopeful behind his glasses that I'll like his plan. Tom is no Jedi. He's a Wookiee through and through, but Wookiee or not, if I walk in with Tom, I won't be alone.

I smile at the Wookiee. "What time are you picking me up?"

It's six o'clock, and I'm just closing down my computer, having stayed late to compensate for the measly amount of work I accomplished today, when the phone rings.

I'm tempted to let it go to voice mail, but I don't have anywhere I need to be and there's only a Lean Cuisine microwave entrée awaiting me at home, so I have nothing to lose by answering. I snatch the phone up. "Roberta Egglehoff."

"Rory?"

I freeze, and then I start to shake.

"Hey, I was hoping I'd catch you in."

It's Hunter. I try to respond but my voice won't come out. Why is he calling me? What could he possibly have to say after last night?

"Hey, are you there?" He sounds a little unsure now.

"Y-yes," I rasp. "Hi."

"Look, I'm sorry I didn't call you earlier today. I meant to, but things got kind of crazy around here. Well, you know how it goes." His voice sounds confident, full of businessman assurance, but underneath I hear a waver of uncertainty. Is Hunter nervous about talking to me?

I give a tinny laugh. "Yeah. I know how it goes."

There's a pause and then Hunter says, "Look, Rory, do you want to go out for a drink or something? Grab dinner? I feel kind of weird about what happened last night. I thought maybe we could talk about it."

I'm so shocked at the invitation that for a full three seconds my heart stops beating.

Hunter must take my silence as a rejection because he says hurriedly, "I understand if you don't want to. I—"

"No!" I blurt out. "I do. When do you want to go? Where should we meet?"

I hear an audible sigh of relief. "How about somewhere kind of quiet? There's a place I know on North Wells. It's not far from your apartment." He gives me the name and address, and after a stop at the bathroom to reapply lipstick and powder—Allison would be so proud—I head over there.

I use the time on the el to fortify my resolve. All last night, I lay awake in bed, miserable because I want to be with Hunter and miserable because I want him to want to be with me. *Me:* the vegetarian, the *Star Wars* freak, the geeky girl who can't even break up with her boyfriend. But

I'm never going to have a real relationship with Hunter if I don't show him the real me. Hunter was brave enough to be open with me—as if he had very much to hide—and I owe him the same courtesy.

So tonight I'm going to be completely open and honest with the men in my life. I'm going to tell Hunter about Tom, then break up with Tom for good. I'm going to tell Hunter I'm a vegetarian, just like the rest of my crazy family, and I'm even going to admit that I go to *Star Trek* conventions and can speak fluent Klingon. I might even mention the extravaganza. If, by then, he hasn't run from the restaurant screaming in terror, maybe there's a chance for us.

The restaurant is in Old Town, my neighborhood. I love this area. It's quaint and cozy, and on my way from the el to the restaurant, I pass dozens of people strolling on the wide sidewalks and sipping cocktails at outdoor cafés. Couples are holding hands, peering in the shops, or admiring the trees and flowers lining the sidewalk, and harried moms and dads are juggling the kids while running last-minute errands.

I spot Luigi's Ristorante up ahead. The wooden display board outside Luigi's advertises deep-dish pizza, hearty lasagna, and cold beer. This is Hunter's kind of place.

Dressed in bold red, I felt powerful and attractive at work. Now I'm just praying I'm not overdressed.

I duck inside Luigi's, mentally preparing myself for the dim, shabby interior, but am again surprised. The neat little tables are covered by red and white checkered tablecloths—real cloth, not plastic—and on each table is a vase with flowers and white pillar candles. The eatery is small and cozy and quiet, despite the fact that it's almost full to capacity. I don't see Hunter right away, so I scan the tables on the floor and those against the brightly painted walls.

"You musta be Rory."

I turn to see a portly middle-aged man in a white shirt, white apron, and faded black pants standing behind me. He smiles and opens his arms. "Welcome to Luigi's!" he says in a voice accented with Italian.

"Yes. How did you know my name?"

"You're meeting *mio amico,* little Hunter."

Little Hunter? "Um—right."

He smiles, showing white teeth. "*Bueno.* You follow me. I take good care of you."

I'm not sure what Luigi means when he says he'll take care of me, but he's already waddling through the restaurant, heading toward the back. I scamper to catch up, desperately scanning for Hunter. The place isn't that big, so I can't understand how I've missed seeing him. Luigi greets just about every customer we pass, and they respond as though he were an old friend. Everyone is so cheery, so upbeat. I'm starting to really like Luigi's.

I've probably passed the restaurant a hundred times, but the plain exterior gives no hint of the warmth inside. The smell of warm bread, ripe tomatoes, garlic, and oregano wafts from the kitchen, candlelight flickers at the tables, and the murals on the walls reflect the atmosphere: robust images of wine and grapes, pasta and meats, men and women talking and laughing.

We reach the back of the restaurant, and Luigi stops and extends a beefy arm to an area just beyond my vision.

"Here?" I say.

He nods, and I swear his eyes twinkle. Raising an eyebrow, I peer around the corner. Hunter's sitting at a small table in a semiprivate alcove hidden behind a short brick wall. For decoration, there's an iron grate between the alcove wall and the rest of the tables, but the iron is covered with climbing vines and flowers, giving the illusion of a private garden.

Hunter stands when he sees me, and my heart beats double time—as it always does when I first catch a glimpse of him. I don't know if it's my imagination, or the intimate knowledge I have of what's underneath those well-tailored clothes, but he looks especially attractive tonight.

With a wink, Luigi lumbers away and I step into the alcove, immediately enveloped by the romantic atmosphere and then by Hunter. He gives me a warm hug, steps back, and gesturing at the alcove, says, "Do you like it?"

I glance around again. One wall has been made to look like a rock outcropping or the inside of a cave, and a small waterfall trickles down the side into a worn marble basin. It's old-style Italian charm all the way. "Like it?" I breathe. "This is beautiful."

Hunter nods and smiles, then pulls out my chair, but I don't sit down immediately. Instead I freeze, staring at him. I'm not going to be able to tell Hunter the truth about me, tonight, maybe ever. I can't take the risk of having him turn away from me, reject me. I want him too much. The look in his eyes just now when he asked if I liked the table, that look of utter vulnerability and quiet strength, pierced my heart straight through.

Hunter glances up at me, hand on the back of the chair. "Rory?"

"Oh, thanks," I finally manage and take my seat. As Hunter takes the chair across from me, I put the napkin on my lap and reach for the glass of water, surprised at how steady my hands are because inside I am a complete jumble. That look. That *look.*

It's the same one he wore in the yearbook picture. How can I disappoint that motherless little boy? I can't be the one to demonstrate to him, once again, that people can't be counted on.

I fell in love with Hunter the first time I saw his vulnerability, picture day, junior year. If the pounding of my heart and the lightheadedness I feel now is any indication, I'm in love again. And I'm in deep.

Chapter 18

"So, how was work?" Hunter asks, moving smoothly into the obligatory small talk. "Anything going on?"

I shake my head. "The usual." A waiter appears with menus and a basket of bread. He's a small man with a thin mustache and a hesitant demeanor. He recites the specials, then scurries away while we make our culinary decisions.

"The chicken Florentine is good here," Hunter says, studying his menu.

"I don't eat chicken—oh!" I blurt out. Then, when Hunter glances up at me, I cover smoothly with, "Ah, I don't eat chicken when—when it has a fancy name. I mean, chicken *Florentine!* Too exotic-sounding. I like to keep my food simple." Inwardly, I wince. I like to keep my food simple? Where the Dark Side did that come from?

"Okay," Hunter says, giving me a quizzical look. I spot our waiter staggering under the weight of a tray loaded with food. It looks like he's going to be occupied for a while, so I have no excuse to delay the inevitable.

"Hunter, I want to apologize for last night." My voice

shakes as I say it, and I look down at the napkin in my lap, gripping the white linen with one hand. "You're being really nice about the whole thing, but if you never want to see me again, I'll understand."

Hunter sets his menu down. "So, what? You think I brought you here to dump you?"

"No." I give him a quick look, release the napkin, and start straightening the silverware. "I mean, I hope not, but I guess I just want to say that I understand if you do."

He reaches across the table and takes my busy hand.

"Rory, I like you."

"Still?"

"Still. I want to see more of you. Get to know you better."

A lump forms in my throat. I'm stuck in a catch-22. The better he gets to know me, the *less* he'll want to see me, especially if he ever saw me in my Princess Leia costume. "But after what I said last night, I thought you'd feel—I don't know—deceived."

Hunter pushes his water glass away and leans forward. "Actually, I'm confused. You said you were a fake and a liar. Why would you say that?"

I stare at my napkin, at the nubbins of white lint the linen has left on my red skirt. Now is the time to tell him. Come clean. About everything. What do I have to lose? "I guess the best explanation for what I did is that I like you so much." I feel my face burning, and I concentrate on picking the lint off my skirt. "And then when you seemed to sort of like me, I kind of freaked out." I look at him, see his brow creased with concentration, and quickly look back down again. "I guess I just didn't want to mess up. I didn't want to blow my chance with you, so I—I—"

Lied. The word lodges in my throat. Say it, Rory. Say it. "I—" My lip starts to tremble.

Hunter releases my hand and nudges my chin up. "It's okay, princess. I understand."

I shake my head. "No, it's not okay."

He puts a finger over my lips. "Stop blaming yourself. This is all my fault."

"*Your* fault?" Now I'm the one who's confused.

"Yeah. Last night was too much too soon. If there's one thing I've learned in life, it's that the things that are most important, the things that truly last, are built on trust." He caresses my cheek and drops his hand. "That goes for relationships, business, politics, everything." He reaches for a piece of garlic bread. "You don't trust me yet. It was too soon for us to go that far. Let's just take it slow." He takes a bite and licks granules of garlic from his lips. "See how things evolve. What do you say?"

What *can* I say? This is Hunter Chase, the man I've always loved, and he's telling me he wants to take this slow. What is that if not male shorthand for "I want a relationship with you"? Am I supposed to answer him with, "Okay, but let me dump my other boyfriend first"?

Not in this light-year.

No! I've talked myself out of telling him too many times. I have to confess now, or I never will. "Before we say anything else—" I pause and try to swallow the lump of dry sand sticking in my throat. "I need to tell you something." I pause again and he nods, eyes dark with concern. "I—I wasn't completely truthful with you."

Where do I start? *Star Wars*? Tom?

Tom.

"Hunter, remember that guy you saw me with at Y and Y? Well, he's—"

"Sorry for taking so long." The waiter bustles into our alcove. He's fumbling in his apron for a pencil and doesn't notice that he's interrupting. "Okay, then." He pulls the pencil free and holds it suspended, like a missile ready to drop and explode on his notepad. "Are you ready to order?"

For the first time I look at the menu and then back at Hunter. He nods, encouraging me to order. I stare at the antipasti, then the insalate, and I can't read a single word. The letters swim together. *Maccarrones de puntzu. Gulurgiones de casu canne al vento.* Where's the spaghetti?

"Would you like to hear the specials again?" the waiter prompts. "The *salmone alle ostriche* is spectacular."

"Ah—" I scan the menu choices, looking in vain for an entrée without meat. *Salmone* means salmon, so I know I don't want that but please tell me *ostriche* isn't the word for ostrich in Italian. What kind of place *is* this?

"How about the veal Marsala?" Hunter suggests. "It's really tender."

"Oh?" Baby cow is not my idea of dinner, but I can't seem to find anything on this menu I *do* consider dinner. The Gnocchi al Cinghiale might be okay. I scan the entrée's description and frown. Pasta with wild boar. Wild boar? Are we in *Africa?*

Time drags and I will the name of an Italian vegetarian entrée to pop into my mind, but my brain's been wiped clean. "How about the chicken Florentine?" Hunter says. "I know you're a little skeptical, but I promise it's delicious here."

"Oh, well, um—" Chicken? Pieces of poor Foghorn Leghorn floating in cream and butter? "Um—" I look at the waiter, and he leans forward, the nub of pencil clutched tightly above his pad.

"I guess I'll have . . ."

The waiter's pencil quivers in his hand.

"The calamari?" Hunter asks.

"The *pollo arosto?*" the waiter suggests.

"No, the . . ." Pollo. Ostrich. Wild boar. My head's whirling.

The men hold their breath, and I close my eyes and say the first thing that pops into my mind. "The chicken Florentine."

With a relieved sigh, a loud one, I might add, the waiter jots down my order and turns to Hunter. Why am I such a coward? Why can't I just tell the truth?

"Very good," the waiter says and pockets his pencil.

He turns to leave, and I shout, "No!" I grasp a wad of his shirt and haul him back. "Wait! I—I can't eat the chicken Florentine."

Hunter is staring at me. Luigi has come out of kitchen and is staring at me. The waiter is staring at me. The noise in the restaurant dies away as guests crane their necks and strain their eyes to get a glimpse of who's causing the commotion.

I look at Hunter. "I have to tell you something." I'm still clutching the waiter's arm and I can feel him stiffen.

"Okay. I'm listening."

"I have to tell you that I'm—I'm—I'm a *vegetarian!*"

My confession rings like a shotgun blast in the restaurant's silence. For a moment, time stands still, then the waiter drawls, "So the pasta primavera then?"

I tear my eyes away from Hunter, who looks even more confused than before, and squint at the waiter. "The pasta primavera," he says. "No meat, the vegetables are fresh. You'll love it."

"Sounds good," I murmur and sigh with relief.

He nods and heads for the kitchen. I put a hand over my eyes, trying to soothe the throbbing behind them. The restaurant's noise level has returned to normal and, after a moment, Hunter takes my hand from my face and holds it in his.

"So, princess, is this the big secret? Is this what you were so afraid to tell me last night? What you lied about?"

I know I should shake my head and tell him the rest. Tell him the serious stuff, but I just don't have the energy. I'd die of humiliation if he walked out on me in front of all these people. I nod dejectedly. "I'm sorry I didn't tell you before, but I didn't want you to think I was abnormal."

Hunter winces. "I wish I hadn't said that."

"But if it's really what you think—"

Hunter cuts me off. "It's not. I was just talking. Talking and not thinking, as usual."

I frown. "But—"

"But nothing," Hunter says. "Rory, I don't care if you're a vegetarian, Unitarian, or an octogenarian. I like *you.* I like that the worst curse word you use is 'blast.' I like how you're so incredibly earnest, that you take everything I say so literally. What you eat or don't eat makes no difference to me."

I blink. "Really?"

"Really." He leans closer and gives me a sexy smile. "You know what else I like?"

A tingle runs from where his fingers touch my hand to my toes and back up again. My hand starts fumbling with my napkin.

"What I really like," he whispers, "is how you react every time I get close to you. I can almost *feel* your heat."

The blood thumps in my head and, as if Hunter's words were a shot of arousal, the blood rushes to my cheeks, my breasts, my thighs.

"Do I make you nervous, Rory?" Hunter murmurs, his voice low and husky.

I shake my head. This guy is too good to be true.

"Good, because there is one thing I *won't* stand for."

I hold my breath. "What?"

"No tofu." He winks, and I give him a rueful smile. I've always known he was perfect. I wish I was perfect for him.

Hunter told me halfway through dinner that he has to go to Cincinnati and St. Louis on business this week and probably wouldn't be back until Friday. He was afraid things might get hectic, so he wanted to "nail down our game plan for the reunion."

The reunion. Tom. My stomach lurches. Keeping track of all my lies is giving me indigestion.

"So, why don't I pick you up around seven? We can grab dinner, and by the time we get there, the place should be pretty full." He grins. "Everyone will have had a drink or two, done the small talk, so we'll be just in time for the nitty-gritty."

"Sounds great," I say, mentally calculating the time crunch. If I get home from the extravaganza at five, that will give me two hours to transform myself from space princess to homecoming queen. No problem.

The real problem will be dealing with Tom. I have to get rid of him. I know how much playing Data at the extravaganza means to him, so I'll go to the extravaganza with him, but I have to tell him it's over. No reunion.

I take a deep breath and smile at Hunter. Everything is coming together for the extravaganza and the reunion. Saturday is the big day. I'll play both Princess Leia and Princess Rory. I'll get my Jedi and lose the Wookiee.

Chapter 19

I stick one more pin into the big, round bun on the side of my head, just to make sure it's secure, and step back for a final appraisal.

Princess Leia *Star Wars* wig in place. Check.

Princess Leia white space dress draped and belted. Yup.

Princess Leia white space boots on feet. I lift the hem of the dress and peer at my space boots. Got 'em.

Princess Leia shiny lip gloss and subtle makeup on face. I frown. Not a top-notch job but good enough for clearance.

Commander, all systems are a go.

I scrutinize my bedroom, making sure I haven't forgotten anything vital, and allow my eyes to rest, just for a moment, on the dress hanging on the closet door.

Allison and I bought it at Marshall Field's weeks ago. It was love at first sight. Allison didn't think it was right for her, but when I tried it on, it was as though the gown had been designed exclusively for me.

It's the classic little black dress in velvet. Allison said there's some rule that velvet shouldn't be worn in the spring, but we both agreed that rule couldn't possibly apply to this dress. It's short and hugs my figure, clinging in all the right places and draping flatteringly in all the wrong. It also shows a lot of skin, stopping a good three inches above my knee, and with only two spaghetti straps to hold it up, it bares my arms and shoulders.

But the best part of the dress, the pièce de résistance, are the teeny, tiny silver rhinestones that dot every inch. From a distance, the dress sparkles, and the rhinestones wink like stars in distant galaxies. The matching wrap is black and sheer, light and gauzy, and also sprinkled with small, twinkling rhinestones.

Looking at the dress, I'm almost as excited about wearing it as my Princess Leia costume. I can't wait until tonight. I'm going to pull my hair up, secure it with a sparkly clip, strap on black heels, drape the wrap seductively around my shoulders, and sweep Hunter off his feet.

There's a knock at the door just then, and I sigh because I know it's not Hunter. It's Tom. He didn't take it too well when I told him I wanted to go to the reunion without him, so I'm not sure what to expect from him today.

I open the door, and there's Tom dressed as Data. "Greetings, Princess Leia," he says in his Data voice. "You are looking most visually appealing."

"Thanks," I say. "You don't look so bad yourself."

Tom really does make an excellent Commander Data. He's so awkward already that it's no effort for him to pull off the androidlike movements and facial expressions. Now he's got the voice down pat, too.

"You're not still mad about the reunion, right?"

"I am—as you humans say—coping."

"Good," I say. "Ready to go?"

"All systems are ready and willing," Tom/Data answers.

Great. If only Hunter could see me now.

The Second Annual Creatures and Features Extravaganza is in full swing by the time Tom and I arrive. As soon as we walk in, Tom spots a group of guys he knows, a motley assortment of Ring Wraiths from *Lord of the Rings* and one Borg from *TNG*. The costume show isn't for an hour or more, so I leave Tom and wander the booths. Within a matter of minutes, I'm glad that I brought only five dollars. There are so many cool things for sale: Han Solo T-shirts, C-3PO radios, Lando Calrissian shower gel. And then there are the limited edition DVDs: director's cut, foreign cut, uncut. I want them all.

Finally I break away, and toward the back of the showroom, I see the booth for Joe's Collectibles and Antiques, but Eddie isn't there. A guy I recognize as his part-time assistant is sitting behind the booth, bored and half asleep. I figure Eddie is busy scoping out the competition. I make a mental note to stop by his booth later if I don't see him around. At the booth next to his, I pause and run my hands lovingly over a foreign version of *ESB*, wondering what Han and Leia sound like in Italian, then glance at my watch and decide I'd better hit the bathroom and head for the stage.

The bathrooms are outside the exhibit area, in a central area of the convention center. When I walk in, there's a gaggle of Counselor Trois ahead of me, an Arwen and, just in front of them, a woman who looks out of place.

She's dressed in a navy pinstripe suit, and she's eyeing the Trois with something between fascination and revulsion. When I walk in, she gives me the once-over, then turns quickly away. She's up next, and one of the Trois and me are still in line when she exits.

"Must be one of the convention staff," I murmur.

"Maybe," the Troi says. "But I think there's another conference going on at the other end of the convention center. She probably got turned around and ended up in these bathrooms instead of the ones down there." The Counselor Troi laughs. "She sure got a shock, didn't she?"

I smile, but for some reason I feel a little uneasy. I glance at my watch, hidden under the costume's sleeve, and note that I still have plenty of time before the show starts. Probably just nerves.

By the time I make it to the stage, I'm nervous and jumpy, and it's a little hard to concentrate when my stomach is queasy and my heart's beating a gazillion parsecs a second.

What if I trip? What if one of my buns falls off the side of my head? Oh, why did I agree to do this? Why did I let Tom and his stupid friends talk me into this?

I see a lot of characters from the newer movies lining up ahead of me and worry that I'm dated. I mean, maybe Princess Leia—the original Princess Leia—just isn't cool enough anymore.

I snort and the Obi-Wan Kenobi in front of me gives me a questioning look. Princess Leia not cool? *What* am I thinking? Of course I can do this. I am Princess Leia. Today, more than ever.

I see Tom a few minutes later, and he waves before heading over to the *Star Trek* grouping area. And then the show's music starts and some guy with a headset and clipboard is hustling the *Lord of the Rings* characters on stage.

That music fades into the soundtrack from *The Matrix,* followed by the *Star Trek* theme, and then I hear the familiar strains of John Williams's score for *Star Wars* and I'm up, standing behind a thin curtain waiting for my chance.

The bright lights and the hundreds of people watching from the sides of the makeshift stage cause my heart to pound and the blood to thrum through my ears at a deafening pitch. I feel my chest constrict, the first warning that I'm about to hyperventilate, and try to calm myself by remembering that I am Princess Leia. Princess Leia does not hyperventilate.

The guy playing Luke gets his cue and strolls out to thunderous applause, and the Han Solo, who's standing next to me, gives me a high five before making his entrance. I watch him swagger onstage, his cocky walk garnering whistles and catcalls from some of the women.

The music on stage softens and the guy with the headset and clipboard gives me an enthusiastic go-go-go gesture, so I take a deep breath and stride regally through the curtain. I walk the length of the stage, turn, nose in the air like Princess Leia, and glide behind the curtain again. Once in the safety of the staging area, I clutch hold of an empty chair and try to catch my breath. The applause had been heady, but not as heady as the fear of messing up and making a fool of myself. Still, it was worth it. I really had felt like Princess Leia. And for just one moment, Princess Leia's poise and beauty flowed into me, and it was a cool, confident Rory striding the catwalk.

The director starts calling everyone together for the big finale, where we're supposed to circle the perimeter of the stage and take a bow. I walk out with the *Star Wars* group, taking my place between Luke and Han.

At the director's urging, we hustle into the bright lights again, and I follow Luke to a spot off to the right. Tom's friend Grant has positioned the characters from *The Matrix* and *Lord of the Rings* in the front, and the cast from the older sci-fi films, like *Star Wars* and *Star Trek*, are on the sides.

Everyone in the audience is clapping as the last of the participants emerge from the curtain, and I'm smiling, still riding high on my newfound self-esteem and thinking that in a few hours I'll be at the center of attention again—this time as the most popular girl at the Lincoln High School reunion. I smile wider, imagining the stunned looks on the faces of Julie Jones, Jellie Abernathy, and the other girls from the Popular Crowd when they see me stride in on Hunter Chase's arm.

I imagine Allison's surprised and, hopefully, pleased expression when she sees Hunter and me together. I'll give her a hug and two air kisses in greeting and promise to explain everything later. Then I'll look up, into Hunter's sapphire eyes, and . . .

I squint at the bright lights and stare hard into the audience. For a split parsec, I thought I saw those sapphire eyes. I shake my head, sure the heat, the noise, and the excitement have got me seeing things. But then my eyes lock on his and the galaxy spins out of control.

All the air rushes out of my lungs, and I stumble back. Oh, Creator. Oh, God. Oh, Dark Side. Light Side. Buddha. Allah. I call on every deity I can think of, and a few I'm not even sure exist, but when I look back at the spot in the back of the exhibit hall, Hunter is still there. He's with three or four other guys, all wearing suits and power ties, all looking out of place, and all obviously having a great time making fun of the freaks in the costume show.

Except Hunter isn't smiling. Hunter is staring at me, and he looks angry and disgusted, and contemptuous.

I catch my balance, with the help of the Chewbacca just behind me, and wonder what Hunter can possibly be doing at the Creatures and Features Extravaganza. He never mentioned attending, and I sure as Darth Vader didn't tell him I'd be here. I lied about ever even going to these things.

I lied. I look into Hunter's burning blue eyes again and know it's over. It's all over. I'm found out, and it's not so much the fact that I'm standing in front of a hundred people, months from Halloween, dressed up as a character from a kids' movie, that's done it. It's the fact that I lied.

My heart aches, and I want to jump from the stage and go to him, but just then Grant comes out and starts to talk. Hunter's eyes flick to Grant, and I turn, too, but I don't register a word Tom's friend is saying.

Behind Hunter a woman who looks vaguely familiar strolls up to the men in the suits. One of the men turns to her, gestures at the exhibit hall—at all of us attendees—and laughs. She nods and laughs with him. I recognize her then; she's the woman from the restroom, and everything clicks into place.

The other conference in the convention center must be some kind of marketing seminar, and Hunter is here for that. He's not here for the Creatures and Features Extravaganza at all. It's just a horrible coincidence that the two events are held at McCormick Place at the same time.

Grant wraps up his speech, everyone takes one final bow, and we start to file off stage. There's no order now. All the participants are just tumbling down into crowds of friends and well-wishers.

I stand rooted to my spot while Han, Luke, and Chewbacca jump down around me. I'm still staring at Hunter, and he's staring at me. And then he breaks away from the clump of suits he's standing with and starts toward the stage. A small glimmer of hope rises in my chest. Maybe I haven't blown it after all. Maybe I still have a chance. Maybe if I'm honest about everything now, if I just explain things, he'll understand. Surely Hunter can see why I'd be embarrassed to tell him about dressing up in a costume contest.

He arrows straight for me, and my heart begins to soar. I take a deep breath, all danger of hyperventilation gone. It's going to be okay. I know it's going to be okay.

And then suddenly I'm torn away from Hunter, spun wildly around, and engulfed in a bony embrace. I try to pull away, to look back at Hunter, but Tom has his scrawny arms around me and he's yelling and congratulating me. Hunter's close enough so that I know he can overhear Tom's loud, adrenaline-filled words.

"We did it, Rory! Wasn't it cool?"

I twist my head to try to get a glimpse of Hunter and, from the corner of my eye, I see that his step has faltered. He's paused, gauging the situation.

"Tom, let go." I struggle to squeeze out of Tom's prison. I push back, but he just holds me tighter and swings me around.

"Hey!" He waves to one of the Ring Wraiths we saw when we came in. "Isn't my girlfriend beautiful? Doesn't she make the perfect Princess Leia?"

The Ring Wraith gives him a thumbs up and a "Yeah, dude," before strolling away, but that's the last thing I register. My breath is short now, my head swimming, all sound muffled like I'm in an underwater tank. And then I really can't breathe because Tom's wet lips are on mine, and he's giving me one of his sloppy kisses.

I give a muffled curse and tear my mouth away. My chest is tight and the room is spinning, but I know I have to show Hunter, somehow—with a look, a gesture, *something*—that this is not what it seems.

But, of course, it is.

With excruciating slowness, I turn my head until my gaze finds Hunter, now standing stock-still in the middle of the exhibit hall. His impossibly blue eyes flash fire, then pain, and he turns away.

"No!" The word comes out on a wheeze. "Hunh-hunh-hunh." I try to wrench away from Tom, but he's spinning me around. I'm getting dizzy and my throat is all closed up. "I can't breathe," I gasp, but no sound comes out. "I cah-cah—" I wheeze, then everything goes black.

Chapter 20

"Just give her some space and I'm sure she'll be fine," a familiar voice says from the darkness. "If you want to help, focus your positive energy. Channel healing thoughts."

I crack my eyelids open. There're only two people I know who would talk about focusing positive energy and channeling healing thoughts while someone is lying on the cold floor of a convention center wearing a Princess Leia costume.

Standing above me, braceleted arms outstretched and full sleeves billowing with every movement, giving her the appearance of a medieval sorceress, is Stormy.

I try to sit up, and she's on her knees in an instant. "Are you okay, Rory?"

I try to speak, but only gasps come out. I gesture instead, an age-old language that sisters understand, and Stormy nods and says, "I think you just blacked out for a minute. You couldn't get enough air and the lights were so hot."

"Here's some water!" Tom rushes up behind Stormy and thrusts a cup at her, spilling half its contents on the floor.

"Thanks." She takes the dripping cup and offers it to me.

I take a small sip. My breath is still hitching, and I can't swallow very well, so a trickle of water runs down my chin. At least it will wipe away some of Tom's spit, I think, and squeeze my eyes shut. I don't waste any time looking for Hunter's face among the small, concerned group gathered about me. I know he won't be there. He's gone. Forever. And I have no one to blame but myself.

And Tom. I glare at him. Blaming him is just a defensive move, but I don't want this to be my fault. I don't want to have to face my lies and deceptions.

"Better?" Stormy asks when I take another sip.

I nod and whisper, "Yeah."

Stormy turns to the crowd. "She's feeling better now. The healing energy worked. Thank you."

A few people in the crowd smile, and the group starts to disperse. A security guard hangs around a little longer, but when I give him a wan smile, he ambles away, too.

Stormy turns back to me, and I make another gesture in sister-language: What are you doing here?

She smiles sheepishly and shrugs. "I'll explain later." She glances back at the anxious-looking Tom. I notice some of his Data makeup has sweated off. His face has large metallic gray stripes broken by patches of his skin tone.

"Right now we need to get you off the floor and home."

Tom leaps forward. "I'll go get the car!"

Stormy gives me a sideways look, and I shake my head slightly. She reaches out to put a hand on Tom's quivering arm. "Why don't you let me take her home? She'll be more comfortable with her sister tucking her into bed."

Tom nods violently, his glasses almost flying off his nose. "Okay. Here, let me help you up, Rory." He takes both of my hands in his and tries to haul me to my feet. My legs are a little wobbly, but I manage to stand. With Stormy following, Tom helps me out of the exhibition room, down the length of the convention center, and to a concession stand with a couple of chairs and tables. He pulls one of the wobbly plastic chairs out for me and I sit. I gently pull my arm out of Tom's grasp, more grateful to be free of his touch than for the support of the chair.

Stormy comes up beside us, looks at me, then at Tom, and says, "You know, I parked kind of far away. In the cheapo parking. Why don't I drive the car to the doors so you don't have to walk so far, Rory? I'll talk to the security guards and get them to okay it."

I think Stormy knows that, given five more minutes to recover, I'd be fine to walk the three-tenths of a mile to the economy parking, but I know what she's doing.

"Good idea," Tom says, sitting down next to me. "I'll stay here with her."

Stormy nods, gives a little wave, and then strolls toward the entrance. Her long, full skirt swirls around her ankles and her jewelry tinkles. Though she isn't dressed as a member of the Rebel Alliance or a resident of Middle Earth, she seems right at home among the hobbits, Cardassians, and Wookiees.

I turn to my Wookiee, dressed as the android Data. He couldn't have chosen a more appropriate character. Poor Data, always struggling to understand humans and emulate them but lacking that key ingredient: an emotion chip.

"Can I get you anything?" Tom gestures to the concession stand. "A Coke? A hot dog?"

I wince. He's just never going to get it, is he? Poor guy. I shake my head.

He looks around at the other vendors. "How about a pretzel?"

"No, Tom." I put my hand on his arm. "Can we just sit here and talk for a minute?" My voice is still a little breathy, but I've pretty much recovered.

Tom shrugs and settles into the chair beside me. "Sure. I'm just trying to help."

"I know you are. Thanks." We sit in silence, watching the space aliens and fantasy world creatures walk by.

"That was pretty crazy when you fainted like that," Tom says.

"I don't think I actually fainted. I think I just blacked out for a moment. Too much excitement, I guess." I think the technical term would be panic attack, but I want to keep this simple. And I don't want to bring Hunter into it. It would only hurt Tom more. Besides, breaking up with him is not about Hunter. It's about me. About me doing the right thing. Something I should have done a long time ago.

"Tom, I've been wanting to talk to you for a while now, but—" I gesture feebly. I could lie and say the time wasn't right, but I want to be truthful. "But I . . . haven't."

I stare at the floor, at the dirty linoleum under the fluorescent convention center lights.

"What did you want to talk about?" There's a slight tremor in his voice, and I realize he knows what I'm going to say. His eyes are anxious and a little fearful behind his wire-rimmed glasses. I sigh. It always surprises me how alike Tom and I are. He's afraid of being alone, just like me.

"I don't think we should see each other anymore," I say quietly, and Tom sits back, bracing himself. "I like you a lot, but not in a romantic way."

Tom nods. "Yeah. I guess I knew that." He looks away, at the line of people buying hot pretzels. He sighs. "So, what now?"

I shrug and bite back a retort. It's annoying that Tom

doesn't even try to talk me out of breaking up. It's like he's just resigned himself to it and has no will to fight for me, for us.

But what do I expect from a Wookiee?

Then I think of Hunter. He didn't fight for me, either, but I don't think that makes him any less of a Jedi. I think it makes me a piece of Ewok shit. Why should either of them fight for me? I'm not worth it.

I glance at my watch. "Stormy probably has the car out front by now. I better go." I stand, and Tom follows.

"Do you want me to walk you?"

I shake my head. "No. I'll be okay on my own." I take a few steps, then turn back to Tom. "So will you."

In the car, Stormy and I listen to a CD of New Age music she's popped in the stereo. Her Honda hybrid chugs along the freeway toward my apartment. My thoughts are filled with Hunter and Tom and the reunion tonight. There's no way I can possibly go, no way I can face everyone alone. Face Hunter.

Stormy snaps the music off. "Did you talk to Tom?"

I don't pretend not to understand. "Yeah. I ended it. I shouldn't have waited so long."

"Was he okay?" She checks her rearview mirror and changes lanes.

I snort. "Yeah. We're a lot alike. Both of us hanging on to the other because we're too cowardly to be on our own."

"You're not a coward, Rory," Stormy says.

"Yeah, I am."

Stormy glares at me. "No you're not. Look what you did today. You got up on that stage in front of all those people. I know that kind of stuff makes you nervous."

I shake my head and wince as Stormy changes lanes

again and narrowly misses clipping the side of an SUV. "That's because it wasn't me. It was Princess Leia. This is going to sound stupid." I fiddle with the material of my white Princess Leia gown. "But whenever I'm scared or unsure, I pretend I'm Princess Leia. I guess it's a way of avoiding dealing with it myself."

"So what's wrong with that?" Stormy takes my exit and slows for a light. "We all play a part sometimes."

"I think I do it more than most." I sigh. "Stormy, did I make a complete fool of myself today?"

She glances at me and grins. "Not a complete fool, no, but I think you definitely added some excitement to the event. The organizers should *thank* you. It wasn't exactly a roller coaster ride of fun in there today. You gave everyone something to talk about."

"Great."

We pull onto my street and the next few minutes are spent looking for a parking spot. When we finally make it inside my apartment, we collapse on the couch. I turn to my sister, "So, if the extravaganza was such a yawn fest, what were you doing there?"

She shrugs. "I don't know. I guess I just wanted to see what all this sci-fi stuff was about. Why you get so excited about it." She picks at a loose thread on the cushion. "I knew you'd be there, and you'd be dressed up and surrounded by all the stuff you love, and I wanted to see you in that light."

Tears blur my vision. "Oh, Stormy. I don't deserve you. I treated you like Star Destroyer refuse last time I saw you. Now you go do something like this. And why?" I throw my arms in the air. "Because you want to *know* me better!" I give her a long hard hug, and she hugs me back just as hard.

"I love you, Rory."

"I love you, too, and I'm so sorry for the way I've been acting and everything I said about you and Sunshine and Dan. I don't know where I'd be without all of you." I pull back. "Especially you. I'm really glad you were there to save me today. I owe you."

She grins. "Does that mean you're going to feed me? I'm starved."

I glance at the clock and see that it's almost six. The reunion starts in two hours.

"Are you going to go?" Stormy asks quietly. "I know how much you've been looking forward to it."

"Yeah, well. I've been acting pretty silly for the last few weeks. Maybe it's time I started living in the present instead of the past."

"I saw him at the extravaganza," she tells me. "Hunter. I saw him see you and then walk away when Tom came up and grabbed you."

I nod, not trusting my voice.

"Is that why you blacked out?"

"Yes," I whisper, clutching my fingers tightly together. "We were supposed to go to the reunion together, but now I've really blown it."

"Maybe if you just call him and explain—"

I give a bitter laugh. "No." I turn to her. "There's nothing to explain. He hates lies and he hates deceit, and I deceived him from the beginning—about Tom, about me, about you and Sunshine and Dan." I turn to her and see the stricken but understanding look on her face.

"He liked me, Stormy. I think he really liked me. But he doesn't know me at all."

"So let him get to know you. Show him the real you."

I shake my head. "I can't. All my life I've been rejected by the Popular Crowd. I can't take any more rejection."

Stormy sits back and crosses her arms. "Then you really are a coward."

"I'm not a coward. This is self-preservation." I bristle. It's one thing if I say it, but no one else is supposed to. And maybe I do have just a little of Princess Leia in me because at Stormy's words, I straighten my spine and stick my nose in the air.

"Coward," she taunts, reclining smugly against the couch cushions.

I jump up. "Going to that reunion tonight would be suicide. The Popular Crowd will snub me, Allison hates me, Hunter will tell everyone what a dork I am, and the whole class will be laughing at me before the night is over. I'll be hiding in the back by the punch bowl."

She shrugs. "At least you won't be here, hiding behind ice cream and another rerun of *Star Trek*."

I bite my lip. How'd she know I'd been thinking about curling up with Captain Picard and a pint of Ben & Jerry's?

"Rory, if you don't go, you'll always wonder what could have happened. You've spent your whole life dreaming how life might have turned out differently if you'd only been popular in school. Don't let this be another 'what if.' Go. Hold your head up and take your lumps. Hunter will respect you more for it."

I give her a long look. For a younger sister, she's pretty smart. "Okay, I'll go, but on one condition."

She raises a pierced eyebrow.

"You go with me. You be my date."

She's already shaking her head. "Nah-uh. I am not going to any high school reunion crap. Even when I was in high school I was too old for it."

I crouch down in front of her, taking her hands in mine. "Stormy, please, I need your support. Just go in with me, and if you really hate it, you can leave. I need you there to force me to go in."

She rolls her eyes, seeming resigned. Then she smiles. "Won't work. I don't have anything to wear, and none of your stuff fits me."

"So go as you are."

She stares at me. "I thought this was a formal event."

"It is, but no one is going to say anything. It's not like there'll be a bouncer at the door." I know I've got her now, so I stand and head for my bathroom to take a shower. I've got to hurry now if I'm going to get my hair and makeup just right.

Stormy shakes her head in confusion and follows me. "Rory, a week ago you were saying that I embarrass you. Now you want me to go to what you've made out to be the biggest night of your life dressed like this?" She holds out her faded gypsy skirt and indicates her ratty hemp sandals.

"Yep." I walk into the bathroom and start to undress. "I've had an epiphany. I think hitting my head on the convention center floor knocked some sense into me." I step back out into the living room and take Stormy by the shoulders. "You are my sister. My one and only sister. I love you, and if Hunter or anyone else thinks you're weird or abnormal or doesn't love you just as much as me, then they can go take a flying leap off the starboard side of the *Millennium Falcon*."

Stormy blinks.

"So are you coming or not?"

"I'll be there, with bells on." She gestures to her feet and the tinkling anklets. "Literally."

Chapter 21

The reunion is at the Drake Hotel, which is one of my favorite buildings in the city. It was built in 1920, and as soon as we pull up, I feel like I've been thrust back into the era of Gatsby. A bellman or valet-type person opens the car door for me and another does the same for Stormy. I glance up and up and up at the classic black and gold awning and the imposing gray edifice of the building, complete with stately arched windows on the first floor, and my heart trip-traps inside my chest.

What am I doing here? The Drake is a palace designed for the Popular Crowd. In high school, I felt out of place at the dances in the smelly school gym.

The bellman/valet clears his throat, and I reluctantly hand him my keys. I blink and see Stormy already standing in the hotel's entrance.

Calm down, Rory. You're not in high school anymore. You're not that geeky teenager huddled in the fringes as if to apologize for her very existence. Tonight I have one last apology to make, but it won't be for who I am. I'll never apologize for being Rory Egglehoff—vegetarian, *Star Wars* freak, sixties love child—again.

I straighten my shoulders, and the doorman nods and smiles at me appreciatively as I approach. Then I see his gaze flick scornfully over Stormy. The weather feels cold all of a sudden, and I adjust the gauzy wrap over my bare shoulders. I hope I haven't made a mistake in bringing Stormy. Not that I care what anyone else thinks—as I said, I'm done with that—but I don't want her to have to listen to snide comments all night.

With Stormy beside me and under the full chill of the doorman's disapproval, I say, "Is there a problem, sir?"

He looks at me in surprise. "No, madam." His gaze strays to Stormy again.

"Good. Then please open the door for my sister. She deserves first-class treatment."

"Of course, madam." He opens the door and gives Stormy a gracious bow. We glide past him into the lobby, and Stormy lets out a low whistle.

"Now I see why that doorman was looking at me like I was tofu on his hamburger. This place is a bourgeoisie wet dream."

"Stormy!" I hiss, but I know what she means. The Drake is gorgeous, sumptuous and ornate. The walls and floors are a rich, vibrant shade of red and, as we ascend the stairs, the huge chandelier hanging in the lobby's center sparkles. I glance down at the tiny rhinestones on my black velvet dress. They're sparkling, too.

A few guests are milling around, but I don't see anyone who looks like they're here for the reunion. It doesn't surprise me, as we're running over an hour late. My limp hair refused to be molded into the style Allison and I had planned, so Stormy finally had to help me pin it up. I found an old rhinestone barrette and added that for show. All in all, I don't think I look half bad. Popular Crowd, watch out.

"Where is this shindig?" Stormy asks. She doesn't look as impressed as me by the decor. Probably imagining all the labor laws abused in the hotel's construction.

I reach discreetly into my small black clutch and tilt the ivory ticket/invitation into the light of the chandelier. "The Gold Coast Room," I read. "It's one of the two ballrooms." We both glance around, looking for a sign to indicate the way, and one of the hotel staff is immediately at our side.

"May I be of service, madam?"

I almost turn to see who he's talking to, then I remember that *I* am "madam." "Uh, we're looking for the Gold Coast Room."

"Certainly, madam."

He gives us directions, and Stormy and I proceed confidently onward. Well, okay, Stormy does. I feel like turning around and sprinting for the exit before the Drake's deferential staff realizes its mistake and boots me out.

Princess Leia. Be Princess Leia.

No. Not tonight. Tonight I'm going to be Roberta Egglehoff. No relying on false fronts and pretty façades. Tonight I'm going to get through this on my own.

We find the Gold Coast Room, and while I gape at the marble floors, the dozens of chandeliers, and the columns of graceful pillars, Stormy checks us in.

She hands me a name tag, and I look down long enough to wince. There's my name and my yearbook picture from senior year. If I needed another reminder that, though I may sparkle, I am no Miss Universe, this picture cures amnesia. I am not a beautiful, fairy-tale princess. I'm just Rory, with limp brown hair, mud brown eyes, and, at best, an *interesting* face.

But that's okay. For once I want to just be myself. At some point I'll have to face Hunter and the lies I told, but at least I won't have to invent more. At least I can stop looking over my shoulder all the time, afraid I'll be found out.

"Should we get a drink?" Stormy whispers, leaning close to me. "I mean, what do you do at these things?"

I glance around the room and take a shaky breath. Most of the people are clustered together, holding wineglasses and small plates and chatting airily. A few brave souls are gyrating on the makeshift dance floor to Alphaville's "Forever Young." I peer at the dancers more closely, at these people I went to high school with. They are *not* forever young. They have beer bellies, wrinkles, and the first signs of gray hair or, worse, no hair at all.

Behind me I hear a squawk, and two women race toward each other and hug. When they break apart, they jump up and down like teenagers. Everyone is trying to recapture their youth, trying to find that elusive golden moment that really exists only in our memories.

"Yeah, let's get a drink," I say to Stormy. "I think I'm going to need one before I start mingling."

But we don't even make it to the bar before a man and woman step in front of us.

"Rory?" The man squints at me through his thick glasses. He has a sweet, vaguely familiar face. "Rory Egglehoff?"

I nod. "Yes?" I still can't place this guy. I look at the woman, hoping for a hint, but she stares blankly, mouth cracked in a pasted-on smile.

"It's me. Gerald," he says and points to his name tag. "Gerald Hoffer."

I glance at his name tag, see the picture, and take a step back. "Gerald! Wow! I didn't even recognize you."

He grins. "Is that good or bad?"

"Good, good," I say. The acne that plagued him when we dated in tenth grade is gone and so is most of the awkwardness. Now he just looks like a nice man.

He indicates the woman beside him. "This is my wife, Lorna."

I shake her hand and she murmurs a hello. I turn to Stormy. "This is my sister, Stormy. She was a few years behind us."

"Rory and I dated in tenth grade," Gerald tells her. "Rory was always the coolest girl in school."

Stormy raises her eyebrows, and Gerald clarifies, "She knew everything about *Star Wars*. A science fiction genius."

"I can't argue with you there," Stormy says. "Excuse me." She pats my arm and indicates the bar. I nod and watch her walk away, then turn back to Gerald.

"And if I remember correctly, *you* were the science fair genius. Did you do anything with all that scientific aptitude?"

"I'm an engineer now. How about you?"

"Accountant."

Gerald grins, "Jeez, we're a boring lot. I always imagined I'd grow up and be a rock star or a film director."

"I wanted to be a princess." My sore heart emits another tiny ache as I say the words. It's almost as though by saying the fantasy aloud, I give the dream up. It's painful, but I have to let it go.

Gerald laughs. "Wow! And I thought rock star was a tough career to break into."

He keeps on talking, telling me something about the engineering firm he works for, but I'm no longer listening. Behind him, standing under a chandelier, his brown hair and bronze skin luminous under the lights, is Hunter. He's talking to a beautiful woman, and she's smiling up at him, adoration in her eyes.

He turns slightly, and I tear my eyes away. He hasn't seen me yet, and I don't want to be caught staring.

"Well, I'd better keep on mingling," I hear Gerald say. I glance at him, and know he's probably noticed that I'm distracted.

"Well, it was good to see you again," I murmur, hardly recognizing my voice. I'm trying desperately not to look at Hunter again. "Nice to meet you, too, um—" I fumble as they move away.

"Lorna," she says, but I barely hear her. My attention is on Hunter again, and this time he's staring at me, those piercing sapphire eyes slicing me straight to the core.

In the nanosecond that follows, a galaxy of options fly through my brain. I could pretend I haven't seen him, turn around and run away, jump out one of the large windows overlooking the lake, fake a seizure . . .

Walk over to him. Apologize.

Hunter's still staring at me, and now the brunette is asking him who I am. He doesn't answer right away, but when he does he keeps his eyes on me. He angles his head toward the brunette, and I see his lips form the words, "Rory Egglehoff."

I'm moving closer, but I'm too far away to hear his voice. Still, seeing my name on his lips jumpstarts my pulse and sends all the blood to my face, flushing it. My legs are heavy and weighted down, but I keep moving. I feel as though I'm trudging through thick, viscous mud, but I slog onward.

Hunter doesn't move, doesn't give me any sign—positive or negative—so I just keep walking across the ballroom that now feels like it's the size of the Milky Way.

When I reach Hunter, I'm so close I can smell the clean scent of his cologne, see the weave of threads in the charcoal suit he's wearing, and feel the tension and anger radiating from him. He still has a cold, formal expression on his face, and though my blood is pounding so hard I'm afraid my head is going to explode, I force myself to speak. "Hi, Hunter."

The small group of people standing near him have quieted, curious as to why he's turned so abruptly to stare at me, and in the silence, my voice rings out like a laser blast.

Hunter says nothing at first. His eyes darken to cobalt, and then he says, "Rory." He gives a short, succinct nod and looks away.

I stand there, feeling inept, unsure what to do next. I want to apologize, but I didn't anticipate having to do so in front of an audience. The brunette standing next to Hunter is looking back and forth between us. I glance at her name tag and see it's Julie Jones.

"Hi, Julie," I say, still staring at Hunter, who is now turned away from me, appearing to listen to a conversation between two guys who look like his old friends Mitch and Cody.

"Hi," she says, and I can tell she doesn't remember me.

I step forward and put a tentative hand on Hunter's elbow. "Hunter?"

He jumps as if burned and whips around to face me. Before I lose my nerve, I say, "Can we go somewhere and talk for a few minutes? I—I want to apologize."

Hunter gives me a look as cold as the blue ice in his eyes. "Don't worry about it."

Everyone is staring at us now, and I recognize many of them. The Popular Crowd. Suddenly, I'm back in the high school cafeteria and have made the mistake of thinking I'm cool enough to approach the Popular Table. That's how they're all staring at me. Like they feel sorry for me. Like my pathetic attempts to ingratiate myself into their clique embarrass them.

And the worst part is that Hunter's looking at me like that, too. The derision is his eyes feels like a thousand daggers piercing my heart.

"Please let me explain," I say, my face burning so hot now that I'm almost on fire.

"There's nothing to explain, Rory. Excuse me." He starts to move away, deeper into the closing circle of the Popular Crowd, but just as I'm about to lose him forever, I hear, "Hunter Chase? Is that you?"

Hunter turns at the woman's voice. We all do, and I almost fall over from shock. It's Allison.

She gives Hunter, and the rest of their crowd, a stunning smile, and they beam back. And why not? With her long, flowing red hair, jade green eyes, and perfect skin, she's still one of them.

"Don't you remember me?" She gives Hunter a playful pout. "I'm Allison Holloway."

"Allison." Hunter smiles and moves forward to greet her, but when she comes to stand beside me, linking her arm through mine, he falters a few steps short. He glances at me, at her obvious show of allegiance, and says, "It's good to see you again."

"You, too. How long has it been?"

"Uh—"

"I haven't forgiven you, you know."

Hunter's head jerks back in surprise, and the Popular Crowd moves in closer. Allison, arm still hooked with mine, gives him a mischievous smile. "Don't tell me you don't remember. I cried for a week."

Hunter's eyes widen, and Allie sighs. "Okay, a day. But to this day, I get all teary-eyed when I think about it."

Hunter looks shell-shocked. "I'm sorry."

Allison tosses her hair, playing the ultimate flirt. "You're sorry? Is that all you can say, after you ruined my Jordache jeans with the rhinestone heart on the back pocket?"

"Your jeans?"

"That's right. Sixth grade." She glances at her enraptured audience and winks at Hunter. "You ran past me, into a mud puddle, and soaked me through. I had to wear *Wranglers* after that. Tragic."

Everyone laughs, and the tension from a moment ago is gone. Even Hunter looks more relaxed, though his eyes flick to mine every few seconds. Allison greets her old friends, giving them quick hugs and bright smiles. Her hand remains firmly on my arm. In a matter of moments, everyone is laughing and joking and recalling old times. Only I am silent. Only I appear to feel out of place. I didn't belong in the company of these minor gods and goddesses in high school, and I don't belong here now.

I try to tug my arm out of Allison's grip. I want to go home, play my *Star Wars* DVD, bury my ugly head in the sand, and disappear among the desert wasteland of Tatooine. But Allison doesn't release me. In fact, she clutches me tighter.

Then, with her free hand, she reaches out and touches the shoulder of the blond she's been talking to. "Kelly, I am so sorry. I forgot to introduce my friend Rory." Allison swivels so that it looks like she is turning to me, but the move is actually designed to pull me forward. I stumble in my heels but manage to grip Kelly's outstretched hand without too much awkwardness.

"Surely you remember Rory," Allison says, her voice exuding confidence. I stare at Allison in disbelief. Why is she helping me?

Kelly squints, glances at my name tag/picture badge, and smiles. "Of course. Rory. We were both in calculus senior year. You always blew the curve."

I nod dumbly, surprised that Kelly Dunvale really does remember me. I'd always thought she was one of the nicer, and definitely one of the smarter, members of the Popular Crowd. But she was still one of the goddesses, while I was an outcast nerd.

"So, how are you, Rory? What do you do now? Rocket scientist?"

I smile and shake my head. "No, actually I'm an accountant."

"Oh, really? What firm? My husband is an accountant."

"Yates and Youngman."

Kelly nods. "Mark works at Spencer and Perlman. So are you married? Have any kids?"

The dreaded relationship questions. With all the turmoil over Hunter, I realize I haven't sufficiently prepared myself for this. I haven't formulated my pat answers, fortified my armor.

Allison squeezes my arm. "No, she's still a swinging single, like me," she says breezily. She's helping me again! I want to cry, to hug her, to scream because I do not deserve a friend like Allison.

"You make the whole dating scene sound like so much fun," Julie Jones says, stepping into our circle, followed by another girl I recognize as Lincoln High's head cheerleader, Kiki Summers.

"I hated it. I was so relieved when I found Allan and we settled down," Julie says.

"I feel the same way," Kiki chimes in. "It's so nice to have

Mike. To have a family and kids, and not have to deal with that whole loud, smoky bar scene."

"Oh, I don't know," Kelly says. "I love Mark and the boys, but sometimes I miss going out. Once in a while it might be nice to go somewhere with loud music, drink too many margaritas, and flirt with a handsome stranger."

"You go, Kelly," Allison says, giving her a high five. "Call me when you're ready to act on that impulse."

Kelly bites her lip and looks sort of shy. "I might just do that."

A few guys enter our circle, and the conversation turns once again to spouses and children, low-cost family vacation spots, and whether public or private school is best. In a matter of seconds, I'm bored out of my mind, and I can tell from her plaster expression that Allison is, too, but she stands steadfastly beside me, supporting me until I make my next move. I'm grateful for her presence and also heavy with the weight of guilt. I can never repay her for this kindness. I will never deserve her generosity.

But even Allison can't make miracles happen, and I'd better make my move toward Hunter soon. He's standing behind our circle, talking with a guy I think is his old buddy Mitch. From their body language, it looks like Hunter's wrapping up the conversation, ready to slip out of the reunion and my life.

I have to formulate a strategy. Searching for inspiration, I tune in to the talk around me, but they've moved on to a discussion concerning car seats, and I find that, just like in high school, I have nothing to add. I stand by Allison's side, mute and awkward, just as I always did around the Popular Crowd in high school.

I wait for the negative thoughts to creep in, but for some reason, they don't. I'm scrutinizing the people around me.

They look like parents, like they drive minivans and spend Saturday nights watching Disney movies.

It's not a bad life. I'm not exactly loving the singles scene, and I can see myself in their place with the right man. My gaze strays to Hunter again. But what strikes me now is that these people are nothing special. They're teachers and lawyers, insurance salesmen and store managers. They're moms and dads, aunts and uncles, daughters and sons. They're not gods and goddesses, and I see now that they never were. They were always just regular people, and it was only my insecurities and those of the other "lower" members of our class that built them up, made them into heroes and heroines.

Staring at Hunter, I realize that my biggest mistake was in making him into some kind of superhero: a Jedi knight who'd save me from my ordinary life then whisk me away on his spaceship. But Hunter is just a regular guy. He's opened up to me, shown me who he really is, and tried to get to know me. But I've been so busy trying to be someone else that, not only did he not see the real Rory, I never saw the Hunter behind the Jedi Knight fantasy.

And worse, I never felt worthy of him. How could a mere mortal like me ever interest a god like Hunter? But he's not a god. He's just a man who thought he found someone he could trust, someone without pretenses, someone he could have something real with.

I glance at Allison, and she gives me an imperceptible nod. Hunter is beginning to make his exit. It's now or never.

I slide away from the group and move toward Hunter. He's just waved good-bye to Mitch, so my timing is perfect. In three steps, I'll be in front of him, and then I can say what I need to. I can explain everything and pray he forgives me, or at least is willing to hear me out.

Two steps and I'm within arm's length of Hunter. He seems to hear me coming, begins to turn in my direction, and then a voice rings out, grating as the whine of the *Millennium Falcon*'s malfunctioning hyperdrive.

"Hunter Zachary Chase!"

I skid to a stop and stare like everyone else. Standing there is a vision in shimmery red. She moves forward, heels clicking powerfully on the marble floor. She's the most beautiful woman I've ever seen.

Embracing Hunter, she says, "God, you're still gorgeous!"

They're both gorgeous, and to watch them together is like a scene from a movie. She takes Hunter by the shoulders and gives him a dazzling smile. "Hunter! Don't say you don't remember me."

He shakes his head, looking overwhelmed by the swiftness with which he's been captured. She's so beautiful, so posh, she must be a model or actress. Her full lips curve into a pout. "It's me, Jellie Abernathy!"

Or she just might be the anti-Christ.

Chapter 22

I start to back away, but my new strappy sandals— the ones I picked out and bought on my own—won't co-operate. The heel of one turns, I stumble sideways, then, in a desperate bid to keep my balance, I reach out and grab the only steady object within arm's length. Hunter Chase.

"Oh, I'm sorry!" I gasp as I find my footing again. Jellie frowns and gives me the once-over. I feel my face flush and then turn even redder when Hunter pulls his arm away. "Hunter, can I just talk to you—" I begin.

"Oh, my God! It's *you.*" Jellie looks at my face then at the picture on my name tag.

Hunter raises a brow. "You know Rory?"

"Of course, silly!" Jellie steps forward, grasps my shoulders and air kisses me. "Robbie, what an incredible dress," she gushes, then whispers in my ear, "Incredibly ugly. What *were* you thinking, dear?" She steps back and coos, "You certainly look different." She says it sweetly for the benefit of her audience, but Jellie and I both know this isn't a compliment. "Older."

As if she's the star of her own Broadway show, she turns her spotlight smile on Hunter again. "But *you*—" Her hand clutches his arm possessively. "*You* haven't changed at all. You're still a hunk. And I bet you've got half a dozen gooey-eyed girls chasing after you." She gives me a pointed look, and I shrink back.

"It's good to see you again, Jellie," Hunter says, but compared to her tropical-island tone, Hunter's voice is Antarctica. "I hear you're getting married. Congratulations." He pulls away from her, but Jellie tightens her grip.

"My wedding! I almost forgot!"

I roll my eyes, trying not to gag.

"Of course, you *must* come. You'll love it. We're having it at the Plaza, and the theme is . . . *illusion*." She draws the U out and waves her hand, indicating some sort of legerdemain. "We're going to have the world's foremost magicians performing. I can't say who yet—top secret negotiations, you know—but suffice it to say you *will* recognize the names."

I'm watching Hunter, and though his face shows mild interest, I can tell he's merely being polite. He's bored with Jellie, disgusted with me, and wants to get away from all of us.

Jellie continues, "And the best part will be the optical illusions—rooms that aren't rooms, mirrors that aren't mirrors—the whole reception room will be shrouded in mist. You know, all white and mysterious."

"Sounds great," Hunter says when Jellie stops to take a breath.

I almost snort. Jellie's dream wedding is comic in its irony. I've spent all of three seconds with her, and already it's clear there's nothing real about her whatsoever. She's nothing more than a pretty illusion.

Hunter places his hand on Jellie's, prying it from his arm. "I hope you have a great time." He gives her fingers a squeeze and releases her.

"Hunter." I step forward again. "Can I please talk to you for *one* minute?"

He sighs. "Rory, we don't have anything to say to each other."

Jellie raises an eyebrow, and I see the gleam in her predatory eyes as she takes it all in.

"Maybe you don't want to talk to me, but *I* have something to say to *you.*" My voice echoes through the cavernous ballroom, and he pauses to look back at me. "I wanted to say this in private, but at this point I really don't have any choice or any semblance of pride, so I'll say it here."

A few of the people milling around move closer, trying to eavesdrop. I see Stormy rushing over, and I'm glad to have her close by. As soon as this is over and done with, we can sprint for the exit.

"I lied," I say to Hunter. "I lied and I misrepresented myself and my family. And I'm sorry." I look at Hunter for a reaction, but he merely stares at me.

"I told you that I'm a vegetarian, but there's more to it. I gave you the impression I ate meat at first because I didn't want you to think I was weird, some kind of hippie type. But I guess I am." I take a deep breath and look to Stormy for support. She gives me a shaky smile.

"I lied about another part of myself, too. I'm a *Star Wars, Star Trek, X-Files* junkie. How's that for a turn-on? I love all that dorky stuff. I've seen the movies a hundred times, read the books, and, yes, I collect toothbrushes with the characters on them. Sometimes I go to the conventions, and I even dress up like the characters."

Hunter nods impatiently. I'm not telling him anything new. I might as well shut up now, but I don't. I have to keep going, purge all the lies to keep them from contaminating my soul further.

"I lied about all that because I wanted you to like me, to think I was cool and sexy, but I have no excuse for lying about Tom." I look down, unable to meet Hunter's eyes. Everyone is staring at me, but I don't care. This is me. This is Rory. If they don't like me, that's their loss.

"Tom was the guy at the Creatures and Features Extravaganza," I continue, swallowing hard at Hunter's stony expression. "He was my boyfriend. I kept meaning to break up with him when you and I started going out, but I never did. I did today, but now it's too late. I cheated on him, and I lied to you, and I'm so, so sorry." My voice wobbles, and nearby I hear Jellie snicker. I'm sure she's enjoying this immensely, but I refuse to cry. I stare at the now blurry swirls in the marble tile and gulp another gallon of pride.

"I lost a chance with someone really great, with someone I really care about. You're smart and funny and talented, and I know I'll never find another person even half as wonderful as you." My voice hitches, and I can't stop myself from looking at Hunter, from ramming home, one more time, what it is I'm losing. Next to Hunter, Jellie sticks her lip out in a mock pout. I hear a few people behind me snigger.

"But I'm *not* sorry for myself," I say, ignoring Jellie and the rest of the Popular Crowd. I just want to get this over with. "I'm sorry because I hurt you." My voice breaks, and I have to look away again. I'm using all my willpower to plug the crumbling dam holding back my tears. "I'm sorry I violated your trust. I'm sorry I let you down. You trusted me enough to let me into your world, and I abused the privilege. I know it's not enough, but I'm sorry."

The room is silent; even the music has faded. I stare at Hunter, willing him to say something, do something. His mouth tightens, and I think for a moment that he might speak, and then Jellie starts clapping.

The hollow sounds ring out, reverberating through the crowded room. "Oh, bravo, Robbie. Bravo. Who would have guessed you had such a flair for the dramatic?"

I tear my eyes from Hunter to stare at her, not sure I believe what I'm seeing, but she's still clapping. Around me I hear tittering, the sound of nervous laughter. Or perhaps everyone is enjoying this? What's more entertaining than watching the school nerd publicly humiliated?

I whirl and start to run. My heels click loudly on the marble flooring, but the thunder of Jellie's clapping and the sound of her laughter batters my defenses as I flee the room. I'm vaguely aware of Stormy behind me, holding my arm, guiding me to the front of the hotel, and then we're out on the street, in the car, and it's over.

Almost over. The next morning, before I can think about it too hard, I tell Dan and Sunshine everything. Last night Stormy convinced me this would be cathartic, but right now it just feels painful and humiliating.

But I keep talking, filling Sunshine and Dan in on the Ultimate Jedi Plan, my fights with Allie and Stormy, lying to Hunter, and cheating on Tom. I tell them about the reunion and Jellie Abernathy, and just as they're really beginning to sympathize with me, I tell them about the day of Sunshine's party.

"I don't know why I did it," I say. My upper lip is quivering, and I'm hoping I don't start blubbering. "I just wanted to be with him so badly. I didn't care about anything else." I look at Sunshine. "I'm so sorry I missed your party. I'll find a way to make it up to you."

She reaches into her pocket and hands me a tissue. "Roberta, you don't owe me anything. All I want is for you to be happy."

I sigh. Unconditional love and support, like always. It's rough, I know, but I suppose I can learn to deal with having such a wonderful, loving family.

"If being with this Hunter makes you happy," Sunshine continues, "what more can I ask?"

I blow my nose loudly. "He does make me happy," I sob. "But I did everything wrong, and now I'm sure he hates me."

Sunshine hands me another tissue, then hugs me. "I've never known you to give up. If you want him, go after him."

"I'm afraid," I whisper into her jasmine-scented hair. "I'm afraid he'll reject me. The *real* me."

Sunshine sits back and brushes a tear from my cheek. "Life is about taking risks, Rory. We put ourselves out there and hope the world will be gentle. Sometimes we get banged around, but without a little pain we'd never appreciate the pleasure." She squeezes my shoulders. "*Live.* Show the world Roberta Joplin Egglehoff. You won't be sorry."

I nod, and then Stormy hugs me, and pretty soon we're all crying and laughing and hugging, and it's a love fest at the Egglehoff residence for over an hour. When we've cried to the point of dehydration and validated everyone's feelings to the point of nausea, Sunshine declares it's time to eat and heads for the kitchen. Stormy stands, but I grab her hand before she can follow.

"I know I was pretty out of it last night, but I thought I heard the phone ring. Did you get it?"

"Yeah, but it wasn't for you." She goes to help Sunshine, and Dan and I are left sitting on pillows in the living room.

"You know, I never realized that taking you to get those Burger King *Star Wars* glasses meant so much to you," he says, sitting forward.

I'd almost forgotten I'd mentioned that in my confession. I guess once I get going, I don't hold back. "It meant everything to me," I tell Dan. "I liked sharing that with you, having a secret between us."

He glances at the kitchen, where Sunshine is talking to Stormy and banging pots. Cupping his mouth, he whispers, "Yeah, thanks for not mentioning the burgers."

"I told you, it's our secret," I stage-whisper back. "Sharing that with you—not the meat, but the experience—made me feel special." I look down and twirl the pillow's tassel. "It made me feel like we had something just between us. Like I was your daughter as much as Stormy."

"Oh, Rory." He leans over and gives me a hug. "You were always my daughter. From the first time I saw you, I loved you."

My heart constricts, and I see tears in Dan's eyes, too. I grab a tissue from the box Sunshine brought in earlier. "I can't start crying again. I'll shrivel up like a raisin. I don't have any moisture to spare."

Dan punches my arm playfully, and then the doorbell rings.

"Dan or Roberta, will you get that?" Sunshine calls. "Stormy and I have our hands full in here."

"I'll get it," I say, grateful for a respite from all the emotional turmoil. I jump up, swiping at my watery eyes and nose. I pull the door open, and Allison is standing there.

"Hi."

I blink, but she's still there.

"Am I interrupting your lunch?" she asks. "Should I come back?"

"No," I finally manage. "No. We haven't eaten yet." With robotic movements, I step back. "Come in. You can join us."

She grimaces. "Great."

"Who is it?" Sunshine calls.

"It's Allison." My voice sounds foreign in my ears. How can I sound so calm when inside I'm a jumble of electrically charged wires?

"I'll set another plate. The wheat berry stew will be ready in ten minutes," Sunshine says.

Allison gives me a horrified look but calls pleasantly, "Thank you, Mrs. Egglehoff."

"Sunshine!" she corrects as she always does, but Allison calls her Mrs. Egglehoff anyway.

"Hi, Allison," Dan hollers from the living room.

"Hi, Mr. Egglehoff."

"We're going to go upstairs for a few minutes, okay?" I take Allison's arm and start for the stairs. As soon as we're in my bedroom, I give her a fierce hug. She almost topples over, but she embraces me back. "Okay, don't say it. You were right about everything. I should have listened to you. And then I was horrible the night you called when you'd broken up with Bryce." I lean back, holding her shoulders. "I wasn't there for you. I'm a terrible friend."

"That about covers it."

"Not even." I shake my head. "Let me get this all out." I swallow and take a deep breath. "And then last night. You stood by me. You were right there the whole time. Tell me what I can do to make all this up to you."

"Rory." Allison takes my arm and steers me toward the bed. "Sit down before you start hyperventilating."

We climb onto the bed, instinctively settling into our usual positions, me at the head and Allison at the foot. How many zillions of times have we sat in this room, on this bed, in these exact spots, pouring our hearts out to each other? Telling secrets and dreams and thinking we'd always be best friends. How could I even think of jeopardizing that?

"Allison, really. I can't lose your friendship. I don't know what happened to me the last few weeks."

Allison crosses her legs. "Hunter Chase happened to you, Rory. You found your Jedi."

And lost him. "But that doesn't excuse the way I acted toward you. The way I treated you. And Stormy. And Tom—"

"Oh, leave Tom out of this," Allison says, waving a hand. "He was never good enough for you, and you're the only one who couldn't see that."

I close my eyes, exasperated. "Why is everyone being so nice to me? *I'm* supposed to be nice to you."

"Rory, I'm your friend. You don't have to make anything up to me. People make mistakes."

"Yeah." I lean back on the pillows. "Some of us make bigger ones than others."

"And don't think I wasn't—I'm not *still*—furious with you."

I fiddle with a loose thread on the bedspread.

"But I figured after last night, you'd suffered more than enough."

I groan. "Ugh. The reunion. I swear, Allison, if I ever run into anyone who was there I'll . . ."

She raises her eyebrows. "You'll what?"

"I don't know, but something bad."

"You'll be fine. Anyone who has the guts to do what you did last night isn't going to shrink from a little embarrassment."

"But I am shrinking, Allison." I scrunch down into the pillows to make my point. "How could I make such a fool of myself?"

"Because you're Rory."

I bury my head and make moaning noises.

"And because you care about people and want to do the right thing," Allison says over my whining. "You wanted to tell Hunter how you felt, and you weren't going to let anyone, not even Jellie Abernathy, stand in your way."

"Jellie," I mumble into a pillow. "Don't remind me."

"What if I tell you what happened after you left?"

I bolt upright. "What?"

Allison gives me a mischievous smile and leans close, assuming the secret-telling position. "After you left and Jellie stopped clapping, Hunter started to leave, too. But Jellie grabbed his arm and was sucking up to him again. You know, hadn't they had such great times together in high school and remember when he took her to this place and that."

I can see the whole thing now. Jellie standing close to Hunter, her arm linked with his, sharing old times. And, of course, he'd remember the times *they'd* spent together.

"So she has her claws on Hunter's arm, and she's telling him that he just *has* to come to her wedding, and that she thinks he'd be *perfect* for a friend of hers." Allison's fluttering her hands around, doing a pretty good job of impersonating the pretentious Jellie. I'm a little surprised. Allison's never made fun of Jellie before.

"And Hunter," Allie continues, "just gives her this look, removes her hand from his arm like it was lint on a swath of velvet, and says, 'Jellie, if your friends are anything like you, I'd rather live the rest of my life as a celibate monk—self-flagellation, hair shirt, and all—than date one of them.' "

"No, he didn't." I grab Allison's arm, digging my fingernails in. "He didn't say that."

She nods. "Yes. He did. And that's not all."

I shake Allison. "What? What? Tell me!"

She smooths her hair, and I bite my tongue with impatience.

"So then he says, 'The only reason I'd attend your wedding is to give my sympathies to the groom. Your wedding is his funeral.' "

My jaw drops. "What did she do?" I whisper.

Allison shrugs. "What could she do? He said it in front of everyone. She tried to laugh it off, and he walked away."

I nod. "Wow. Hunter really put her in her place."

"Oh, that's not all," Allison says. I blink in disbelief. Not all? What more could there possibly be?

"As he was walking away, he turns around and says, 'Oh, and Jellie, the way you kiss, we should really start calling you Jelliefish."'

"No!"

"Yes! Lame but effective. You should have heard Jellie shriek."

"I wish I had." I flop back on the pillows again. "Are you still going to her wedding?"

"Are you kidding?" Allison throws a stuffed Ewok at me. "She's a complete bitch. Even the Plaza and Vera Wang isn't worth putting up with her. Besides, she treated you like crap. Last night and probably in high school, too." She frowns at me. "I'm still waiting for that story."

I smile. "Thanks, Allison." I stare at my ceiling for a long moment, trying to picture Hunter taking Jellie down a notch. I wish I'd been there to see it. "Allison?"

"Hmm?" She's picked up an old *Star Wars* comic book and is flipping through it.

"Why do you think Hunter did that with Jellie? I mean, he didn't have anything against her."

She shakes her head, giving me a look that says, "You are the biggest nerf-herder this side of the planet."

"Because he likes you, Rory. Because he didn't like seeing you treated like that."

I roll onto my stomach. "Yeah, well, I guess that's over."

"Don't be so sure," Allison says, and before I can ask what in the Dark Side she means by that, Sunshine calls us to brunch.

Chapter 23

"Yeah, but the problem I have with Oprah," Stormy tells Allison as Sunshine dishes out a heap of her famous tofu carob mousse, "is that she's contributing to the American crisis of conformity."

Allison is sitting cross-legged next to Stormy in our living room. As usual, the whole family has gathered in a circle, reclining on the big, plush pillows. In the center of our circle are the leftovers from brunch: wheat berry stew, roasted red pepper hummus, and homemade pita bread. Allison raises a brow at Stormy. "Crisis of conformity?"

"Yeah. Take her book club as an example." Stormy accepts a bowl of mousse from Sunshine. "By advocating that we all read the same books, the books *she* deems acceptable, Oprah contributes to the plague of conformist thinking infecting our country."

Sunshine hands Allison a bowl of mousse. Allie takes it without looking and murmurs, "Thanks." She sits up, and I can see a familiar look on her face. It's the one she gets when she tries to explain to me, for the hundredth time, the importance of moisturizing.

"But Stormy," Allison says, her tone painfully patient. "No one *has* to read those books, and the good thing about the book club is that it's gotten a lot of people reading who wouldn't normally open a book."

Stormy points a spoon at Allie. "Yes, but *what* are they reading? Don't the selections just reinforce the capitalist—"

"Stormy!" I hold up my hands. "Enough already. She's remodeling the woman's TV studio, not endorsing her as the next candidate for president."

"Great," Stormy says through a mouthful of mousse. "All that money, and what does she choose to do—"

We all groan, even Sunshine, and Stormy finally laughs. "Okay, I'll give it a rest."

Sunshine hands me a helping of mousse and stares into the serving bowl. "I always make too much."

Dan grins. "That's okay. I'll take seconds."

"Oh, no, you won't." The doorbell rings, interrupting Sunshine's impending lecture on Dan's eating habits. We all look at one another. "Are you expecting anyone?" Sunshine asks Dan.

He scoops up a spoonful of mousse. "Nope." He takes a bite of the mousse and closes his eyes like a cat with a bowl of cream. "And I'm not getting it, either. They can come back when I've finished my mousse." He winks at me. "*Both* servings."

Sunshine frowns and puts the bowl on the table, but as she turns toward the door, Stormy puts a hand on her arm. "Why don't we let Rory get it?"

I'm immediately suspicious. "Why?"

"Sunshine's been cooking all morning." Stormy shrugs. "Give her a break."

So why don't *you* give her a break? I think. I don't like the look in Stormy's eye. Something is up.

But everyone is looking at me, waiting for me to move, so I push my bowl of mousse aside, stand, and, for the second time that day, answer my parents' front door.

And almost slam it again.

Hunter is standing on the other side of the storm glass, holding a bouquet of red tulips. "Hi," he says.

"H-h-h-hi."

We stand there for a long moment, the glass door between us, and then he says, "Can I come in?"

I nod but don't move to open the door, and finally Hunter does it himself. I step back to allow him inside, and immediately my senses shift into warp drive. He smells so good, and he *looks* so good, and though I'm not touching him, I know he *feels* good.

Thank the Creator I let Stormy talk me out of wearing my sweats and prodded me to put on a little makeup. I'd dressed in my favorite jeans and a new white top with a scoop neck edged with flirty lace. Come to think of it, Stormy had the outfit lying on the bed for me when I emerged from the shower. Hmm.

"Who is it?" Sunshine calls.

Hunter glances past me toward the living room, where I can hear the clink of spoons as everyone eats dessert.

"A—a friend," I answer.

"Well, does she want to come in and have some carob mousse? I've got plenty left."

I look at Hunter. He looks at me. "I could go for some carrot mousse."

I laugh. "It's *carob,* not carrot, and since I know it's your favorite, I'll warn you the mousse has tofu in it."

"Mmm." He rubs his stomach. His tight, hard stomach.

"Healthy." He looks back at the door. "But I don't think it's right to hoard all that great-tasting tofu. Do you think there's enough for one more? I've got Dave in the car."

"Dave?"

"Yeah. I talked him into coming with me." He grins. "I told him he had to console me on the way home if you wouldn't talk to me."

"If I wouldn't—" I shake my head, unable to fathom what I'm seeing. It's Sunday afternoon, and Hunter is standing in my parents' hallway, holding a bouquet of flowers.

"Brought you some flowers." He holds them out, and I take them automatically.

"But how did you know I'd be here?"

He winks. "A little bird told me."

I frown. "So, so . . ." I still can't seem to put the pieces together. "You *wanted* to see me? I mean, after last night and everything I did . . ."

Hunter puts a finger on my lips. "Let's talk about that in a little while. Right now let me get poor Dave out of the car."

"Okay."

Hunter goes to fetch Dave, and I dash to the half bath to check my hair in the mirror. I flip on the light, prepared to be terrified at my reflection in the mirror. But when I see myself, I don't immediately start primping in an attempt to mask my flaws. Instead, I stare at my reflection in the mirror.

I like what I see. I like the girl in the mirror. She looks happy, confident, attractive. Not like a dork at all. Sure, her eyes are tinged red from crying and her T-zone is in desperate need of powder, but with her hair flowing loosely at the neckline of the feminine blouse she shopped for herself, she looks . . . pretty. And for the first time in her life, she *feels* pretty.

Turning off the light, I wander into the living room. "Where'd you get those gorgeous flowers?" Allison shrieks at the same time Dan says, "Are you okay?" and Sunshine looks past me and asks, "Where's your friend?"

Only Stormy doesn't say anything or seem surprised. I give her a considering look, but then I hear the door open again and Hunter and Dave's voices in the hallway. Sunshine rushes to greet them, I follow, and a few minutes later the men are propped up on pillows, eating mousse with the rest of us.

I hold my breath for the first fifteen minutes, waiting for something to go wrong, but nothing does. In fact, after a little while, it doesn't even seem so strange to have Hunter here, in my home, talking to my family and friends. He seems to fit right in.

He doesn't even blink when Sunshine pours him a neon green wheat grass smoothie or when Stormy argues that technology has made the Western world subservient slaves to a cold, inhuman master.

Finally I catch Allison's eye and give her a desperate look. She nods and smiles, then a moment later suggests Hunter and Dave join us girls for a walk. Sunshine says that's a great idea, Stormy concurs, and we're practically pushed out the door and onto the porch.

It's a warm, sunny April afternoon, and immediately Dave and Allison wander off. Their disappearance is none too subtle, and I wonder if there isn't more than courtesy to account for Allison and Dave's eagerness to leave us alone. They head down the driveway, walking side by side, and as I watch, Allison's shoulder brushes against Dave's and she smiles up at him.

"So what do you think of my attempt at matchmaking?" Hunter asks, moving closer to me. He nods toward the driveway. "The first time you mentioned Allison, I knew they'd hit it off."

It's a struggle, but I drag my thoughts away from Hunter—how good it is to have him here, how much I like to be with him—and try to pick up the thread of conversation. When I do, the mousse I've just eaten hardens in my belly. "So, is that why you came, then?" I look down at the faded doormat on my parents' porch. "To set Dave up with Allison?"

"One of the reasons," Hunter says. "But not *the* reason."

I look up, hopeful again, but he frowns at me and crosses his arms over his chest. "You know, Rory, we really have to do something about this mental block of yours. You can't seem to wrap your head around the idea that I *like* you."

My heart trips at his words, but I try to remain calm. "I'm sorry. It's just so hard to believe. I liked you for so long in school, I guess you became sort of like this symbol of all that was unattainable to me. You were like the Holy Grail or—" I feel my face grow hot. "A Jedi Knight," I whisper.

"Well, I'm not a symbol, and I'm sure as hell not Luke Skywalker. I'm just a guy. A regular guy who wants to get to know you. The *real* you."

"That's another thing." I look down again. "After all the lies I told you, I thought you'd never want to see me again." I glance up at him. "I mean, aren't you mad?"

"Hell, yeah, I'm mad. I'm pissed."

"Oh." I take a step back, stumble on the steps of the porch, and almost tumble over. Hunter catches me and pulls me to safety. But when I'm righted again, he doesn't let go. In fact, he drags me closer.

"You should be more careful," he murmurs, wrapping

his arms around my waist. "I'll come off looking like the bad guy if I have to strangle you in your hospital bed."

Since he runs a hand up and down my back as he says this, I'm not too worried. "So the truth comes out," I say on a shiver. "You came here to throttle me."

"Among other things." He kisses me gently on the mouth. When he pulls away, I'm tingling all over.

"Does this mean I'm forgiven?" I say it in a low, sort of sexy voice, trying to be flirtatious, trying to hide how desperate I am for him to answer yes.

He wrinkles his brow. "Let's just say you're on probation. I understand why you lied, but I'm not happy about it, and I'm not sure how much I can trust you."

I nod. "That's important to you, I know. I'm sorry."

Hunter shakes his head, cutting off my apology. "No more being sorry. Just be Rory." He grins and I groan.

"That was bad."

He shrugs. "Okay, so I have a lousy sense of humor. I told you I wasn't perfect."

"Could have fooled me," I mutter.

Hunter laughs, and I huff.

"What's so funny?"

"The expression on your face reminds me of how you looked last night."

"Why does everyone have to bring that up?" I try to pull away, but Hunter won't let me go.

"You were so determined to talk to me, so determined to set things right. You had this don't-mess-with-me glint in your eyes, and when you turned on me and Jellie, I almost saluted."

"It didn't feel like that to me. I felt like an idiot."

"You *are* an idiot," Hunter says and squeezes me when I stiffen. "But I like that about you. I like that you were willing to embarrass yourself in front of half of the class of ninety just to do what you thought was right."

I look down and shuffle my foot. Hunter stares at me for a long time. "You do realize you went a little over the top?"

I bury my head in the curve between his neck and shoulder, secure now that he's not going to disappear.

"Did you ever think about telling me all that in private?"

I glare up at him. "I *tried,* but—"

"I know, I know. I blew you off. Shit, I should have known better, especially after that vegetarian scene you pulled in Luigi's."

I bite my lip. "I didn't mean to make a scene—at Luigi's or last night. I just reacted. I wasn't thinking."

"I know." He kisses my nose. "And that's why I like you, princess. The real you has no pretenses. And when you stop trying so hard to impress me, and let me get to know you better, I think I'm going to like you even more."

I shake my head. "You're going to think I'm a dork. I mean, look at my crazy family."

"Is any family normal?"

"What about my *Star Wars* obsession?"

"They're great movies."

I narrow my eyes at him. "So does that mean the next time there's a sci-fi convention you'll be my date?"

"You mean go inside?"

"That's usually the way it works." Out of sheer mischief, I push it further. "You'd make a great Mr. Spock. Or what about Chewbacca? My friend Eddie even has a costume you could borrow."

A look of pure horror crosses Hunter's face. He stares at me, opens his mouth once. Twice. Then explodes, "No way in hell am I putting on pointy ears or a hairy body suit. Look, princess, I'll drop you off outside the convention center. I'll buy your ticket, even, but I'm not going in. Those things creep me out." He squeezes my waist. "We don't have to like all the same things. I scream at the TV and throw the couch cushions when the Bulls are losing. But I don't expect you to get that involved in basketball."

"That's a relief," I say under my breath.

"So, no alien conventions for me, and no basketball for you. Deal?"

I nod. "Deal." I give him a playful smile. "But what about TV movie marathons? There's a *Star Wars* one next month."

He gives me a pained expression. "I don't know. There'll probably be a game on at the same time."

I grin. "That's what picture-in-picture's for, right?"

He groans, then jerks to attention.

"Hey! That reminds me." Hunter releases me and looks around. "Where's Dave?"

"A *Star Wars* movie marathon reminds you of Dave?"

"No, no." He jogs down the porch steps and heads toward the mailbox, where Dave and Allison are pretending not to be watching us. Hunter says something to Dave, and Dave nods, then Hunter pulls his car keys from his pocket and disables the alarm on his SUV.

"Come on, Rory." He waves. "Field trip."

"Field trip?" I stand rooted in place, staring at him. "What are you talking about?"

"It's a surprise. Just get in the car."

I look at Allison and Dave. Allison shrugs and Dave grins. "Go on, Rory," Dave calls. "If the principal comes looking for you, we'll cover."

I'm not often spontaneous. Okay, I'm not *ever* spontaneous, but I figure for Hunter I can make an exception.

"So where are we going?" I ask a few minutes later as he turns onto Sheridan. "It looks like we're going to campus."

My parents' house is only about ten minutes from Northwestern, and up ahead I can already spot some of the university's taller buildings.

"You'll see," Hunter says, and when I try to press him further, he turns on the radio. Appropriately enough, it's tuned to an eighties station, and Modern English is singing "I Melt with You." I look over at Hunter and smile. He takes my hand, his warm skin making *me* want to melt.

"How did you know where to find me today?" I ask.

"Your sister." He brakes for a light.

"Stormy? I don't get it."

"I called your house last night and she answered."

"She said it wasn't for me!"

"She told me you were sleeping."

The stoplight changes to green, and he turns into a strip mall.

"You called last night, and Stormy didn't wake me up? I'm going to *kill* her!"

Hunter pulls into a parking spot. "Whoa, princess. Don't blast her yet. She told me that she wasn't going to wake you because you were upset and needed your rest, but if I really wanted to try to work things out, you'd be here today."

I roll my eyes. "Yeah, that sounds like Stormy."

"She's tough." Hunter shuts off the engine. "When I hung up with her I felt guilty for making you feel so bad."

"*You* felt guilty?"

He chuckles. "I know. And I was half afraid to come to see you today. Stormy told me if I wasn't serious about you, if I was just going to hurt you, not to bother. That girl scares me." He grins.

"She's harmless."

He raises a brow.

"Well, most of the time." Harmless, but confusing. We're about as close as two sisters can be, yet she's continually surprising me. Daily, I realize I don't understand Stormy nearly as well as I think I do. Stormy made it clear she considers Hunter a shallow jock. If that's true, then why did she tell him where to find me?

I smile. Maybe I understand her better than I thought. Stormy would deny it to the bitter end, but this is proof positive that my little sister—the crusader, the cynic, the disillusioned activist—has a romantic streak.

"Yeah, well, you may say she's harmless," Hunter mutters, "but I figure I better keep my intentions honorable, just in case she decides to put a hex on me or something. So, here we are." He gestures to the stores in the strip mall. There's a video store, a fast-food place, and a dry cleaner, but I don't see anything special.

I give him a quizzical look, and he points to the store right in front of us. I bend down to read the sign above. "The Junk Shop," I say and look at him. "What's this?"

Hunter climbs out of the SUV. "You'll see."

I follow him inside and almost turn around again. It looks like a dollar store after a nuclear attack. But worse.

There's junk everywhere—stacks of mismatched plates, bins of sponges and other household cleaning supplies, and coating everything, a three-inch layer of dust and grime. There is *nothing* I want in here, but Hunter heads straight for the clerk behind the ancient register.

"Hi. I'm Hunter Chase. I called a week or so ago, and I think you're holding some items for me." He turns around and grins at me. I arch a brow. He's acting pretty weird.

Wait a parsec. He can't have—

I glance around the shop again, this time really studying it. No, no sci-fi stuff. No *Star Wars* collectibles. The clerk, an older woman with a haggard face and thin lips that look as though a cigarette should be hanging from the tips, mutters and reaches under the counter.

She pulls out a paper bag and hands it to Hunter. He takes it and grins at me.

"So, what's in the bag?" I ask. I swear, Hunter is being so weird. "Memorabilia from high school? A Lincoln letter jacket? Your long-lost MVP trophy?"

Hunter just keeps on grinning.

"That'll be ten-fifty." Her voice is deep and gravelly.

"Give me a second," Hunter tells her. "I want to be sure I got it right." He hands me the bag. It's relatively light, and it clinks when I take it.

Oh, Creator. It *clinks*. My heart is pounding and I feel light-headed all of a sudden.

"Open it," Hunter says.

I peer inside the bag and gasp, then gasp again, unable to catch my breath. Breathe, Rory. Breathe. With trembling fingers, I pull out first one, place it reverently on the counter, then reach for the other Burger King *Star Wars* glass. And, amazingly, they're the two I'm missing: Luke and Leia from the original movie and Han and Luke in the Tatooine desert.

I stare openmouthed at Hunter. "How did you find these? I've been searching for years." I pick them up, turning them over in the light, looking for any chips or cracks, but they're nearly perfect.

"Obviously not in the right places."

"Obviously." I glance around the junk shop again. Who would have thought? But that's the lesson I keep forgetting: Appearances can be deceiving. The dumb jock might be a really deep guy inside. The school nerd might be a real party girl. It's what's inside that counts.

"So, you want them or not?" the woman asks.

Hunter looks at me.

I stare at the glasses, stare at the picture of Luke, the Jedi Knight. Then I look at my own Jedi. He's still waiting for my response, and I see in his eyes the little-boy vulnerability I fell in love with. And under that vulnerability is strength, intelligence, character, and—love? Definitely affection.

I look at my Jedi, and I see Hunter. Not the quarterback, not the homecoming king, not Mr. Popularity. Hunter.

And he's looking at me.

With infinite care, I place the glasses back in the bag and hand them absently to the clerk.

Hunter's watching me, still waiting for my answer. I step forward and take his face in my hands. Our eyes meet, and everything else in the universe fades away. I place a soft, tender kiss on his lips and whisper, "Yeah. I think I finally found what I'm looking for."

Want More?

Turn the page to enter
Avon's Little Black Book —

the dish, the scoop and the
cherry on top from
SHANE BOLKS

Everything I Need to Know I Learned from *Star Wars*

1. **An arrogant, stuck-up, scruffy-looking nerf-herder can be a good thing!** Hey, if it's good enough for Princess Leia, it's good enough for me. Han Solo might have been a scoundrel, but he always came through. A guy with some scoundrel in him keeps life interesting.
2. **Protect your friends, even if the Empire is going to blow up your planet.** I made the mistake of choosing a guy over my friends only once. The guy turned out to be a self-centered jerk. When we broke up, my friends were the ones who got me through.
3. **Pay your debts or Jabba the Hutt will come after you.** Han Solo made the mistake of waiting too long to pay off bounty hunter Jabba and ended up encased in carbonite and hanging on the wall of Jabba's palace. I've seen the best of friends come to blows over a loan. When I borrowed money from my mom and had to clean the kitchen floor on hands and knees to work off my debt, that was the end of my borrowing days.
4. **Impersonating a deity isn't always wrong.** Remember the Ewoks from *Return of the Jedi?* They looked adorable, but that didn't stop them from trying to roast Han, Luke, Chewbacca, and R2D2 for dinner. C-3P0 saved them by pretending to be a god. There are times I am a goddess: in the classroom, on the highway, and in an argument.

5. **Looks can be deceiving.** Back to those teddy bear Ewoks. One moment you're hugging the little guy, the next he's stuck a spear in your gut. I have a friend who looks perfect on the outside. When I first met her, I would have changed places with her in a second. When I realized she had problems like everyone else, it was a letdown. I realized that there really is no one who's perfect.
6. **Any reason to party is a good one.** When I was fourteen, I threw a birthday party for Harrison Ford. I baked him a cake, lit candles, and made my family sing happy birthday to his picture.
7. **The more you read, the more you know.** I've read *Star Wars, The Empire Strikes Back,* and *Return of the Jedi* at least ten times each. I've read *ESB* over twenty.
8. **Technology is overrated.** The first time *Star Wars* came on TV, I recorded it with a little silver tape recorder and microphone. This was before VCRs, or at least before I had one. I listened to that recording—all sound, no video—until I wore the tape out. I know every whirr and screech in the movie.
9. **Free enterprise is good!** I sold all my *Star Wars* action figures, ships, and other memorabilia when I was twenty-five. I made almost $200.
10. **"If money is what you love . . . that's what you will receive."** Han Solo got this scathing remark from Princess Leia when he balked at going up against the Death Star. But in the end, Han cared more about his friends and doing the right thing than money. I could make a lot more money in the corporate world than I do as a teacher and a writer, but that's not the right thing for me. All the money changing hands on Wall Street wouldn't make me happy if I had to do something I hated day after day.

My First Book

It's obvious I was always meant to write this book. When I was about eight, my mom gave my sister and me each a copy of *My Book About Me.* To complete the book, I had to—among other things—count how many teeth I had, how many windows in our house, write what I wanted to be when I grew up (I wrote "nurse"), and write an original story. This is the story I wrote, typed but uncorrected (Hint: Luce=Luke and lavers=light sabers).

STAR WARS

Leia said Han don't go

Why you love Luce

I don't love Luce

Yes you do

I was afraid to admit I was trying to make you jelles

And that's why you kissed Luce

But . . .

No I am not fineshed you want me to believe that

Yes

Well I'll tell you what Leia if you love me kiss me and well get marryed and for get about Luce and besides hile probably go back to Yoda

But then well hurt Luces feelings

I know you love both of us well we will half to have a contest with our lavers

No shouted Leia I know you want to kill Luce so you can marry me well I'll never marry you I rather marry a wokie

I rather go!

No don't go

Yes

No

Yes Good buy

Stay

Ok

But I love you

I now

What about Vater

I don't know don't you know he is dead

Scary, that is, hmm? The funny thing is that when I was telling my younger sister about rediscovering that story in my book, she informed me that I'd actually also written the story in her copy of *My Book About Me.* If you have a younger sibling, then you understand that he or she frequently rewrites history with you cast in the role of the villain. I mean you pour hot wax on someone once, and you never hear the end of it. But when I accused my sister of practicing her revisionist form of history once again, she whipped out her book, turned to the story page, and showed me another story titled Star Wars.

It was suspiciously similar to the above story, not only the content but also the handwriting. Now, if those stories don't give some early insight into my future then nothing does. My younger sister says all these stories show is that I was bossy and domineering, but I find it telling that when most kids copy other kids' papers, I wrote two stories and pretended one was someone else's. Or maybe I just wanted to see my story in as many "real" books as I could.

Top Ten Things You Wish You Didn't Know About Me

1. I actually like to get up at five in the morning. Any later and I've wasted half the day.

2. I suck at math. I still use my fingers. My dad helped me with all the accounting stuff in the book.

3. I tell people that the only TV I watch is *Queer Eye for the Straight Guy,* but sometimes I watch the Nick and Jessica Newlyweds show on MTV.

4. I'm a really *bad* driver. I've had four accidents—all my fault. In the first, I totaled two cars, and that was four days after I got my license.

5. I'm named after Shane Gould, Australian gold-medal Olympic swimmer. She's a woman. But I don't have a middle name. In second grade, I told my teacher that my middle name was Teresa and that everyone called me that. When my mom came to Open House, the teacher kept talking about Teresa, and my mom had to ask who she meant. I got in double trouble for that one.

6. I was five feet three inches in third grade. When I walked into the classroom, the kids thought I was the teacher.

7. I majored in opera my first semester at college. I changed majors because I had a huge crush on my Intro Psych professor. Dr. Lewis, mmm.

8. My hero is Dian Fossey, advocate for the gorillas in Rwanda.

9. In high school, my friends and I adopted names for ourselves. There was Jezebel (me), Alanna, Starr, and Rhapsody. One night we were listening to Depeche Mode, and we took a safety pin and carved our sign, a circle with a cross in the middle, on each other's wrists.

10. My first real kiss was with a guy named Butch. We were in summer school together. We turned off the lights and kissed in the classroom during lunch. He was a helicopter-kisser. Yuck, but I got to wear his letter jacket.

THE LONGHORN GAZETTE

Ms. Bolks Practices What She Teaches

by Christopher Coleman, Staff Reporter

Wazzup, Longhorns? It's your homie, Crazy Chris with another look inside Longhorn High School. You know I'm a player, but I ain't playing when I tell you we got a genuine author in the house. Wave your hands in the air for Ms. Bolks, sophomore English Teacher.

CHRIS: Hi, Ms. B. So, first question. Why'd you fail me? Haha. Just kidding. (Sort of).

MS. BOLKS: Chris, I don't have a lot of time, so . . .

CHRIS: That's cool, G. No worries. Real first question: Why did you become a teacher? Was it so you could torture us students?

MS. B: Um, tempting as that idea is on days like, well, like today, I became a teacher because I couldn't pass up a job where I'd be paid to spend all day talking about what I love—literature and writing.

CHRIS: Yeah. You do a lot of that. You give a lot of homework, too, Ms. B. What's up with that?

MS. B: I can't cover everything in only 55 minutes. Especially when certain students come in late every day.

CHRIS (LOOKING AROUND, INNOCENTLY): Yeah, um, but back to homework. Were you a nerd in school or something?

MS. B: No. I was a Goth.

CHRIS: Oh, yeah, like Tiger Woods. He da man!

MS. B: *Goth,* Chris. Not golf. I was into vampires, Depeche Mode, and nonconformity.

CHRIS: Now we're talking!

MS. B: I used to wear black lipstick and spike my bangs to six inches. I measured.

CHRIS: But you weren't a nerd, right. Ha-ha. Okay, so do you have favorite students (cuz I sure ain't one of them)?

MS. B: No, I like all my students.

CHRIS: Yeah, but are there any guys you like more than others? You know (waggling eyebrows) . . .

MS. B: Chris, I've got a lot of papers to grade. Are we done?

CHRIS: Couple more questions, Ms. B. Just chill. Okay (looking at notes). I read your book.

MS. B: You did? Really? The whole thing?

CHRIS: Um, sure. There's not like a test or anything, right?

MS. B: Not yet.

CHRIS: So, in the book, Rory and her freaky family are veterinarians. Are you a veterinarian?

MS. B: No, I'm a teacher.

CHRIS: Yeah, but do you eat meat?

MS. B: Oh, am I a *vegetarian*?

CHRIS: Yeah, that's what I said.

MS. B: Actually I am a vegetarian, but I'm not as radical as Rory's family. Not anymore, anyway.

CHRIS: So, you don't eat hamburgers?

MS. B: I don't eat meat.

CHRIS: What about chicken?

MS. B: No. Chicken is meat, and I don't like the idea of an animal dying to please my palate.

CHRIS: But hey, what if you saw a dead chicken, like it had been hit by a car? If it was dead already, would you eat it?

MS. B: Would I eat road kill? No.

CHRIS: That's cool. Yeah, I wouldn't either. Did Jason and Mike tell you I did, cuz they always up in my Kool-Aid.

MS. B: Chris, I'm not in your Kool-Aid. Are we done?

CHRIS: Almost. In the book—which I *did* read—Robin—

MS. B: *Rory.*

CHRIS: That's what I said. Rosie likes this boy who doesn't like her. That ever happened to you?

MS. B: Yeah, actually it did. When I was in middle school I liked this guy named David Wald, but he didn't know I existed.

CHRIS: So, what did you do? Did you flash him? That would get my attention.

MS. B: No! But I did do something a little psycho.

CHRIS: Aww. Ms. B. I knew you had a gangster side. Tell us what you did.

MS. B: He liked this other girl, so I cut letters out of the newspaper and pasted them to paper. The note said something like, "Christy isn't good enough for you." Then I secretly put it in his mailbox.

CHRIS: Tight, and then what?

MS. B: That's it.

CHRIS: Oh. Yeah, look at the time. Last question. You're not married, right?

MS. B: What does that have to do with anything?

CHRIS: Well, Coach Anderson isn't married either. I thought maybe I could hook you two up. Give him your digits.

MS. B: Thanks, Chris, but no.

CHRIS: No worries. Respect.

Okay Longhorns, that's the 4-1-1 on Ms. B. Get jiggy with her English class in room 227. Aight?

I Have a Confession to Make . . .

. . . I have a split personality. It's nothing serious, but every once in a while, I think I'm in Regency England and I start addressing people as "my lord" and "my lady." Whenever I do this, I call myself Shana Galen, and I start to write about earls and daughters of dukes. My latest "trip" resulted in *When Dashing Met Danger,* available now in your local bookstores.

Alexander Scarston, Earl of Selbourne, may be wealthy, devilishly handsome, and one of England's most eligible bachelors, but as far as lovely Lucia Dashing is concerned, the man is a scoundrel—one who makes her heart race, even as her own safe, stodgy fiancé leaves her feelings cold—but a scoundrel nonetheless. However when Lucia's twin brother vanishes mysteriously, she must turn to Alex for help and convince the fearless and arrogant earl that he needs her and her inspired plans.

As a secret agent for the Crown, Alex has mastered the ability to mask his identity and his heart. When he realizes that his nation's future depends on his finding the missing youth, Alex risks all by exposing innocent Lucia to his world of secrets and subterfuge. The impulsive lady delights in courting certain danger for the first time in her young life—yet nothing will prove as perilous as Alex Scarston's kiss!

SHANE BOLKS

SHANE BOLKS is an award-winning writer. She teaches sixth-grade English and battles the Dark Side in the form of comma splices and dangling modifiers. She didn't attend her high school reunion, fearing no one would recognize her without the black lipstick, dog collar, and spiked hair. These days she prefers cashmere to combat boots and Shakespeare to the Sex Pistols, but algebra is still mystifying. Read more—about the author, not algebraic equations—on the Web at *www.shanebolks.com*.